NATALIE SHAW EVJEN

Leapfrog Press
New York and London

Wolfpack
9 8 7 6 5 4 3 2 1

First published in the United States by Leapfrog Press, 2025

Leapfrog Press Inc.
www.leapfrogpress.com

Cover and text design: James Shannon and Prepress Plus, India

ISBN: 978-1-948585-286 (Paperback)

The Forest Stewardship Council® is an international non-governmental organisation that promotes environmentally appropriate, socially beneficial, and economically viable management of the world's forests. To learn more visit www.fsc.org

We make every effort to make sure our products are safe for the purpose for which they are intended. For more information see our website or contact our EU Authorised Representative, EAS Project OU, Mustamäe tee 50, 10621,Tallinn, Estonia, gpsr.requests@easproject.com

LEAPFROG GLOBAL FICTION PRIZE

Past Winners of the Leapfrog Global Fiction Prize

2025: *Little Mice* by Tara Crowe*
2024: *Magic Boy* by Michael Konik
2024: *Wolfpack* by Natalie Shaw Evjen*
2023: *Istanbul Crossing* by Timothy Jay Smith
2023: *The Aves* by Ryane Nicole Granados*
2022: *Rage & Other Cages* by Aimee LaBrie
2022: *Jellyfish Dreaming* by D. K. McCutchen*
2021: *But First You Need a Plan* by K L Anderson
2021: *Lost River, 1918* by Faith Shearin*
   My Sister Lives in the Sea by Faith Shearin*
2020: *Wife With Knife* by Molly Giles
2019: *Amphibians* by Lara Tupper
2018: *Vanishing: Five Stories* by Cai Emmons
2018: *Why No Goodbye?* by Pamela L. Laskin*
2017: *Trip Wire: Stories* by Sandra Hunter
2016: *The Quality of Mercy* by Katayoun Medhat
2015: *Report from a Burning Place* by George Looney
2015: *The Solace of Monsters* by Laurie Blauner
2014: *The Lonesome Trials of Johnny Riles* by Gregory Hill
2013: *Going Anywhere* by David Armstrong
2012: *Being Dead in South Carolina* by Jacob White
2012: *Lone Wolves* by John Smelcer*
2011: *Dancing at the Gold Monkey* by Allen Learst
2010: *How to Stop Loving Someone* by Joan Connor
2010: *Riding on Duke's Train* by Mick Carlon*
2009: *Billie Girl* by Vickie Weaver

* Young Adult | Middle Grade Fiction

These titles can be bought at: https://leapfrogprize.org/shop

For GG, who said, "Why not?"

CHARACTER RUNNING PLAYLISTS

CAT 🟢 ·|||·||·|·||·||·||·|||·

JOSIE 🟢 ·||·||||·||·|·||·||||||·

MILE ONE
CHAPTER 1
CAT

Seven months.

It's how long it took me to learn to ride a bike. To save up for a pair of Chuck Taylor platform high-tops. To grow out my bangs after my best friend, Blythe, dared me to chop them off with a pair of Fiskers.

In seven months, Bill Harker's cornfield outside of town – the one I'm currently driving past in the back seat of Dad's truck – goes from billowing green ocean to endless white void to stubbled wasteland.

It's enough time to fall apart, and enough time to put yourself back together again.

Theoretically.

Coming home is surreal, but not because of how much has changed or what I've forgotten. It's the feeling that I never left. Like I blinked and somehow the past seven months – 227 days – evaporated into nothing more than a dream.

The chipped and faded *Plain City – A Place with Space!* sign welcomes me like a trusty, if slightly unhinged, old friend. We pass the Thompsons'. The Reids'. The Chattertons'. The red swing hanging from the walnut tree on the corner. The vacant lot next to Fuller's Family Market, where all the neighborhood kids used to meet for night games in the summer.

Everything is exactly the same, just as I left it.

It's me who's supposed to be different.

**

Meri is on the front porch painting her toenails when we pull into our driveway. Her frayed cutoffs and yellow tank show off her late spring tan, freckled like a bronzed robin egg.

To add to my list of things that haven't changed, Meri's phone is pinned between her ear and right shoulder. She ends the conversation with whomever she's talking to – Paul, no doubt – and slips the phone into her back pocket. A bright smile erupts across her face as I open the passenger door and step outside.

"Pennygirl, look! It's Cat!"

From this angle, it looks she's talking to a medical supply grab bag rather than an actual person – tubes and Velcro straps and monitors – but I know Penny's small frame is somewhere beneath it all. Meri bends down to kiss her forehead, the only unobstructed part of her face.

I walk up the porch steps to meet them as Dad pulls my suitcase from the back. As I get closer, I see tufts of Penny's hair sticking up above the pillow. Without her wheelchair and the traveling hospital room, it's easy to see she and I were dealt the same deck of cards, from the Shultz side – straight dark hair, long nose, sharp chin – while Meri, with her red curls and perfectly proportioned everything, is all Anderson. As I climb onto the porch, Penny finds my face and flashes me a big, heart-melting smile. I still don't know if she truly recognizes me even when I *haven't* been gone for seven months, but there's something about the sparkle in her eyes that makes me hopeful she does.

Meri pulls me in for a long hug. When she steps back, I see the same look on her face that Mom and Dad wore when they picked me up. Like there's something on the tip of her tongue but she doesn't want to upset the balance of the universe by saying it aloud.

2

"Supper ready, Mer?" Mom says.

Meri seems as relieved by the distraction as I am. "Go see for yourself. I might just survive college after all, Mom."

"That's jumpin' the gun, ain't it? Gotta taste it first," Dad teases, winking as he hauls my suitcase past us.

Inside, I see that the house has been deep cleaned and the table is set. Unless it's Sunday or someone's birthday, dinner is served buffet style – no frills, load up your own plate and find an empty chair. Today, though, there's even a vase with fresh-cut flowers as a centerpiece.

Mom rushes to the kitchen, and I follow Dad into my room. He sets down my suitcase and tousles my hair. "Good to have you back, Sis."

Sis. The nickname I can't ever seem to outgrow.

He leaves, which I appreciate, and I sit on the edge of my bed, breathing in the scent of my room. Everything is coated with a fine layer of dust that seems to glow in the fractured sunlight peeking through my blinds. My eyes land on a picture of me and Blythe, taken just a few weeks before I left for New Horizons. I remember pulling it from the stack of photos I'd just gotten developed, thinking it was one of my best pictures. Now, I'm almost horrified by my jutting cheekbones, the glazed-over vacancy of my eyes.

Mom calls out. I head back into the kitchen to see everyone already sitting up, so I hurry to my chair and close my eyes. Dad says grace. I can tell they're determined to make dinner seem as normal as possible by their play-by-play commentary: *"Just the right amount of spice in the meat, Mer." "No olives? You can't eat a taco without olives." "This is our last bottle of salsa. Those tomatoes better hustle up."* Even Penny seems to join in, her unintelligible grunts and babble matching the volume of the conversation. I smile and nod like I'm paying attention, but it takes every ounce of my concentration to put the food in my mouth and chew. I try to imagine braless Ms. Reid and her saccharine smile, repeating affirmations about food being our friend and loving ourselves.

After just a few minutes, Meri sets her fork and knife on her empty plate.

"Full already?" Dad asks. "Your food wasn't *that* bad. Get another."

Meri's eyes shift. "Oh, um, Paul's picking me up –"

"Whoa, whoa, whoa, your sister's home after being gone for near a year. You're not going anywhere."

My face gets warm. "Oh, it's fine, she doesn't need –"

"Your Dad is right on this one, Merideth," Mom cuts in. "It's a family night."

Meri's eyes shift, avoiding mine. "You're right. I wasn't thinking."

I clear my throat and stand up. "I'm actually pretty tired. I was just going to go to bed anyways."

"Cat, honey –"

Before Mom can finish, I hurry to my room and shut the door. The heat in my face pools around my eyes and my vision blurs, but I give my head a shake, willing the tears to reabsorb back into my skull.

To distract myself, I unzip my suitcase and sort through the contents. At the bottom, hidden beneath stacks of clothes, lay the artifacts of my time at New Horizons: a plaid journal, Mom's letters, some pictures I watercolored during art therapy. I spot the blue mug I made in pottery class and pull it out, turning it over and over in my hands. I was so proud of it last week, but now all I can see are the fingerprints in the finish and how lopsided it is.

There's a knock on my door, a soft click as it unlatches. Mom's face appears in the crack. "Can I come in?"

I nod but don't look at her. She sits beside me on the bed.

4

"Did you make that? It's so pretty," she says, motioning to the ceramic atrocity as I start stuffing the smashed stacks of clothes into my dresser.

"They said it might be hard at first," she continues. "You've got to lean on us, Cat. That's what we're here for."

There's no stopping the tears now. Soon I'm sobbing, complete with trembling shoulders and weird squawking noises I can't control.

She wraps her arms around me, brushing the hair from my face. "When New Horizons called last week, they were so impressed with how far you've come. Said you were their model resident. But this is a marathon, love, not a sprint. Things always seem harder when you can't quite see the finish line."

I wonder if she realizes the irony in what she's saying. This all started with a New Year's resolution to "get healthy." Blame it on puberty, I guess, because I never felt out of place in my body until I started getting hips and a chest. And unlike Meri, who has always been curvy in all the right places, mine suddenly looked awkward and out of proportion. I stopped recognizing myself in the mirror. The only solution, it seemed, was to go for thin. To get into those size zeros, like Blythe, who – as fate would have it – has been praying for boobs since the third grade.

So I started exercising. Nothing too intense, just a short daily jog down my street and back. Cut back on junk food. But no matter what I did, I somehow still felt empty inside. Still got hit with that nauseating wave of self-loathing every time I looked in the mirror.

The first time I tried to purge, I was positive it wouldn't work. Thought I'd stick my fingers down my throat, gag a little, forget the whole thing. When it *did*, I felt … proud. Like, sure, I'm not as pretty and talented as Meri, or as thin and outgoing as Blythe, but – hey, look, vomit in the toilet – I finally did *something* right.

I didn't do it all the time, at least not at first. Just after big meals or the occasional milkshake indulgence. I guess it seemed easier than counting calories, especially when people would say, "But you don't need to watch your weight" every time I turned down a slice of pizza.

More than how it made me look, I liked the way it made me feel inside. Powerful. In control.

I spent the next few months in the "honeymoon phase," as Ms. Reid would later tell me. Thinking I'd finally figured out the secret to accepting myself.

It was September – seven months later – when I realized I was in trouble.

When I went from having all the control in the world to none at all.

**

Mom hugs me tighter, and for a moment, the tension in my shoulders releases. "We're going to get through this, hon." She pulls back and meets my eyes. "Pretty soon it'll be –"

She's interrupted by a series of all-too-familiar beeps coming from the living room.

I forgot how loud those beeps are.

"Hey, Deb?" Dad calls out to her.

Our eyes lock, and in that micro-fraction of a second, I see her pain, her apology. "I'll be right back, honey."

I smile, trying to reassure her that it's okay. That *I'm* okay. That none of this is her fault.

Because it isn't.

She's only been gone a minute when another face reappears in the crack in my doorway. Meri's. "Can I come in?"

I nod and wipe the last few stray tears from my cheeks. She sits down, wrapping her arms around me, her sweet-pea-scented lotion working its palliative magic.

"Sorry about dinner," she says. "I honestly just figured you'd want some alone time. You haven't been by yourself since you left, right? Like, even to *pee*?"

"Nope."

"Man. And *I* complain when Mom busts into the bathroom while I'm showering to grab something."

I force a laugh, accepting her peace offering. "I honestly don't care if you go to the party, Mer."

She hugs me tighter. "Eh, Paul can fend for himself for a night. Probably needs a break from me, anyway."

We sit there for a few seconds, comfortable and quiet.

Finally, Meri pulls back. "Netflix marathon? You have so many shows to catch up on. Aren't you *so* lucky to have a sister who saved every must-watch for you on your profile?" She cups her hand behind one ear. "Can I get a *Thank you, Meri*?"

"Thank you, Meri," I say, feigning spite.

"You're the best sister ever, Meri."

"You're the best sister ever, Meri."

She's joking, of course. And that, I think, is what makes it hurt the worst.

CHAPTER 2

JOSIE

"Thought we should chat about next year," Coach Davis says, tapping a ballpoint pen on his palm and twisting back and forth in that vinyl swivel chair all the teachers have. The man can't sit still.

"You think?" I tease, which he deserves.

"Yeah, whatever happened to *procrastination is abdication*?" Sergio adds, and we exchange a smirk. It's one of Coach's favorite catchphrases.

It's the last hour of the last period of the last day of school, and the two of us have been begging Coach for a captains meeting for weeks now so we can make a game plan for the first half of summer. There's some CHSAA rule that forbids high school cross country coaches from doing any coaching until July 16, which means we're on our own until then. We're not even supposed to call ourselves a team – it's a "summer running club," in case anyone asks, which they won't because it's cross country and no one gives a shit. It's really up to us, the captains, to make sure the team gets enough mileage in to be ready for speed training once bona fide practices start.

I've been chomping at the bit ever since the announcement about Plain City moving into 5A – the same division as Aspen Ridge, the high school cross country equivalent of the Jokic-era Nuggets, minus the fact that they're a bunch of snobby white girls. Barbies, the kind that come with the dreamhouse and the pink convertible and all the ridiculous accessories. Except we're in Colorado, so what I really mean is ski lodge and Subaru and Patagonia gear.

People I meet at big races always think I'm making it up when I say I'm from Plain City. Not the part about me being from there, but that it's an actual town. I mean, I get it – a name like that doesn't do itself any favors. The guy who came up with it, some Scottish (Swedish?) pioneer turned beet farmer, was no doubt referencing how flat it is, but the other definition of plain works just as well: The cow-to-human ratio is about five to one, the cornstalk-to-human ratio is about five *million* to one, and the biggest news story since I've lived here was when they put in the stoplight at the corner of Center and Main.

What's funny to me, though, is that Plain City is to Denver what Denver is to the rest of the world – a bunch of Podunk nobodies.

It's a fact my father, who is dead to me, reminds me of often. Which I guess is a big reason why I still proudly claim this shithole town.

"Speaking of next year, check this out," I say, pulling out an issue of *Runner's World* from my backpack. Mom got me a subscription last year for Christmas, and the front cover of the latest issue had me shrieking so loud Mom ran into the living room wondering whether someone had been murdered.

Five girls in baby-blue uniforms, arms crossed and heads cocked unnaturally to the side, smile up at us. "*It's a Team Thing*" is stamped in cursive lettering across the front.

Of *course* Aspen Ridge would get featured on the front cover of *Runner's World*, wearing smiles I've never seen on any Aspen Ridge runner in real life. Truthfully, I've always felt gratified by their surliness. They might be able to steamroll everyone, but they never seem to be having fun while doing it.

"Hey, Jo?" Coach says.

"Have you read this? I mean, *obviously* Aspen Ridge is the top-ranked high school team in the country," I say, ignoring him as I flip to the article. "Nike *flies* them to national meets. If we had that chance, we'd turn heads too. Listen to what Coach Hendrich says." I make my voice go all pompous 60-year-old man. *"The reason we've been able to be so successful is because of the culture of excellence we've built here. The kids who come to us know they can achieve more than what's available to them on a local or even state –"*

"Jo," Coach interrupts, more firmly this time, and I suddenly realize I don't like the look on his face.

"What?" I ask. "Don't tell me they changed their minds about letting us into 5A."

Even though Plain City High School is in the middle of nowhere, we're not actually that small of a school since everyone from all the farm towns within a 30-mile radius gets bused in. Consolidation, I guess they call it. It takes an hour to drive from one side of the school boundaries to the other. We've actually had the numbers to be in 5A for years, but they must have thought we couldn't hack the competition because of our demographics, which is a fancy word I happened to learn in Coach's history class last semester.

And proving people wrong might just be my favorite thing.

Coach shifts. Stops twisting in his chair, tapping his pen.

I freeze. Sergio and I exchange another glance, but neither of us are smirking anymore.

"Did I ever tell you my wife is from Denver? Never wanted to live in a small town."

My heart starts pumping ice.

Coach's lips press together in a thin line. "She's going to apply for graduate school this fall. There aren't any opportunities for that out here. My in-laws have offered to help out with the kids as we ... you know, make the transition."

"But you love your job." I regret the words as soon as they come out of my mouth. They sound so ... desperate.

His eyes gloss over. "I *do* love my job, Jo. But I love my family, too. They've made a lot of sacrifices these past few years for me to chase my coaching dreams. It's time for me to make some of their dreams possible, too."

I feel Sergio's gaze on me but don't return it this time.

Coach clears his throat. Continues. "I'll still be around this next season. The application process doesn't start until fall, and it'll take me a year or so to line up another teaching gig. I considered waiting until after State was over to tell you, but I didn't want you to feel tricked, like I was keeping this a secret. I want the team to be as prepared as possible for the transition."

Sergio sighs and brushes his dark hair from his eyes. "Man, Coach. Not what I was expecting. Cool, though."

For being one of the fastest boys on the team, Sergio's never been one to put up much of a fight. A bit *too* nice, in my opinion.

Coach looks at me, clearly waiting for my blessing.

Which I refuse to give.

He leans forward and rests his elbows on his desk. "I'm sorry if this took you off-guard, but I don't think it's as big of a deal as you might be thinking. You'll both be juniors this season – two more years and you'll be moving on, too. And whoever they hire as my replacement will probably be 10 times better than I am, anyway."

"Oh, right. Because people are lining up for miles to move to *Plain City* so they can coach *cross country*," I say with as much acid as I can muster. "You've told us a million times what the program was like before you took over. That they had to *beg* teachers who'd never run a day in their lives to

11

coach the team."

"Might be different now. Look what they'll be inheriting. You guys have built yourselves quite the reputation." His calm makes the ice in my veins start to boil. "Besides, I'm sure you'll both have college scholarships already lined up before this year's out. I promise, Jo, time's going to fly. One season is the blink of an eye."

"Then why can't *you* stick around for just one more?"

I'm fully aware that I'm being unreasonable. That asking him to stick around until the two of us graduate implies we're the only people he cares about on the team. I might as well be asking him to lock a garbage bag of banana peels in the closet for a year and dump it on my younger teammates instead.

He shakes his head, exasperated but also wearing that tiny smile he gets whenever I'm being stubborn. Which is basically all the time.

I might be a pain in the ass, but it's why I'm the fastest girl he's ever coached. Top 10 fastest of *any* runner, boys or girls.

The bell rings. My sophomore year of high school is officially over, ending in the shittiest way possible.

He takes a breath, opens his mouth to speak, but I don't give him the chance.

"I'll send in the summer mileage reports," I say, avoiding his eyes as I stand.

"Jo –"

"Have a great summer!" I say with fake enthusiasm.

I don't wait for Sergio. Don't turn around as I reach the door.

"See you in July," he calls after me.

Yeah, I think to myself as an idea begins forming in my mind. The tiniest flicker of hope. *See you in July.*

CHAPTER 3
CAT

"Let's just go over for like 30 minutes," Blythe says. "I swear we'll leave if it starts getting weird."

I'm sitting on the chenille rug in Blythe's bedroom, looking through her earring box as she tries on her fourth outfit. I'm trying not to seem annoyed, but this wasn't what I (or Mom, I assume) had in mind when Blythe invited me over for a girls' night. I wonder if Mom would even let me hang out with her anymore if she knew Blythe was the one who casually suggested I try purging.

"Matt will be there," she says in the same voice you'd use to bribe a three-year-old to pee in the toilet.

"Me and Matt aren't a thing anymore. We never *were*."

"Whatever, you guys kissed."

"Only because he found out I've liked him since fourth grade and he knew I was an easy target."

She sighs. "Sometimes you just have to get back on that horse and ride, Cat. You're going to have to face everyone at school, anyway."

"Just *try* to understand how it would feel to face the entire grade after all this, B. Everyone knows. They probably think I'm crazy."

She rolls her eyes. "No one thinks you're *crazy*. And anyways, so what? There's a very fine line between crazy and intriguing. Come on, you're overthinking it."

I'm not convinced. But because Blythe always wins, clear back to the first grade, when she convinced me to hide a kitten under my bed (*"I promise, your mom will never find out"*), a few minutes later we're walking down a dark road, past the train tracks, into Kelli McGillis's backyard. It smells like camping and mosquito candles, and way back in the empty field behind her house I see about 30 people silhouetted against the orange light of a bonfire.

Every muscle in my body tightens, but there's no backing out now. Blythe grabs my hand and pulls me forward. "Come on. Everyone's going to be so happy to see you."

It only takes me about two minutes to figure out why she was so eager to come. Tyler Hicken is practically drooling all over her, alternately tickling her sides and sticking a stalk of hay into any gap he can find between her skin and clothes. She keeps swatting him away but it's so annoyingly obvious that she likes it. I guess he must have broken up with Amanda Ostler. Or if he hasn't, they'll be broken up as soon as she hears about this.

As for all the people who were supposedly going to be "so happy" to see me, they're glued to their phones, avoiding eye contact like I'm a foreign exchange student no one wants to get stuck in a conversation with.

The thoughts start creeping in faster than I can reason them away: *Way to permanently screw up your life, Cat ... Everyone's judging you ... You'll never fit in anywhere again.* In some ways, the thoughts are like old friends, familiar and easy, slipping into place like well-worn jeans.

Eventually, Blythe must notice how miserable I am. She shakes Tyler off and links arms with me. "Just be yourself," she whispers.

Funny how she doesn't seem to realize "being myself" is precisely the problem.

Like a puppy, Tyler follows her over and puts his arm across her shoulders. His attention momentarily shifts from her to me, eyes growing wide with realization. "Wait a sec ... whoa. You just, like, disappeared last year."

Blythe swats his arm, this time not so playfully.

Sure, Tyler and I have never been BFFs, but I sat right behind him in English in seventh grade and let him cheat off me on the bell quiz pretty much every day. Not only that, but I know his middle name, his football jersey number, and that he got a Remington hunting rifle for Christmas two years ago.

Perhaps more humiliating than everyone knowing where I've been is the possibility that no one has even noticed I've been gone at all.

I turn away from them and head back toward the road. Blythe jogs to catch up. "Cat, Tyler's an idiot. I swear, everyone's been asking me when you'll be back, and –"

She stops talking when we see the outline of a boy and girl walk around the house, hands held. Even in the darkness, I instantly recognize the boy's wide linebacker shoulders, his crop-cut hair.

Matt.

Matt, with Chelsea, a pretty blonde who has gone out with at least half of the boys in our grade. They almost walk straight past us, but at the last second Matt does a double-take.

"Didn't know you were back," he says. Chelsea glances back and forth between us, clearly confused as to why he'd be speaking to me.

"Yeah, a few days ago," I say, forcing a smile.

"Oh. Cool."

"Yep."

"Well, guess we're gonna ..." He motions to the fire.

"Yeah, sure."

As soon as their backs are turned, I lose the pretend smile and continue toward the road.

"Okay, I am *so* sorry," Blythe says, keeping pace. "I had no idea they're going out."

"It doesn't matter. I just want to go home."

She sighs dramatically, grabbing my arms. "High school wasn't supposed to be like this, Cat. I need my best friend back."

"Looks like you've been doing just fine without me."

And I mean it. While I've been gone, Blythe's social status has clearly been on a steady incline. She made the freshman cheer squad, which was especially weird since she got to be mentored by Meri. And ever since I've been home, she's been talking nonstop about people we never really hung out with before I left for New Horizons. It's almost like I was the leash holding her back.

She slaps on her famous puppy-dog eyes, the ones I know are going to get her out of so many speeding tickets someday. "Don't even say that. You know I've missed you like crazy. I just wish things could go back to the way they were again."

"But that's just it," I say. "Things *can't* go back to the way they were."

Blythe is basically allergic to taking things seriously, so the look that takes over her face catches me off-guard. For a second, I forget she's driving me crazy. I see the girl who taught me to tie my shoes and waited next to me in the skating rink when I broke my arm. The one person alive who knows all my secrets.

She just becomes B again.

"Cat, I didn't mean ..." she says quietly. "I would never say anything that ..."

I pull her in for a hug, mostly so she can't see the tears filling my eyes. "It's not your fault. I don't blame you."

When we break apart, she grabs my hands. "*Real* girls' night tomorrow, okay? And I promise, no sneaking off or anything."

"Deal. Seriously though, Tyler *is* an idiot, B."

"Maybe. But a *hot* idiot." She flashes me a sly smile. "Come on, I'll walk you home."

"I'm fine. Just call me tomorrow."

I'd probably be scared to walk home alone in the dark if I hadn't done it almost every night of my life since I was seven. If either of us isn't at home, our parents just assume we're with the other, knowing we'll come back when we're bored or hungry or tired. Not much to worry about in a place like this. It'd be a little harder if either of us lived on a farm or acreage on the outskirts of town, only accessible by highways and dirt roads, but both our families live in one of the few actual neighborhoods in Plain City. Takes me five minutes to get from my house to hers. I could do it in my sleep.

The moon is just coming up over the mountains in the distance, and other than the early summer crickets, it's dead quiet. The perfect setting for a little my-life-is-a-pathetic-nightmare ruminating.

I'm just crossing through the park off Center Street when faint voices and the pattering of footsteps break the silence behind me. I turn around to see the outlines of a dozen or so figures running down the road toward me. I'd call it a stampede, but in reality it's more like a flock of birds, swerving in unison to the right and left, shape-shifting like an amoeba.

As they cross under a lamppost, I realize it's a bunch of shirtless, mop-headed high school guys, laughing and joking around like they're enjoying the whole thing. Some unfathomable Friday night leg-powered joyride.

Whenever I used to run, I did it for the pain, did it because I hated doing it. Punishing myself was the point.

The boys don't seem to notice me as they pass. I watch until they disappear back into the darkness, until the silence once again reminds me just how lonely I am.

CHAPTER 4

JOSIE

I must take too long to get my locker cleaned out because Ziggy leaves without me. Surprise, surprise.

It's whatever. I probably would have walked home anyway. I'm feeling fragile and shaken after the bomb Coach just dropped and I'm not sure I can handle the scent of Ziggy's car (think: warm, rotten death) or his best friend Vinnie's incessant phallic jokes or their death metal shattering my eardrums. Or, worst of all, Ziggy's casual cruelty.

One more year with the douchebag.

I exit out the gym doors, which spits me out in front of the soccer fields.

Big mistake.

The memory floods my mind: summer break, two years back, the morning of soccer tryouts. Mom pulling the car alongside the curb, squeezing my knee, saying she was proud of me no matter what. Me, scoffing, knowing she was only saying it because she didn't think I had an actual chance of making the team.

And I knew I could. That I *would*.

I believed back then that my invisibility was just a side effect of being in middle school. That as soon as people my age finally grew out of their shallow pettiness they'd stop judging me by my hand-me-downs and our double-wide trailer. That they'd start seeing my true potential.

I'm smart, you see. Smart, and driven, and gritty as hell.

I was the girl in elementary school showing up the boys

out on the field during recess. The girl lapping everyone during the mile in PE. The girl who once ran 15 miles to Bald Mountain just because Ziggy said I couldn't.

Soccer was my passion, but Mom couldn't afford to put me on a comp team, so I did AYSO until they couldn't get any more parents to volunteer to coach. After that, I'd hang out at the park and jump in any pick-up game that formed, then spent three or four hours a night practicing skills in the field next to our trailer park. Not ideal, but I figured if I worked twice as hard as everyone else it would make up for my lack of formal training.

And I killed it at tryouts. Came in top five on all the sprints, made a spinning heel kick goal right in front of the head coach. I was stronger, faster, more accurate than 90 percent of the other girls.

So two hours later, when they taped up the list of the girls who'd made the first round on the front of the locker room door, I couldn't understand why my name wasn't on it.

They'd already started the second round when I walked back outside, my Goodwill cleats in one hand and Ziggy's old football duffle slung over my shoulder. Two full hours remained until the time I'd told Mom to pick me up ("There's no *way* I'll get cut before the second round, Mom"), so my options were to call her or do the walk of shame past everyone who'd avoided the ruthless blade of the first ax already scrimmaging out on the field.

And I couldn't bring myself to do either.

So I just sat on the steps and stared out at the girls in their shiny new cleats and perfect ponytails, high-fiving and calling each other by ridiculous pet names. They'd been playing together since kindergarten, maybe even before that, their tickets punched with their parents' money.

I didn't even realize I was crying until I heard a voice behind me.

"You all right?"

I wiped my eyes and whipped around to see a middle-aged guy with a scruffy, gray-speckled beard and a pen behind his ear. Based on his T-shirt and joggers, I figured he was one of the assistant soccer coaches I hadn't seen yet.

"It's *bullshit*," I spat at him, not even caring if it got me referred to the administration for another school counselor intervention where they would no doubt try to adultsplain to me how to *"be in control even when the world feels out of control."*

"I outplayed all those girls," I said.

His eyes went from confusion to sympathy. And as he turned his gaze out toward the field, I somehow knew that he understood.

"You know," he said, looking back at me, "I'm scouting athletes myself."

**

There's no one out on the field today. I walk almost painfully slowly along the perimeter, kicking pebbles through the diamond-shaped holes in the chain-link fence.

For most people, saying goodbye to a coach probably isn't that big of a deal. The soccer girls have probably been through a dozen or more, once you factor in club teams and all the different layers of high school – freshman, JV, varsity.

And if Coach were only a coach to me, this probably wouldn't be a big deal to me, either.

But he's not.

And this isn't just a team.

The anger that's been slowly climbing my spine like a fuse finally reaches the mortar. I wind up and kick a fist-sized rock so hard it gets lodged in one of the holes, leaving the fence trembling and clanging against itself.

Him leaving isn't an option.

Which is why I have to convince him to stay.

Forget how the team is like family – how he's filled in the gaps in all our lives, helped us face our parents' messy divorces and our small-town bullies and even our family members' deaths, once or twice. All that aside, Coach is a *competitor.* And I know that in all his years of coaching, there's one goal he hasn't yet accomplished.

Winning a state championship.

Coach grew up like me. No money. No dad around. Nothing but his own perseverance to get him where he wanted to go. It's one reason he's worked so hard to build this team here – an emphatic middle finger to all the people who've been doubting him his whole life, telling him he won't succeed.

So if there's anyone who hates Aspen Ridge and their Nike warm-ups and national ranking and pretentious *look at the dynasty we built* bullshit more than me, it's Coach.

And if we can do the unthinkable, get ourselves on the front page of *Runner's World,* there's no *way* he'd be able to walk away.

There's time for making his wife's big-city college dreams come true.

It just can't be next year.

CHAPTER 5

CAT

We're sitting on the bottom left corner of the football field bleachers, waiting for the graduation to start. The administration reserved the spot just for our family, since it has a wheelchair ramp and is out of the sun. It's a nice day – low 70s, no wind – but even so, Penny is doing her I'm-not-happy cry, and I don't blame her. I sometimes fantasize about how glorious it would feel to be able to scream at the top of my lungs whenever I feel like it.

Finally, the principal – an extremely nerdy bald man who unfortunately always sounds like his nose is plugged – comes to the microphone. "Welcub, freds and fabily of the Plade City High School graduadig class!"

It's actually pretty remarkable this guy survives being surrounded by teenagers every day.

After a few more barely intelligible remarks, a slideshow begins to play on the white screen that's been set up over one of the endzones. The very first photo is one of Meri in her cheer uniform, waving her pom-poms at the camera. After a few more cheering football crowds and couples dressed up for some dance, she's back again, flashing that perfect smile. I wonder how many brokenhearted boys are currently being tortured in the crowd. By the time it's over, I think I've seen her 20 times – at the state science fair, in her tennis gear, the moment she and Michael Mitchell were crowned prom king and queen ...

It's no secret that my sister is the goddess of Plain City High School.

In the movies, the popular kids are always mean – shoving people into lockers, knocking down their lunch trays, torturing their little sisters. Meri missed the memo on all that, I guess. I mean, sure, she'd never pass up the opportunity to embarrass me in public, and she still makes semi-discreet kissy faces whenever we run into a boy from my grade. I'm not saying she's a *saint*. But I could have done a lot worse for an older sister.

Part of that, I'm sure, is that she's genuinely a nice person. But another part is circumstantial. When Penny was born, we lost Mom. Not literally, of course; I mean that there just wasn't enough of her to go around anymore. And as we all transitioned into this new dynamic, our new life, Meri naturally began to fill in the gaps.

She knows full well that I need her, that I rely on her more than most people do their older sisters. Which, in some ways, I think I resent more than anything. Like, sometimes I almost wish she were catty and self-absorbed.

Because it would have made it a whole hell of a lot easier to watch her drift away, out of my life.

**

An eternity later, after an off-key choir performance and a few droning speakers, the principal starts reading names. *"Thobas Abbot ... Verodica Arrigtod ... Becky Aslad ..."*

Penny moans like one of those life-size Halloween decorations. The people around us try, and fail, to suppress their irritation, offering pitying smiles, which Mom deflects with her own well-practiced sorry-not-sorry face.

My brain is mush by the time we get to the S's, but I catch a second wind when they call Meri's name. I'm certain it's not my imagination that the cheering is louder for her than anyone else.

When it's finally over, we go to the big wolf monument in

front of the main entrance of the school to meet her. Meri and her friends hardly even acknowledge us – they're too focused on posing for pictures for one another's phones. Eventually, she does look our way, but Mom says, "Take your time," even though I can tell Dad's getting antsy. Meanwhile, I try to focus on the inanimate objects around me so I don't catch the eyes of anyone from my grade who's also there waiting around for a sibling.

When she and Paul finally make their way over to us, I realize I don't remember ever seeing her so happy. It surprises me; I guess I assumed she'd be at least a *little* sad to leave all this behind.

Her kingdom. Her dynasty. *Us.*

"Picture!" She pulls us together. "Paul, here, take it for us."

He takes the phone from her hands. "A little to the left, Mrs. Shultz. Cat, crouch down next to Penny. Perfect. Now, everyone say … 'Peace out, PC!'"

I smile as big as I can.

**

We eat dinner at The Prairie Mill. It's the fanciest restaurant in Lyman, which is the next city over and technically still a glorified town, but at least they've got a Walmart. Everything tastes like it's been soaked in 10 gallons of butter. I barely make a dent in my steak, and discreetly drop my roll underneath the table.

When we get home, it's time for presents and pie before Meri heads off to the big graduation party, an all-nighter PC's student government puts on every year at the civic center.

I give her the lame blue mug I made at New Horizons because I have no money to buy her anything else. She says she loves it but I can tell she's just being nice.

Mom and Dad give her a phone, a used iPhone a few

generations back but still an upgrade. She thanks them profusely until Dad finally says, "Don't you got somewhere to be? You only get one high school graduation night."

Meri practically jumps out of her chair, as if she's been waiting for their blessing to get the hell out of there. Mom and Dad watch her race down the hall, eventually remembering I'm still at the table.

"We were thinking you could have Meri's old phone, Cat," Mom says as she starts gathering our pie plates. I only ate a few bites, but I've done a good job of spreading the remnants around so it looks at least half gone.

I remember when Blythe got a new phone for her birthday last summer. I was insanely jealous. Now, though, I don't know what I'd even *do* with a phone, even though I'm the only 15-year-old alive without one. I have no friends to text, and I already know me and social media would be a bad combination.

"You're going to need it once school starts up and you start getting involved with clubs and all," she adds.

Ah. Those proverbial "strings attached."

The upcoming school year and its accompanying activities, or lack thereof, is a daily topic of conversation. It's no secret Mom believes "getting involved" is the key to success and happiness. My lack of interest in any sports or clubs or musical groups has always been a touchy spot for us, and though she'd never say it, I think she blames my introversion for my eating disorder.

The problem is I'm not like her or Meri.

"I ran into Mr. Edwards in Lyman last week," she continues, clearly undeterred by my eye-rolling. I'm about to say something glib about how it's a wonder Mr. Edwards is still alive (which is remarkable, considering he was *her* drama teacher at the old high school however many eons ago), but I decide on a gentler approach. "I'm just not into acting and all that, Mom, remember?"

"He says they're doing *Oklahoma!* for the fall musical this year."

Oh, please, no, I think to myself.

"Well, you never know until you try. Might surprise you what you get out of it." She puts one hand on her hip, directs a playful smirk toward Dad.

I can predict the soliloquy that's brewing, could probably even chant along verbatim, as if it were my story to tell.

Which I guess it sort of *is,* in a way. Would I even be alive if it hadn't happened?

The extremely short version goes like this: Dad, Plain City's resident rebel-without-a-cause cowboy, was madly in love with Mom, the Meri of the class of '98. Delusional with love, he signed up for the school play just to be close to her, then worked his tail off to land the role of Curly when he found out the two of them would get to kiss. Yada yada yada, the whole harebrained scheme worked, and they lived happily ever after.

Ish.

Being real, though, it *is* sort of the perfect love story, if it weren't about my parents and therefore inherently disgusting.

Luckily, I'm saved from hearing it for the thousandth time by the creak of the front door opening. We all know it's Paul, who doesn't even bother knocking anymore.

His voice echoes through the kitchen. "Ready, Mer?"

Mom and I follow Dad as he pushes Penny's chair into the living room. Meri, in a sparkly top with a short white skirt, has already met Paul by the stairs. She looks stunning, her red hair falling over her shoulders in loose, perfect curls. After a couple minutes of small talk, Dad sends them off with a final "I know where you live, buddy" pseudo-joke that poor Paul has probably heard a thousand times since he and Meri started dating. When the door shuts, everything is quiet. Dad goes back into the kitchen to finish the dishes; Mom pushes Penny's chair into the bathroom to begin their nightly routine.

I head to my room and lay back on my bed, my thoughts fluttering between all the unknowns of high school, Meri leaving for college, Blythe and Tyler. There's the unmistakable feeling of change in the air – which is what I want, what I *need* – but right now it's hard for me to see where I fit into it all.

Before I know it, my body is jerking awake, and I'm hit with that fuzzy feeling you get whenever you accidentally fall asleep and aren't quite sure who or where you are when you wake up.

The glowing red numbers on my alarm clock help me get my bearings: It's 10 minutes to midnight. I debate between going back to sleep and getting up to brush my teeth, but ultimately decide on neither. Instead, I go to the window, pull open the latch, and climb outside. The roof shingles feel like sandpaper on my bare feet, and the May wind whips my hair in tangles and sends goosebumps up my arms and legs.

Midnight roof escapades were Meri's idea, back when we shared this room. It was the day after Penny was born, 10 weeks earlier than she was supposed to be, and between her abnormal development and prematurity, the doctors gave her a 20 percent chance of surviving. Grandma Lynn, who – bless her heart – I'm not totally convinced ever actually raised kids, came to stay with us. It was July Fourth, and Meri and I both begged her to take us to the city park to see the fireworks just so we could feel a *tiny* slice of normalcy, but she fell asleep watching *Matlock*. So instead, we climbed on the roof with a package of Oreos and a handful of Otter Pops and watched the fireworks from there. After that, we'd come out at least once a week, playing cards, watching for falling stars, hypothesizing about the mysteries of the universe.

At least once a week … until Meri started high school.

It wasn't intentional; she moved out of my bedroom and into the basement, which naturally made spur-of-the-moment rooftop visits more difficult. And then, of course, she got busy with friends and activities and Paul. We'd find spare nights here or there, make plans ahead of time, but the magic waned as I began to feel, more and more, like she was doing it as a favor.

Tonight, I've been out on the roof for less than five minutes when headlights cut through the darkness and a car pulls into our driveway. Not until it's parked do I realize it's Paul's green pickup.

I scoot myself back up toward the window, wanting to get inside before they see me, but Meri's voice floating out the open truck window stops me.

"You know what I'm saying is true, though …"

"Oh, do I?" Paul says, sharper than I've ever heard him talk to her before.

"It doesn't have to be like this."

"Are you kidding me? Yes, it *does*, Mer. It's all or nothing. You *know* that. I can't do anything else."

She climbs out and shuts the door. I don't know if I've ever seen her look so defeated. So broken.

Without another word, Paul revs the engine and speeds away.

She disappears beneath the eaves, onto the porch directly beneath me. I listen for the sound of the front door opening and closing but hear crying instead.

I again consider sneaking back inside – the last thing I want is for her to think I was intentionally, and quite literally, eavesdropping – but I can't bring myself to leave her like this.

"Meri? You okay?"

She comes back out onto the driveway and looks up, her tears reflecting off the moonlight. "Save me a spot up there."

Two minutes later, the window slides open behind me. She sits down and holds out a package of Red Vines. She's no longer crying.

I take one with no intention of eating it. "Great party, huh?"

"It actually was. Until Paul and I broke up."

Even though I just saw the whole thing, hearing her say the words out loud still sends a jolt through me. The two of them have been best friends since sixth grade, and when they finally started dating sophomore year, it seemed like all of Plain City was cheering them on. The perfect small-town high school couple – football captain, head cheer-leader, straight-A students. Nice people, on top of all that. Their eventual wedding has basically been an inevitability ever since. Paul calls me and Penny his "kid sisters," Blythe regularly comments on how adorable their future babies will be, and Mom makes random comments about how hard it will be to go from having Shultz as a last name to Kowal-czuk. Even Dad, despite all his fake threats, tolerates Paul.

"How did it … I mean, *why* did he …?" I don't even know what to ask.

"It was me. Well, I guess technically he was the one who casu-ally dropped his offer to play at CMU. I just suggested maybe we should take a step back. Slow down a bit. He said …" She stops herself. "Well, you heard what he said. All or nothing."

"But you could still call each other. Come home and meet up on weekends." I feel myself getting hopeful as I say it. Maybe I won't totally lose her after all.

But she shakes her head. "We'll be four hours apart; it'll be too hard. Anyway, I know Paul, and he's going to meet other girls. Even if he denies it now." She hugs her knees to her chest. "And if I'm being honest with myself, I know I'm going to meet other guys."

I've envied her and Paul for as long as I can remember –

29

the way they can laugh about nothing together, the look she gets in her eyes whenever he walks into the room. "But you guys are perfect."

She doesn't answer. We watch the stars for a bit, then finally she lets out a small, wistful laugh. "Remember when the window jammed and we couldn't get back in?"

I smile. "And that time we jumped off into that huge snowdrift?"

Then, like she's been reading my mind for the past 12 hours, she says, "This is always going to be home, Cat. No matter where I end up."

"I know," I say, even though I don't.

"Promise me something, 'kay? If things start getting bad again, call me. Won't matter if I'm in class, or at a party, or making out with some hot college guy …" She bumps my shoulder playfully. "I'll answer and find a way to help."

We haven't talked about my eating disorder, not ever. I feel a mixture of relief and shame, and ask myself, for the billionth time, why I couldn't have been born strong and talented and confident like her. Why I felt I needed to resort to something I knew all along was bad for me and would hurt the people I love.

"I promise," I say, grateful the darkness is hiding my face.

CHAPTER 6

CAT

If I had to sum up the last year of my life in one word, it would be this: shame.

I'm not talking embarrassment or regret, not referring to the normal, "whoops, screwed up again" feeling I'm sure most normal teenagers feel every day.

Eight months ago, I almost made myself disappear. There's a jagged scar on the back of my scalp that reminds me every time I wash my hair.

It was intentional, and it was an accident. A cry for help, and a way to tell the universe, and everyone in it, to leave me alone.

Most people don't know about purging disorder. Less intriguing, perhaps, than its better-known cousin, bulimia – no secret bags of Cheetos stuffed under the front seat of the car, no disappearing boxes of donuts. Just the paralyzing, obsessive fear of food, and a willingness to do just about anything to keep it out of my body.

I will forever be grateful to New Horizons for saving my life, but once I started feeling like myself again – or, at the very least, *human* – I was more than ready to leave. But coming home has been harder than I ever expected. There, everything was controlled and monitored: I ate the snack that arrived at precisely the same time each afternoon, knew exactly how many calories would be in dinner each night. Had a therapist and a nutrition coach basically at my disposal. Support groups each Monday and Wednesday night, which, as much as I secretly judged the other girls and their city girl sob stories, helped me feel at least a little less insane.

And I'm realizing how naive I was in thinking the transition back to real life would be seamless. That being surrounded by the people I love would be enough to ground me.

I *want* to be home. Want to stop causing Meri and Blythe and my parents grief and pain and worry. Want to be a normal 15-year-old girl.

Which is why I feel myself start to panic when I'm doing normal 15-year-old girl things – shopping for school clothes, watching TV on the couch, undressing for a shower – and a familiar, haunting voice, at once quiet and shrill, starts whispering once again in my ear.

**

A week has passed since graduation. Meri is putting on a brave face, but we can all tell she's hurting after the breakup. She overcompensates by going into a mad frenzy she calls "getting ready for college."

I'm in my room when I hear a heavy thud against my door, followed by a quick knock. "Just went through some more stuff. Take a look and see if you want any of it," Meri calls from the other side.

This is the third box of hand-me-downs she's given me to look through. I open the door and haul it into my room, dumping the contents on the floor: a few shirts, a pair of white Reeboks, a flannel backpack with some empty three-ring binders covered in ballpoint pen doodles.

I pull a small wooden box with a rose carved into the top from the pile. It's full of jewelry. I sort through the necklaces and earrings and bracelets, most of them gaudy and cheap looking, but one small charm on a metal chain – a silver wolf, chin raised and howling – catches my eyes. I pick it up and join the clasp behind my neck.

I go to Meri's room. She's sitting on her bed sorting through stacks of pictures.

"Did you mean to put this in the box?" I lift the charm away from my neck to show her.

She nods. "It was from Hazel. She gave one to the whole squad last year after she decided not to come back from maternity leave. A goodbye present, I guess."

"You don't want it?"

She shakes her head. "I doubt I'd ever wear it again. Looks cute on you, though. Maybe it'll bring you good luck now that you're *officially* a silverwolf."

I was already harboring the superstition that if I wear Meri's stuff, the universe will get confused and start sending me some of her cosmic energy, so I thank her and, of course, keep it on.

I go back to my room and keep sorting through the pile. Most of the stuff is already pretty worn out, but I hang up what's salvageable in the closet and toss the rest in a pile so Mom can donate it to the Goodwill in Lyman. When I get to the white Reeboks, I turn them over in my hands a few times, deciding to discard them since the most athletic I get these days is walking from my bed to the living room couch.

But I'm stopped by a memory: me, sulking in the darkness as I walk home from Kelli McGillis's party a few weeks ago, the herd of rail-thin, way-too-cheerful boys running past.

I push the thought out at first. After all, running was what started this whole thing. My gateway drug, so to speak. At New Horizons, they warned us that people recovering from eating disorders sometimes substitute exercise for starving or purging, and that it can be just as dangerous. Sometimes even more so.

I even remember fighting with Mom about my running habit back when my parents knew I was struggling with disordered eating and body dysmorphia but thought that with a few heart-to-heart conversations they could turn the boat around. Before they realized it was already sinking.

But with my demons, undead and restless as I gain back a few medically prescribed pounds, something has to be done, and I can see only two options: Tell my parents, or figure it out on my own. And the thought of going to Mom, who is helping Meri get ready for college on top of all she has going on with Penny – after all she's *already* done for me – seems beyond selfish. Borderline narcissistic.

I have to learn to live with myself at *some* point, don't I?

It's just jogging, I tell myself.

I slip on the shoes and tie the laces. Tiptoe into the hallway, spying Mom in the kitchen stirring something over the stove. I'm certain I can make a clean break outside until I hear Mom's voice as my fingers touch the doorknob.

"Where you headed, Sis?"

Despite my best rationalizing, the pit that settles in my stomach validates what I know deep down: Mom would never approve. She'd say I need to give my body and mind more time to heal before starting up any new "healthy habits," especially ones that got me where I was in the first place. I can picture her response now, head cocked, a rueful smile on her face. *"It's just too soon, honey."*

"Just … outside." I meet her eyes, which are full of guilt-inducing sincerity.

"All right, well, dinner's in an hour or so."

"I'll be back in."

I step out and shut the door behind me. It's the kind of early June afternoon that hasn't quite decided whether it's spring or summer yet – warm sun, cool breeze that seems to blow the heat off before it can soak into your skin.

I take a few steps down the driveway but can't bring myself to go any farther. Mom could come out looking for me at any time. Could be watching from the front window.

I drag myself back to the porch swing and sit down, letting my legs dangle as I rock back and forth.

It's not that I'm doubting my idea. In fact, the more that I think about it, the more certain I am that burning off some of this anxiety with a little mild exercise is not only okay but necessary, even. The next step in my healing. It's just that I don't want to give Mom and Dad any more cause to worry. I want to be able to make this choice on my own, to prove to them – and to myself, if I'm being honest – that I can handle it.

If only there were some other way.

If I'm going for discreet, mornings are really my only opportunity. Dad leaves for work around 5 a.m. and Mom and Meri sleep in until at least 9 – Meri because she's usually been out late with friends the night before, and Mom because she gets up four or five times a night to help Penny. The thing is, though, Mom and Dad's bedroom is right next to the front door, and the hinges creak like a police siren. There's no way I could sneak out without waking her up.

I keep swinging, staring aimlessly around the yard, soaking in the fresh new green, the blooming flowers. June, the month when everything roars back to life after the long winter, is my favorite time of year. Leaves sprouting, clematis vine starting the ascent up Mom's white trellis –

Mom's white trellis.

I jump off the swing, backing up onto the lawn until I can see the juncture where the trellis meets the roof. *My* roof.

Of *course*.

I know it will hold because that time Meri and I locked ourselves out of the window, we climbed down that trellis, laughing the whole way, so we could get the spare key out of the garage. Meri even used it to sneak out a few times.

The butterflies in my stomach start flapping their wings right as a real-life monarch flutters past my face.

It's a sign. I'm sure of it.

**

When I wake up the next morning, thanks to another Meri hand-me-down – a digital watch with an alarm that I figured would be less ear-splitting than the alarm clock on my dresser – I'm significantly less thrilled about my "brilliant idea." Still, I force myself out of bed, eyes half closed as I pull on last year's PE clothes and lace up the white Reeboks. As stealthily as possible, I slide open the window and climb outside.

The breeze that hits my face is like a much-needed shot of caffeine. I tiptoe across the roof, then grab hold of the trellis, trying to avoid stepping on Mom's clematis plant as I climb down. When I get to the bottom, I freeze, waiting for a door to open, for someone to call my name, but all I hear is the rooster squawking in my neighbor's back pasture.

I walk to the end of the driveway and stop again, looking behind me to check for any faces peeking through blinds.

They hang still, undisturbed.

I head north because it's the opposite direction from the high school. Yes, it's early, but it seems like there's always something going on at the fields – soccer tryouts or football practice or cheer camp. For a variety of obvious reasons, I don't feel like having an audience.

My goal is to make it to the stop sign and back – half a mile, three quarters max – without stopping.

Since there are no sidewalks on our street, I hug the edge of the pavement and do my best to stay out of the weeds growing like a hedge outside the shoulder lane. After only a few hundred feet, my legs feel heavy and I have a sharp pain in my side.

There are three houses between me and the stop sign, with a couple hundred yards between each. *Just make it to the closest one*, I coax myself. I do, then tell myself the same thing with the next house. Then the next.

It takes me way longer than it should, but I finally make it. The spit in my mouth has turned into cement and I can hear my heart pounding inside my head, but as I turn around I can see Dad's prize walnut trees in the distance, beckoning me home.

The way back is just as painful, but with the end in sight, it seems more manageable somehow. When I pass the mail-box of our next-door neighbor, I pick up speed, driving my burning legs forward and swinging my arms like a half-delirious boxer.

Ten strides from our property line, I hear a car behind me, and I cut into our yard just as a red beater passes with a honk. It's impossible to know if it was a friendly "hello" honk or an "out of my way, idiot" honk, but either way I'm too tired to care. I collapse on the lawn beneath the trees, staring up at the blushing sky through the branches. Sweat pours off my face, stinging my eyes and making my lips taste like potato chips.

I look over at the house. The blinds are still closed. No signs of life.

I turn my gaze back up to the tree branches, lying still as my gasps subside, my sweat cooling until it is indistinguishable from the morning dew.

CHAPTER 7

JOSIE

The first practice of the summer, I'm up before the sun.

Mom doesn't usually get off from the drugstore until midnight and there's no way in hell Ziggy would wake up early to drive me to practice, so I run there. Might seem ironic to run to cross country practice just to do *more* running, but I actually don't mind. It's roughly three miles – a decent warm-up and 15 extra miles a week I can add to my mileage chart. Plus, I like the time to be alone, to clear my head. The team is great and all, but they're not exactly what you'd call "chilled out."

By the time I hit the road, the June sunrise is creeping over the horizon, turning the sky the color of a ripe peach. There's something sort of magical about observing the plants in the farm fields each morning, noticing how much they've grown in one day's time. Like you could almost sit and watch it happen if you were patient enough.

I've been taking it pretty easy the past two weeks to recalibrate after an intense track and field season – I took fourth in the mile and second in the 3,200-meter at the state meet, not terrible – so it feels amazing to finally be able to burn off some of my pent-up energy. At this point, running almost feels more natural than walking. My body's default setting.

As I jog into the high school parking lot, I see 10 or so terribly parked cars crisscrossing over the neat white stall lines painted onto the asphalt. I can't help but smile. A miniature revolt – our own little way of flipping off the world.

I jog over to the huddle of girls, ignoring the immature outbursts coming from the boys who have gathered a few yards away. A dozen eager smiles greet me.

I'm not exaggerating or trying to brag when I say I built this team. I have a gift, see, for noticing people the rest of the world doesn't: the quiet girl in PE who isn't breathing hard after running an eight-minute mile; the shy new move-in with legs that could have been designed by Nike; the skater chick, the very personification of potential energy.

The common denominator is that all of them knew the sting of being invisible. All I had to do was invite them to join our little Island of Misfit Toys.

Of course, none of this would have happened if Coach hadn't invited *me* to practice after the soccer tryout fiasco. It's like some magical spark was lit that day, a flame that keeps burning as long as you feed it.

And I guess that's the heart of the problem: Coach is the one holding the candle.

"Yo," I say, taking the space they've created for me in the circle. "Where are the –"

I'm interrupted by the guttural sound of a car on the verge of breakdown. I turn to see a red sardine can on wheels putter into the parking lot.

"– freshies," I finish, smirking.

The freshies, a quintet of girls from farming families, are the real reason we placed second at State last season. Tough as nails, they've spent their entire lives working their asses off from sunup until sundown.

Lucky for us, they were looking for a way out of afternoon farm chores.

The car parks and they jump out of the car.

"No *way* they gave you a driver's license," I tease Lucy, the oldest of the bunch.

"Technically, it's a permit," she says, "but what's the

difference?"

"No one's safe with you guys on the roads."

"Can't call us freshies anymore, Jo," Millie, the team's unofficial court jester, says. "We're sophomores now, remember?"

"You'll always be the freshies to me," I say, bumping her shoulder with mine.

More people trickle in. The boys hurl a few playful insults at us; we toss some right back. Jack, Millie's counterpart on the boys' team, pulls up blasting some early-aughts indie band out his open windows. Pretty soon everyone's dancing, laughing, tossing a Frisbee around. It's fun to see everyone happy, and necessary because it's what keeps people coming back each season.

But also, we've got work to do.

"All right!" I yell. "Gather up!"

I climb on top of Lucy's car and take a seat on the roof. Sergio eyes me quizzically, but I return it with a look that says, *Trust me.*

"Last year was huge for Plain City Cross Country. Second place for the girls' team, the highest this school has ever gotten in any sport." Everyone claps and cheers, but I see a few boys covertly roll their eyes – we've been rubbing our second-place finish in their faces ever since State. "And moving up to 5A this season, we're looking at another big season. The stakes are higher. The competition faster. But the silverwolves are gonna rise up, 'cause that's what we do."

There's more applause. I make my face stone serious. "But there's something you all should know."

Sergio flashes me those eyes again, but I ignore him.

"This is Coach's last season."

There are gasps. Inaudible chatter.

I keep going. "Now, Coach is the one who saw potential in us when no one else did. He's the one who pushes us day in and day out to be our best, to set our goals high, to never give up until we've reached them. I mean, he's ..."

More of a father to me than my real dad.

"He's done so much for this team. And we have to win State this year. For *him*."

People nod, and my confidence snowballs. I've always kicked ass with team speeches.

"Now, Aspen Ridge isn't just another team. At the girls 5A state race last year, all five of their scorers finished before most other schools had a single runner across the line: 1,2,5,6, and 9, for a total of 23 points. *Twenty-three*. The lowest in Colorado cross country championship history. But the truth is they're fast because they're *spoiled* – meals prepped by nutritionists, their own private trainer, a Nike sponsorship that gets them free gear none of them actually need. But you know what? I've never seen any of them smile. Maybe they can afford to wipe their asses with dollar bills, but they don't have heart. And I would give *anything* to show them what heart can do for a team."

I've considered what I'd say to the team a hundred times since Coach broke the news to me and Sergio. What I decide to leave out, right now, at this moment, is the part about how if we can beat Aspen Ridge, the best team in Colorado, the best team in the *nation*, that maybe he'll decide to stick around.

It sounds more noble this way. I refuse to beg.

My teammates' faces are resolute. I see fire in their eyes.

"Reality is what we decide it is," I say. "From now on, we talk about this championship as if it's *fact*. As if it's already happened. But it can't just be in our minds. We're going to have to recruit big time. Find those secret weapons at PCHS – people no one's noticed before. I *know* they're out there. Our strength is our depth, so your job is to reach out to anyone and everyone you think might have potential. Go

41

door to door if you need to."

I take a deep breath, because the success of my plan hinges on how they receive what I'm about to say next. "But most importantly, we've got to put in the work. Push ourselves like never before. So we're gonna do seven miles today."

Seven miles on the first day of summer practice is insanity, but to my amazement, no one complains.

With my army behind me, we start to jog.

CHAPTER 8

CAT

I escape the house for a jog every morning that week, sneaking it in during that narrow window between when Dad leaves for work and everyone else wakes up.

It feels amazing. And just like I predicted, the voice in my head gets quieter, less menacing. By Friday, I barely notice it at all. Like I'm back to my pre-purging self again, or at least close enough.

I'm almost to the corner when I get passed by the same red car that honked at me on Monday. It brakes in the middle of the road, then reverses.

The window rolls down slowly. A girl with thick brown hair and sunglasses leans out. Four other girls, one in the front passenger side and three in the back seat, crane their necks to look at me. "You're running the wrong direction."

I wipe the sweat from my forehead with the back of my hand, hoping my shifting eyes are doing enough to convey my confusion. I have literally no idea who this person is or what she's talking about.

"Jump in," she says. "Practice starts in 10 minutes."

"Practice?"

"Cross country practice!" a girl with bright pink hair shouts from the back seat.

I know that cross country has something to do with running, but beyond that, I'm clueless.

"Oh, I'm not really a runner."

The driver lifts her glasses on top of her head. "This is the second time I almost killed you with my car," she says. "You're *obviously* a runner."

"It's not what it looks like," I say, still trying to catch my breath.

"You *aren't* running, then?"

"I mean, yes, I'm *running*. But I'm not a *runner*."

She smirks. "My name's Lucy. You a freshman?"

"Cat. I'll be a sophomore this year."

Her face lights up with surprise. "Hey, us too. Never seen you around. You go to PC? Or are you, like, homeschooled or something?"

"Something like that. Just for last year though. I'll be going to PC in August."

She eyes me quizzically. "Seems like I would've seen you around. You go to Carver Middle?"

I shake my head. "Radcliffe."

"Ah," she says, nodding in realization. "Radcliffe."

I can tell from her face exactly what she's thinking. I'm fully aware that Radcliffe is seen as the most uppity middle school around here, but I don't think that's necessarily fair. Sure, Dad does all right for money with his general contracting business, but it's not like we're rich or anything. Besides, pretty much all of our extra money goes to medical stuff for Penny.

Or medical stuff for *me*. I don't even want to think about how much it cost to send me to New Horizons.

"You?" I ask.

"Proud Brown Bengal, through and through," she says, holding a fist to her chest in mock reverence as her friends crack up around her. "Messing with you. Middle school blows."

If Radcliffe had an opposite, it would be Brown. It's the middle school where all the "troubled kids" come from,

44

though I'm living proof there are exceptions. I've heard Mom and Dad talk about it at our neighborhood's annual block party, the drug busts and TikTok vandalism challenges and lunchroom fights.

Another car pulls up behind her. "Hurry, before I piss someone off."

I open the back door and squish myself next to the three girls, stunned by her command and even more stunned that I'm obeying it.

The high school is just a three-minute drive from where she picked me up. Lucy introduces me to everyone: Bea, the tall redhead sitting shotgun; Alma, curly haired and compact; Sophia, with sparkling eyes, perfect teeth, and long black hair pulled into a ponytail; and Millie, the one with pink hair and a mouthful of braces. Based on the very passionate way they sing along to the radio for the rest of the ride – the car is so old there's nothing more than an old AM/FM tuner – it's evident they feel equally as chilled out as I feel awkward. Other than the 10 minutes I spent in Kelli McGillis's backyard, my social life has been basically nonexistent since I got home. Blythe keeps inviting me to stuff, but I have zero motivation to go to parties with her, especially now that I know she'll just be drooling all over Tyler the whole time. The last time she called, she told me the two of them made it to "second base" and I dry-heaved.

We pull into the parking lot, which is empty except for a few terribly parked cars and a couple dozen people in shorts and tank tops. "Come on," Lucy says, unbuckling her seat belt. "I'll introduce you to everyone else."

She takes me around to meet 15 or so girls, who offer me half-interested hellos, spouting off their names before any of them have a chance to sink in. The last has a tousled pixie cut and serious, coffee-colored eyes. "And this is Josie," Lucy says. "She's captain."

Josie is a sight. Tall, angular, imposing. Definition in her arm muscles that could rival half the football players in my grade. She sizes me up.

"Jo, this is Cat," Lucy says to her. "I almost killed her with my car while she was out running. Twice."

Josie's eyebrows shoot up. "*Who* signed your permit, Luce?"

Lucy ignores the clearly rhetorical question. "She's a freshie, like us. And by freshie, I mean sophomore, of course."

Josie meets my eyes. It's uncomfortable holding her gaze. "Welcome," she says. "Glad you came."

Didn't really have a choice, I think.

More people arrive, and soon they're all chatting and laughing about stuff I have no context for, giving me time to play fly on the wall. I recognize only two girls here: one with regrettable acne who I remember from my middle school PE class two years ago and a stringy-haired blonde I've seen around town, who I only remember because she wears mismatched clothing that usually features a unicorn or some other mythical creature.

I'm surprised I don't recognize more. I thought I'd been to enough of Meri's school events to recognize most people who go to PC, by face if not by name. But whoever they are, they clearly have lots of energy. It's not even 7 a.m. yet, and they're essentially having a dance party in the parking lot.

I glance over at the mass of boys congregating a few yards away. I assume they're the same ones who ran past as I walked home from Kelli's party – how many shaggy-haired guys can there be in Plain City who would want to spend a Friday night running? Inexplicably, they look even more gangly and stretched out in the daylight.

"Hey, Josie, where's Serge? Wear him out last night?" one of the boys calls out. The rest double over, laughing.

Josie rolls her eyes. "Let's warm up!"

Everyone starts to jog. I consider making a break for home – it's less than a mile away – but Lucy jogs up along-side me, smiling wide.

As we make the first curve around the side of the school, I'm acutely aware of the speed difference between them and my usual pace. I feel like I'm sprinting.

We all merge onto a narrow sidewalk, which forces the boys closer to us. "Josie and Serge, sittin' in a tree ..." one of them sings to a chorus of laughs and smooching noises.

"Grow up, dickweed," the stringy-haired, mythical-crea-ture-wearing girl shouts back, which momentarily stuns me. I barely hold my laugh in.

"Attagirl, Gretchen," Bea says.

We make it back to the corner of the parking lot and everyone starts stretching. I try my best to follow along. Millie, whose pink hair is already a disheveled mess, scoots next to me. "So, newbie, what's your fastest 5K?"

"5K?"

She laughs. "You have no idea what you just got yourself into, do you? That's how long our races are. Five kilometers. Three-point-one-something miles."

"Like, *every* race is that long? There's not different lengths?"

Her face takes on an *aren't you cute* look. "Oh, sweetie. That's track and field, in the spring. There's just one race in cross country." She must see the horror on my face because she taps my shoulder consolingly and adds, "You'll get used to it."

I'm trying to understand what would ever in a million years possess anyone to join this sport when a low hum pulls my attention to the entrance of the parking lot. A moped coasts over to the group and parks near the stretching boys. When the driver pulls off his helmet, a cascade of blond surf-er-boy waves falls to his shoulders.

"Cheeto!" the boys yell in unison.

"His name's *Cheeto*?" I ask Millie.

"Well, his real name's Charlie, but everyone calls him Cheeto," Millie says.

"Why?"

"Dunno. The boys are idiots and make up dumb nicknames for each other. Usually food or some random word from a song." She begins counting off on her fingers. "Let's see, there's Scorcho, Dewser, STD …"

My eyebrows shoot up and she laughs. "Super Tanner Dixon. Like I said – idiots."

Two other boys stand and belly-bump Cheeto/Charlie. He laughs and shoves them away. I can't help but notice the gaping armholes in his cutoff T-shirt exposing his biceps and chest. Cheeto, it seems, is one exception to the whole skin-and-bones thing. And not in a bad way.

I force myself not to gawk.

Josie gives a loud PE teacher whistle, which quiets the chatter. "Goat Run today. Little break after all the miles we put in this week."

Cheeto? Goat Run? A boy who tolerates (prefers?) being called STD?

"Who died and made you boss?" one of the boys shouts. "Serge is our captain, and we make our own rules."

"Sergio's bailing hay today, so by default, I'm in charge. But fine by me if you want to do your own thing. You make your own rules, we'll keep winning races. Including" – she shoots them a wry smile – "the state championship."

∗∗

There's no way in hell I'm going to make it three miles even if there's a rabid dog chasing me. So my plan is to minimize embarrassment. Stay on the outskirts, drop down to a walk when no one is watching. Maybe even run home, if I can lose their attention long enough.

"All right, ladies," Josie says as we start to jog down the road, taking over the whole left lane. "You know the drill. Someone starts falling behind, we circle around to get them."

Scratch *that* plan.

Everyone around me is chatting like we're on a nice, leisurely garden stroll while I feel like an astronaut with the empty light flashing on my oxygen tank. I wonder why I couldn't just have said no to Lucy. Passivity is one thing, but it's something else entirely to be complicit in your own kidnapping.

We turn left at the stop sign and onto a dirt road closed off by a green farm gate. One by one the girls climb over.

Josie catches my eyes. "Don't worry, the farmer's chill. We do this all the time."

I climb the rungs and jump to the other side. With everyone safely across, we start back into a jog along the dirt path, passing a cluster of slanted sheds pieced together with scraps of sheet metal and mismatched lumber. Beyond them, 15 or 20 brown goats look up at us with bored eyes, their jaws moving in slow, exaggerated circles.

At least the Goat Run mystery is solved.

The dirt path soon disappears beneath a carpet of knee-length grass, and we spread out, more bounding than running, leaving behind snake-like patterns in our wake. The field dead-ends at a creek bank, forcing us to turn right and run parallel to the water, pausing only when we need to climb over a fallen tree trunk or step around a bog. After a few minutes, the back of everyone's legs are speckled with mud.

I realize that between dodging trees and listening to them debate the ending of some new fantasy series on Netflix, I've forgotten how much my side hurts.

I hear the boys' voices just before they emerge from a

grove of trees on the other side of the creek.

"See, the boys talk a big game, but they still listen to you, Jo," Bea says.

"Yeah, well, they did Taog just to spite me."

"Taog *is* better," Millie says.

"It's the exact same thing!"

"Yeah, but the view changes when you do it in reverse."

Josie scoffs.

"Goat Run's about as scenic as it gets around here," Lucy says to me. "Gotta enjoy it when you can. We usually run Stink Dairy or Dead Deer."

"Dead Deer?" I manage to ask between gulps of air.

"The boys named all the runs," she says. "Stink Dairy goes right past Beutler Farms, and if you've ever been over there, well, you know how it got its name."

"And we literally found a dead deer on Dead Deer once," Millie says. "Don't worry, it's completely decomposed by now," she adds as if to reassure me.

We stop in front of a rusted metal pole about a foot wide laid across a farming canal intersecting the creek. I'm grateful for the break, but the relief is short lived – I realize we're stopping because we have to cross it. Which wouldn't be a *huge* problem, except that whatever's flowing in the canal more closely resembles split pea soup than water.

"Then there's the *type* of run we're doing. We've got names for those, too," Bea says as she starts to cross, clearly unfazed by the toxic sludge. "Goose chase is fun. Circuits are okay, depending on if they're timed and how many push-ups and crunches you have to do between laps. Fartleks, though …"

I look from face to face, trying to find some hint of suppressed amusement. "You're messing with me, right?"

"It's fart-*lek*, not fart-*lick*," Millie says, doubling over. I'm not sure how the single vowel change is significantly better, but I don't say anything. "Man, it's nice not being the newbie anymore."

"Don't forget intervals, Luce," Bea calls over her shoulder. She's already halfway across the pipe, her arms outstretched like a tightrope walker.

"No one's allowed to say the word 'interval' until Coach gets back in July!" Millie shouts.

I'm funneled into line between Millie and Lucy, hoping that balancing on the pipe is as easy as the girls in front are making it look. "There's so much to teach you," Millie says, looking back at me. "But right now, let's focus on the most important thing."

"Which is?"

"Never touch the pipe. Not with your hands, anyway."

"Why?"

Millie points to the boys, who are now stopped on the other side of the pole. Their T-shirts swing like tails from the back of their shorts, and a few of them have mud handprints on their bare chests as if it were warpaint. "These idiots think it's fun to pee on it."

Bea stops a few feet from the canal bank. "Out of our way, weirdos."

"Maybe you should get out of *our* way," says the one referred to as Scorcho, arms folded across his puffed-out chest. He's flanked on both sides by boys nodding in agreement. It reminds me of Peter Pan and the Lost Boys.

I'm expecting a standoff. Instead, his scowl turns into a mischievous smile. "You ladies in for a jump?"

Millie, still balanced on the pole, looks back at Josie like a kid begging for candy in the grocery line. "Pretty please? Think of how hard we worked this week."

"Yeah, we need to cool off," Lucy adds, even though it's not even 8 in the morning and we've been in the shade pretty much the entire time.

Josie rolls her eyes. "Fine. But you're all going to get a

parasite one of these days."

Much to my relief, Bea and Millie cross back over the pipe, saving me from a potential slime bath. The boys follow, some of them jogging across, fearless and surprisingly graceful. We backtrack through the trees together until Scorcho veers sharply to the right, leading us to a still section of the creek canopied with cottonwood trees so dense that hardly any sky peeks through. Hanging from one of the limbs is a rope with three knots.

Scorcho jumps in first, then two other boys. One of them tries a flip, his arms and legs flapping wildly in the air before landing in a belly flop. Even Josie can't hold back a laugh.

"What happened to ladies first?" Lucy says, taking the rope from another boy as he's about to go. Without hesitating, she jumps into the air, letting the momentum take her as far across the water as possible before she drops down.

When the rope swings back, Cheeto catches it and holds it out for me.

"I'm okay." On top of having absolutely no desire to jump in, it would be pretty hard to explain to Mom how I woke up with sopping wet clothes that smell like a fish tank.

A short boy with laughing eyes and a smile that takes up most of his face comes up behind him. "Come on, new girl. Live a little."

"She has a name, Jack," Bea says.

"What is it then?"

"Cat," I say.

"Cat what?"

"Shultz."

His smile broadens. "Shultz, huh? You Merideth Shultz's kid sister?"

I feel my cheeks get warm. Even here I can't escape Meri's shadow.

"Think you could get me a date?" Jack continues. A few

boys around start snickering.

Bea scoffs. "There is no way in *hell* Merideth Shultz would ever go on a date with you."

"Oh, yeah? Well, she probably hasn't seen this bod ..." He pulls down his basketball shorts, revealing chalk-white thighs and black boxers covered with red lips. The girls all groan in disgust while the boys double over, laughing. He takes the rope and does a backflip into the water, thankfully pulling the attention with him.

"You remember the streaker at the homecoming football game last year?" Cheeto says. It takes me a second to realize he's talking to me.

I shake my head. "Oh, no. I wasn't there, actually."

"Freshman?"

I wonder how many times I'm going to get asked that question over the next few months. "Sophomore."

He looks surprised, but thankfully doesn't inquire further. "Anyway ... it was him." He points to Jack, still flailing in the water, eliciting laughter and catcalls.

I make a mental note to ask Meri about it today. "Did he get in trouble?" I ask.

"Didn't get caught," he says. "Never does. They don't call it a Jack Attack for nothing."

Jack climbs onto the bank, the wet fabric of his underwear clinging to his legs like a second skin. "Can't really say I'm sorry I missed it," I say.

An adorably crooked smile crosses Cheeto's face. "Gotta find some way to entertain yourself when you live in PC, right?"

He grabs the rope as it swings back toward us, holding it out to me once again. Again, I shake my head. He shrugs, then glides over the water, jumping in with barely even a splash.

That's when I see Josie sitting on a fallen tree trunk across from where Cheeto was standing. Watching me. She looks startled that I've noticed her but smiles.

"You did good today," she says.

I figure she's just being nice. "If barely survived is good, I guess."

"You kidding? Most newbies end up a mile behind at their first practice. We didn't have to circle around for you once."

I'm not sure how much credence to give her compliment, but I say thanks. In the awkward silence that follows, I notice a ray of sun peeking through the branches. It has to be past 8 by now, and every minute that passes increases my chances of getting busted.

"I better get back. Chores and stuff."

"You remember the way?"

I nod. It's not the getting lost that I'm worried about so much as the jogging that whole distance over again. But at least I can stop and walk without feeling self-conscious.

I turn to go.

"Hey, Cat," she says. "Can we expect you back tomorrow?"

I've been so focused on surviving the morning that I haven't even thought about tomorrow. But just like with Lucy, there's something about Josie that makes me not want to disappoint her.

"Yeah. See you then."

CHAPTER 9

JOSIE

Since Coach can't actually coach us until mid-July, we developed a system for staying honest in our training by sending him our weekly mileage reports. Everyone who hits 500 miles by the start of the school year gets treated to a big steak grill-out in his backyard the day before the first race, which, this year, is also the first day of school. We call it the Five-Hundred-Mile Club. Last year it was just me, Bea, Lucy, and Sophia who got it on the girls' side, but I'm pushing to have at least half the team there this summer.

Keeping track of everyone's mileage is one of the captain's duties, but honestly I'd probably do it even if I didn't have to. I'm a numbers person. I like how straightforward they are. Words are too subjective, take too much guesswork.

I finish tallying Millie's report (complete with a spaghetti sauce stain and a corner ripped off, not surprisingly) and move it to the bottom of the stack. The name on the top of the next paper spurs an unexpected lurch in my stomach.

Cat Shultz.

I have nothing against Cat Shultz. Or at least I *shouldn't* have anything against her. She's been perfectly nice and has done all the workouts without complaint. In fact, for being new at this, as she claims, she's running at a pretty remarkable pace already. As in could be a factor on varsity.

Which, if I'm being honest with myself, is the problem.

I don't know the Shultz family personally. But I do know her sister, Meri. Know *of* her, I should say. I also know they live in one of those newer neighborhoods with garages bigger than my entire house. They're one of the established families who've been in Plain City for generations, the kind of people who get elected to city council and run the PTA and invite each other to their smarmy Christmas parties. And I also know that these people, as good as their intentions might be, don't seem to realize that *other* people live in Plain City, too. That sometimes single moms lose their job and are forced to shoot out applications for every available pharmacy technician position within a 50-mile radius, and the only one that works out is at a drugstore in the middle of their nowhere town, forcing the entire family to move against their wishes.

So no. I don't have anything against Cat *personally*. But it just feels like ... like she's changing lanes. Like she could play anywhere she wants on the whole damn playground, and we have this one lame set of monkey bars, and I just don't get why she feels the need to play on them, too.

The phone rings, loud and obnoxious, from the front room, where Ziggy and Vinnie are playing some slasher video game.

Zig and I share Mom's old phone, which basically has to stay plugged in at all times or it'll die. I hardly ever use it, anyway. The only place I go is practice.

It rings again.

"Turn off the ringer!" I yell.

It rings again. Then again.

I storm out of my room and squeeze between the coffee table and the couch, maneuvering myself around their legs, which are blocking my way. Ziggy's eyebrows furrow as he cranes his neck to look around me, as if I'm the one inconveniencing *him*.

"Douchebag," I say. I go to hit reject, but stop when I see who's calling.

Dear Old Dad.

We saved him as that in our contacts to be ironic, of course. He's not dear, and he's not that old. He and Mom had us when they were way too young to be procreating.

I glance over at Zig, noticing the crunched-up beer cans peeking out from under the couch. They've been less and less discreet about their drinking the last couple months. Vinnie's dad straight-up buys it for them. Mom has tried to put her foot down, but ... it's complicated.

I know we'll just have to call him back anyways – Mom always makes sure we do – so I click accept and put the phone to my ear, trying to swallow my irritation. "Hello?"

"Jojo!"

"Dad." I say it just like that. Not as a question. Not as an exclamation. Just a statement of fact.

Yes, you are my father. No, I'm not happy about it.

Ziggy finally stops playing and looks over.

"How's it going over there?" the disembodied, blood-chilling voice says.

Few things annoy me more than the way Dad refers to Colorado as "over there." As if it's some foreign place where he didn't live for 26 years of his life.

"Oh, you know. Good." It's a constant balance trying to make sure he knows we are fine without him while at the same time making sure he doesn't forget that he ruined our lives.

"Good, good," he replies. "Hey, is Junior there? Why don't you put me on speaker?"

Spoiler alert: Ziggy's real name isn't Ziggy. It's William Junior.

And he will seriously mess up anyone who calls him that.

William Senior – or as I like to call him, the person who supplied the other half of my DNA – lives in New York City now. He left five years ago for a job interview and never came back. What started out as *can't quite afford to move you all out here quite yet* became *keep an eye on the mail for those divorce papers.*

Mom still thinks he'll come around. That he'll get tired of big city life and come back to us.

I catch Ziggy's eyes. He narrows them and shakes his head, and I shrug as if to say, *What am I supposed to do?*

I turn on speakerphone.

"You there, Junior?"

Ziggy glares at me, teeth clenched. "What's up?"

"Hey there, bud." I'm validated, if only slightly, by the discomfort in his voice. "Just wanted to share some exciting news. Marigold and I are engaged!"

Ziggy and I don't agree on much these days, but right now I can tell we're feeling the same conglomeration of disgust, horror, and fury.

As if the moment couldn't get any worse, the storm door rattles and in walks Mom. Smiling, probably because she was excited to surprise us with the two boxes of Dominos carry-out she's holding.

The next moment happens in slow motion. Like a glass vase falling from a very high shelf.

It shatters before I even have time to reach for it.

"The wedding's going to be in September. I'm going to fly you both out here, get you out of that hellhole for a few days."

The smile disappears, taking with it the color from her face.

This tells me he didn't think it was important to tell the woman who still doesn't understand why he left, who is still *incomprehensibly* in love with him, the news before this phone call. Which reminds me, for the millionth time, that he's the douchiest douchebag of all time.

I end the call without saying goodbye. Take the pizza from Mom's hands, set them on the coffee table, wrap her in a big hug. Play parent to my broken mother, a role I admittedly hate but take on because I love her.

I'm surprised to feel other, stronger arms around both of us. The slight aroma of cheap beer doesn't even phase me right now.

Nothing quite like a common enemy to bring a family together.

CHAPTER 10

CAT

Two weeks in, and Mom and Dad still don't have a clue.

It's almost scary how easy it's been. Every morning is the same routine: Wake up, climb down the trellis, run to the school, run home, hide behind Mr. Dawson's hedges while I scan the yard, climb back *up* the trellis, throw my sweaty hair in a bun, and voila: I'm safe in my room, ready for the day to begin with a solid half-hour buffer between my parents and my secret.

So far, my plan seems to be working. My weight gain has plateaued. Visits from my ultra-loyal wraiths are growing fewer and farther between. I'm actually *hungry* sometimes, and can eat to satisfy it without driving myself crazy. I wouldn't go so far as to say I'm excited for practice in the mornings, but I don't dread it, either. It's not exactly the social scene I'm used to, but the cross country kids are nothing if not entertaining. The other day, Millie pantsed Scorcho in front of the whole team, which escalated to a bunch of the boys chasing around the freshies and trying to force them to smell their armpits.

Blythe, no doubt, would call them freaks.

The first couple days I was almost embarrassed by their odd rituals – spitting off Thompson Bridge every time we run past, hosting funerals for their old running shoes – but I have to admit there's something liberating about acting like a 10-year-old again. Most recently, they've been trying to teach me how to "banshee cry." Apparently, right before the final sprint at the end of every race, they all scream at the top of their lungs like madwomen. In theory, it gives them an extra boost of energy to pass competitors, but based on the facial expression of the old lady outside hanging laundry while they demonstrated for me, it's more likely the runners around them are momentarily paralyzed out of pure shock that someone would do something so weird in public.

But they're weird *together.*

That's their whole thing. Unity. Josie says it's the reason they've gotten so competitive against the bigger city schools. In a group you can work together, encourage each other through the tough parts of races. There's nothing worse, she says, than running alone.

The Wolfpack, they call themselves, like some secret mafia code name.

What I can't figure out is how it can possibly stay like this once the racing begins. Once they become both teammates *and* competitors. Only one person can win, right?

I remember watching some nature show a few years back. The camera followed an actual wolfpack around a frozen tundra in Russia as a British guy narrated a play-by-play of their lives. The animal version of *The Kardashians.*

The pack was so orderly. So human-like. Which is why it was so disturbing when the wolves in the pack suddenly turned on one of the members, sending him away, bloody and limping. According to the British guy, away to die.

I wonder: Are humans really that much different?

**

"Pizza and Frisbee tonight at Meadow Park in Lyman. 6:30."

Serge's announcement during stretches barely registers. Outside my illicit morning practices, I still haven't done anything social since Kelli's party. And as much as I find myself growing more and more endeared to these people, I wouldn't go so far as to call them my *friends*.

"You wanna go?"

It takes me a minute to realize Lucy is talking to me. "Oh, um … I've never really been that into Frisbee."

"Hold up, hold up. It isn't just Frisbee; it's *ultimate* Frisbee," Lucy says. "The nerdy love child of soccer and football. I can give you a ride if you want."

The freshies – the irrational collective nickname for Lucy, Bea, Sophia, Millie, and Alma, who are actually *not* freshmen – all turn to look at me.

I shake my head. "It's okay."

Millie pouts. "Why not?"

"I just …" I can't think of a good excuse without telling them an outright lie. Beyond not really feeling like this is my social scene, which would undoubtedly hurt their feelings, the truth is that if Lucy comes to my house to pick me up, my secret is out. How would I explain to Mom where I met a bunch of random high school kids?

"She's probably got her *real* friends to hang out with." Bea's face takes on the same expression as Lucy's did when she found out I went to Radcliffe. A look that says, *You think you're better than us.* Which, when I realize it's actually not that far from the truth, makes me feel terrible.

"No, it's not that …"

Suddenly, I have an idea.

"Could you pick me up here at the school? My parents are weird about me riding in cars with teenagers." Probably not far from the truth, either. "But, like, I totally trust you."

Their faces light up. Millie cheers.

Lucy smiles. "I'll swing by here at six."

**

Mom doesn't ask too many questions when I tell her I'm going with Blythe to a party. Even though I've been eating and generally less on edge than usual, I've basically been a hermit. And as much as I don't really want to go tonight, I realize creating some semblance of a social life is part of proving to her that I'm better. That she doesn't need to worry about me anymore.

I walk over to the school and wait on the curb, keeping my head down in case I'm spotted by any potential informants. I don't have to wait long before I hear the honk of Lucy's car. Music blares from the open windows.

"Jump in!" Lucy calls. "Sorry, you'll have to share seat belts."

I squeeze in, trying not to imagine the look on Mom's face if she knew what I was doing.

"Sorry about the smell," Lucy says. "Today was my turn for stable duty."

Away from the rest of the team, without all my energy focused on trying to keep up, I'm finally able to observe the dynamics of the freshies' friendship. So far, I've had the most interactions with Millie and Lucy, since they're the most outgoing. Millie is a shock jock in the best way, the kind of person you want around when you're feeling down and need a pick-me-up. And Lucy is the unofficial mother hen of the group, the oldest and most mature, with a natural confidence that exudes in everything she says and does.

Sophia, Bea, and Alma are more reserved, but I think I'm slowly figuring them out, too. Sophia is the Disney princess type, generous to a fault and either oblivious to her good looks or just really good at pretending to be. Alma seems to be the peacemaker, happy as long as everyone is happy, too. And Bea is the most like Josie: tall, serious, intimidating. I'm not saying I'm scared of her, but I'm certain I don't want to get on her bad side.

When we get to the park there's already a group gathered under the pavilion. I hardly recognize anyone without their sweaty workout clothes – at 7 a.m., with everyone having *literally* just rolled out of bed, there's an inherent uniformity to how we all look at practice.

Tonight, I get to see everyone's "true selves." As to be expected, Gretchen is wearing a sparkly unicorn T-shirt, and Becca, the poor acne-covered bookworm I also recognized on the first day of practice, looks completely different with her hair curled and a little makeup on.

Then Scorcho drives up in his beat-up SUV. When he steps out, I almost laugh. He's dressed almost entirely in black. A handful of earrings line the perimeter of his right ear, and one of his nostrils is adorned with a tiny silver ring. The goth vibe is unexpected, but when I think about it, it totally makes sense.

He pulls out a stack of Little Caesars pizzas from his back seat while everyone fishes out crumpled dollar bills from their pockets. I'm glad I didn't think to bring any money since it gives me a reason to turn down the slice that Jack tries to give me. There are still some foods I just can't stomach.

"You don't want pizza?" Jack says, clearly shocked.

"I didn't bring any cash."

"Psh. No one cares, just take a piece."

"It's okay."

He shrugs. "Suit yourself, new girl."

The pizza disappears in a matter of minutes, leaving behind a nauseating stack of empty, grease-soaked boxes.

"All right, let's get the game going," Scorcho yells. He and Serge start yelling out names, and it takes me a few seconds to realize they're picking teams. I prepare myself to be one of the last, and I'm not wrong. It comes down to me and a mousy girl who I assume must be an incoming freshman.

Scorcho looks between us and sighs, as if deciding between scrubbing the toilet and changing the litter box. "I'll take Little Meri Shultz."

I jog over, trying to brush off the nickname as Scorcho begins spouting off instructions. I don't understand most of what he says, but luckily Lucy and Bea, the two girls Scorcho chose first, break down the rules for me. It seems simple enough: You're allowed three steps forward with the Frisbee, a drop is a turnover, and a catch in the endzone equals one point.

Playing, however, is less simple.

Before I know what's happening, the Frisbee is whizzing back and forth on the field, sometimes so fast I lose track of it. The boys on the opposing teams, who were laughing and playing air guitar together just minutes before, might as well be mortal enemies. There's shouting. Cussing. A tense argument about whether or not Jack intentionally head-butted someone.

Other than a few pity throws to the more athletic girls like Josie and the freshies, the game is 100 percent dudes only. I don't think anyone has even *looked* at me.

Finally, after Scorcho ignores Bea (who was wide open, waving her arms wildly in the endzone) and instead gets intercepted on a risky pass to Jack, Josie stops the game.

"Okay, this is ridiculous."

Scorcho rolls his eyes. "We'd pass to you *females* more often if you'd take the game seriously."

"That's bullshit and you know it."

"Oh, yeah? Well, if you think you're being so *underutilized*, why don't you prove it? Guys versus girls. And if we win, bitching about not getting passed to enough is eternally outlawed."

Josie looks around, meeting a few of our eyes. "What do we think, ladies?"

The rest of the girls don't even hesitate before congregating on one side of the field. The boys move to the other. Most of them are laughing in a *you asked for it* kind of way, but some look annoyed. "No women next time," I hear someone mutter.

Josie motions for us to huddle up. "Here's the plan: short passes, good defense on the cherry-pickers. They think this is going to be so easy they'll be throwing long. If we can avoid quick scores and wear them out on defense, we can totally take them."

We all nod, but I'm not sure how convinced I am.

"We need a totem," Millie says, looking around briefly before pointing to the wolf dangling from the chain on my neck. "Cat's necklace."

Josie's eyebrows raise in mild annoyance.

"We all have to kiss it," Millie says. "I mean, only if it's cool with you, KitKat. Also, it needs a name. Olga?"

I know it's mostly a joke, but I can't help but feel proud, both for my necklace's new nickname and my own. I'll take anything over Little Meri Shultz.

"I mean, it *is* lucky," I say, playing along.

"That settles it." Millie reaches over and brings the charm to her lips. One by one, the other girls follow suit. All except Josie, who just shakes her head like we're her obnoxious little sisters.

"Are you guys *making out* with that necklace?" Jack calls out, tapping the Frisbee impatiently on his thigh, waiting near the midfield line. "Could you get any weirder?"

"Only if we were more like you," Bea says as we break our huddle and scatter in front of him.

He rolls his eyes. "We'll throw off to you first, since we're *gentlemen.*" He bows dramatically, then tosses a high floater. Lucy makes the catch and passes to Millie, who drops it. The boys pick it up and score immediately on a long throw, just like Josie predicted. "Someone stay back near their endzone," she says as we regroup on the other side. "Distract them, break up their passes, whatever you can do."

Staying back and out of the way sounds just fine to me, so after the throw-off, I jog to the other side, watching the action from a distance. The girls up playing offense stick to Josie's plan, zigzagging down the field. Several of the boys converge on Millie, which frees up Bea to sprint to the endzone. Millie throws up a Hail Mary, and without anyone guarding, Bea bounds into the air for the catch.

"Got lucky," Scorcho says on the boys' retreat.

We throw off, and the boys seem more determined this time, as if Bea's score gave them permission to actually try hard. I tail Sergio, who seems to be their go-to for long catches. When I spot someone taking aim I sprint in front of him, waving my arms in the air just as the Frisbee is about to make contact with his hands. It hits my palms instead and falls to the ground.

Jack, breathless from his sprint to the endzone, gives me a slow nod. "Dang, new girl."

When the Frisbee makes its way to the backfield again, I'm ready. I stick with whoever's in the endzone, waving my arms in front of their faces and jumping to break up passes, only losing the *teensiest* bit of focus while guarding Cheeto.

The game continues, back and forth, until the sun disappears behind the horizon. Josie makes a catch that evens up the score, 10 to 10.

"It's getting dark," Sergio says. "Next point wins."

Millie throws it off, making it halfway down the field before Jack intercepts and throws a quick long-ranger to Scorcho, who I see eyeing Sergio in the corner of the endzone. I sprint over.

The Frisbee climbs above us, wavering slightly as if trying to decide which way to go. I know I can't outjump Serge, who is built like an antelope, but I stay in front of him, keeping my feet in line with his. When it starts to drop, I stick my arms up and leap into the air with everything I've got.

It happens so fast that the burning sensation in my hands doesn't fully register until I hear the high-pitched cheers and low-pitched groans around me. I'm too stunned to react for a few seconds, but suddenly Josie is motioning for the throw a few feet away. A baby toss, but I'm happy to get it out of my hands before I can mess anything up. Josie passes to Alma, who then throws another all-or-nothing pass into the endzone. It heads straight for Lucy, who fakes out a defender on the right, goes left, and comes up with the catch.

We race to the middle of the field, celebrating like we just won gold at the Olympics. Everyone hugs and high-fives, and I get a good share of the praise.

The only person who doesn't make it around to say good job to me is Josie. I try to shrug it off, telling myself she probably didn't even realize she'd missed me.

"Guess you all aren't going to be so cynical about Olga now, huh?" Millie says.

"You can keep kissing Olga all you want, Mill," Josie says, ruffling her hair like she's an overgrown puppy. "But we don't need luck."

CHAPTER 11

JOSIE

I know that right now is for building up base mileage. That if we push too hard before the actual season starts, we'll peak too soon.

But my legs are itching.

Just once, I tell myself.

"How does everyone feel about a time trial today?" I say as everyone's stretching.

Their eyes get big. "You're joking," Millie says. "It's not even July yet."

"Come on, it'll be fun," I say. "Once isn't going to hurt. Plus, it'll be good for the new runners to get a feel for the course and have a chance to practice their pacing."

Like Plain City generally, our home course is pretty boring. Two laps around the soccer field, across the street to the city park, up the berm, around the tennis courts, then finish on the track. Three miles of sheer boredom, unless you've got something to think about, like how close you can get to last season's PR.

"You're captain," Bea says. "We'll follow your lead."

I jog over to where the boys are stretching. "Girls are gonna race this morning. You guys in?"

The boys cheer. But as I'm heading back toward the girls, I hear Sergio call out my name.

He jogs over. "Coach said no tempo work until he gets here."

"It's just once, Serge."

"I don't like it. This is when we're supposed to be working on running as a pack. We have plenty of time to race each other once the season starts."

"No one's forcing you to join in. You're captain of the boys; do what you want."

He sighs, and I know I've put him in a tough spot. It's clear the boys are eager for some healthy competition, and Sergio backing out will make him look weak.

"One time, Jo. And if you try to pull this again, I'm telling Coach."

"Fine," I say, feigning annoyance. In truth, I'm just glad he's not going to out me for this.

**

We line up at the start. Twenty-three girls. Twenty-seven boys. Ragtag as we are, we're a sight all bunched up together.

"Remember, this is a friendly," I announce, still using soccer lingo even though I've all but given up the sport. Sergio's comments have started to sink in, and I don't want this to cause any early rifts that I'll have to explain later to Coach. "No pressure. Just do your best; work together like we've been practicing. That's what makes us the force we are, yeah? 'Wolf-pack' on three, ready?" I stretch out my arm. Everyone forms a circle around me, following suit. "One, two, three!"

Fifty hands shoot into the air. *"Wolfpack!"*

Those goosebumps. They never fail.

"All right, on your marks …" I yell.

Everyone crouches.

"Get set …"

Freezes in place.

"Go!"

**

It feels amazing to push as hard as I want, to hold nothing back. A nuclear reaction flowing from my core into my extremities. Every part of me feels the rhythm of my stride, like a broken clock finally ticking at the right pace.

I take the lead of the girls almost immediately. Sergio, Jack, and Cheeto fly ahead, but I'm fully aware I have no chance of beating the three of them. There are certain injustices built into human DNA that even I can't outwork or outsmart.

I'm on my second lap around the soccer field when I break the cardinal rule of running – I look over my shoulder – to see the freshies not 50 yards behind me.

Normally, this wouldn't bother me. They need to step up this year if we're going to have any chance against Aspen Ridge. Closing that gap is what we've been working for all summer.

But someone new is with them.

Cat.

Something snaps inside me, releasing a hit of anger, jealousy, fear – I'm actually not sure *what* I'm feeling, exactly, only that it shouldn't be there. Cat is my *teammate*. If anything, I should be thrilled to have a new asset on the team, someone else who stands a chance of challenging Aspen Ridge's varsity runners.

But I'm just … not.

I kick it up a notch, letting the bad feeling propel me forward. And as I'm circling the school for the last half mile, I allow myself one last glance over my shoulder to make sure I've put enough distance between us that even if Mo Farah were trailing he wouldn't be able to catch me.

The three boys who've already finished are cheering at the line. I surge as if it were an actual race, clicking my watch to stop the time. After a few big breaths, I check my wrist.

18:47.

I laugh. Only 10 seconds slower than my PR, which I got at State last year – 150 other elite runners pushing me and all the adrenaline my body could produce.

It's a good sign.

"C'mon, ladies, let's go! Bring it in!"

I look up to see the boys clapping the freshies in. Cat has fallen slightly behind, but after the five of them finish, they all join the cheering to help bring her across the line.

She's clearly pushing hard. Chest heaving, face contorted in pain. Her dark hair, braided in one long plait behind her back, swings behind her from side to side like a metronome.

I force myself to clap, too. "Let's go, Cat! Push all the way through. You look amazing!"

Truly, she does.

Fluid, rhythmic, graceful. Absolutely *killing* it, especially considering how recently she started running. I can't wrap my mind around how quickly her speed and endurance have developed. It wasn't until we were well into the racing season last year, months of training behind us, that the freshies started showing their full potential.

Cat finishes and laces her fingers behind her head, pacing in a circle.

More people start to trickle in. We all stand around and cheer until everyone has finished. It's Wolfpack code: Once you've finished running, you automatically become cheerleader until the last person on the team has crossed that line. It's not like any of the *actual* cheerleaders would ever come to a meet to cheer us on.

I go through the motions, clap and spur on and wave my arms like any good captain should, but out of the corner of my eye I'm watching Cat get high fives and congratulatory slaps on the shoulder, all the while telling myself what a miracle it was that she walked onto the team right when we needed her.

CHAPTER 12

CAT

The week before July Fourth is hot and sticky. Our mileage has been incrementally increasing since practices began a month ago, and today is my new record: eight miles without stopping. I'd probably be pretty proud if I could think of anything else right now other than how I'm about to die of thirst.

We're just about to run past Fuller's Market – our last possible hope for water until we get back to the school – when, much to my relief, Alma asks for a break.

At the last second, Josie veers us inside. "Better make it quick," she grumbles.

We're in line for a drink when someone points to a flier advertising the annual Fourth of July 5K race pinned up on the bulletin board behind the fountain. "A hundred bucks each to the top male and female runner," Sophia points out, her bright red nails tapping the flier. "All yours if you enter, Jo."

The Plain City Freedom Festival is the biggest – okay, the *only* – event the city sponsors each year. There's a parade, a talent show, and a Greek souvlaki dinner, which probably at some point had significance. It's got *obscure small town* written all over it. Every year, my family always goes to watch the fireworks at night – minus the week Penny was born, of course – but I've never seen the race. I don't think I ever even realized they *had* one. This is the first time in my life when I haven't lumped competitive running in the same category as disc golf and professional bowling.

"You guys know Coach's rules. No racing until school starts," Josie says.

"Think of the new Adidas you could buy with $100," Lucy goads.

Josie looks like she's going to say something, but Millie cuts her off. "We know, we know, Jo. *You don't need fancy shoes to be a badass.*"

**

We're on our way back to the school when Lucy pulls up beside me. "We're all gonna go sleep over at my grandma's in Colorado Springs and crash their big Fourth of July race," she whispers. "You should come."

"Crash their race?"

"Yeah. Just race without signing up."

"I thought Josie said –"

"Psh. It's a dumb rule. No one will find out."

"I don't think I'm ready."

"You hung with us at the time trial."

"Until I *didn't.*"

"You're way overthinking that. You did fine. *Amazing.* And anyway, it's just a glorified excuse to get out of Plain City and hang out in Springs for a night."

An uncomfortable pang radiates from my chest. Ever since the summer before fifth grade, Blythe and I have slept out on her tramp together the night of July 3. We paint our nails like little flags. String red, white, and blue beads onto necklaces. Light sparklers. Blythe hasn't mentioned it yet, I'm assuming because she has plans with Tyler.

But Mom and Dad don't know that yet.

I know that going with the freshies will require several layers of deception. That each element of the scheme – driving two hours with a girl who doesn't even have her license yet, sleeping at a random grandma's house with a bunch of high school kids I don't really know that well, and running in a three-mile race – has the potential to get me grounded for a month.

Maybe it's my buried loneliness talking, or the thought of Blythe spending our night with her village-idiot boyfriend, or the sudden awareness of how much of my adolescence I forfeited at New Horizons, but I suddenly realize how much I *do* actually want to go. "You're sure you want me to come?"

"What, you think you're our charity case or something?" she says, smirking. "Of course we want you there."

When my eating disorder first developed, I quickly learned that if I resisted food for long enough the hunger pains would go away. I guess my brain got tired of being ignored and would just stop trying.

Eventually, though, I'd have to eat something. And the moment food hit my tongue the pain would return, even stronger than before, as if all my organs were caught in a death match inside me, fighting for resources.

Turns out, there's more than one way to starve yourself.

**

I'm in my room packing my duffel bag when Mom peeks her head around my bedroom door.

"Why don't you have Blythe come here this year?" she asks, leaning up against my door frame.

"*Because*, Mom. She has a trampoline. And a firepit."

She gets a sad smile on her face. "Well, come home if you need to. We'll leave the spare key under the mat."

I feel an instant stab of guilt at all the ways I'm not being truthful with her. Heat rises up my neck, bringing with it a spurt of surprising courage. "I've been thinking about school and all that. What would you think about me, like, trying out a sport?"

My hope is immediately crushed by the expression on her face. "Oh, honey … I don't know. It would depend on the sport, I guess. Do they have a bowling club, maybe? Table tennis? Ms. Reid talked to us for quite a bit about signs to watch out for, things to be careful of. I think it's best to stay away from anything too intense for right now."

"Yeah," I say as my stomach twists into a thousand knots. "I get that. Totally."

She gives me an apologetic smile, which I try to return with the most understanding, genuine, trustworthy smile I can muster. If she only understood, I'm positive she'd feel different. I'm happier, healthier than I've been in years, doing exactly what she wants: getting involved, making friends, doing normal teenager things.

Minor deceit is all part of that, right?

I make a mental note to turn off location sharing on Meri's old phone.

**

Lucy picks me up at the school. Just like Frisbee night, I squeeze into the back seat with Alma, Millie, and Sophia – Bea claims her long legs entitle her to permanent shotgun status – and we head toward Colorado Springs.

Compared with Plain City, Springs is the Garden of Eden: thick aspen groves, meadows of wildflowers pinned against a stunning mountain backdrop, everything green and alive. Whenever I come with my parents, either accompanying them to one of Penny's appointments or supporting Meri at some regional school competition, we always make sure to plan a hike or a park visit or shopping at the Citadel.

Lucy's grandma, however, clearly lives in a *different* part of Springs.

Lucy drives to the outskirts of town, pulling into a neighborhood with tiny box-shaped houses, dandelion yards, and teenagers strutting around in hoodies even though it's 90 degrees outside. She stops in front of the driveway of one with peeling white paint and a window pane patched with cardboard and duct tape.

Knowing what they're already inclined to think of me – rich and privileged – I try not to show any signs of alarm on my face.

Lucy unlocks the door, and we carry our bags inside. The inside is decorated just like Grandma Lynn's house, with knickknacks and photos and slightly crooked crucifixes covering every inch of wall space, everything tinted with the same faded earth tones. It even smells the same, musty and ancient, except here there's a mouthwatering aroma of Mexican spices mixed in. The sound of feet shuffling on the carpet precede the appearance of a short, pillowy woman with permed gray hair in the entryway.

"*Abuelita!*"

All five girls rush toward her. She hugs them, pinching cheeks and squeezing their sides as she shoots off a string of melodic, rapid-fire Spanish. I smile, but can't help feeling like an outsider.

Finally, the old woman motions toward me, her gesture accompanied by a Spanish phrase I feel I should be able to parse.

"This is Cat," Lucy says, smiling back at me. "She just joined the team."

My stomach flip-flops. I haven't told them yet that I'm not actually *joining* the team. That this is just a summer thing; that I'm here because of a chance encounter that spiraled way out of control.

Her grandma eyes me suspiciously for a few seconds, then

breaks out in a wrinkly smile that shows in every inch of her face. She waves me toward her, pulling me in for the best hug I've ever had in my whole life.

"Come eat, *niñas*," she says, leading us into the kitchen.

We sit around the table as Lucy's grandma sets still-steaming bowls and plates in front of us. Black beans, shredded meat, sauteed vegetables, rice. Crumbly white cheese and corn salad. A stack of tortillas at least 30 high.

My stomach rumbles, but it's joined by a twinge of anxiety. One facet of my illness is an aversion to eating in front of people. I mean, I'll *do* it. I don't have a choice at home. Mom and Dad were instructed to record the food I eat in a diary like I'm diabetic or something, although they've kind of started to slip since things have been going well and I haven't made any sort of effort to remind them. But I definitely don't *enjoy* it. The best comparison I can come up with is how it would feel to pee in a public bathroom without any stalls. Like, sure, peeing's a necessity, something we all do to stay alive, but that doesn't mean it's not embarrassing.

Most of the time when food has been involved with the cross country crew I've been able to avoid causing any sort of scene – like the time at Frisbee when I didn't have cash for the pizza, or the donuts someone brought for after practice which I conveniently didn't have time to stay for.

Lucy passes out plates and the freshies dig in, making satisfied moans and licking their fingers. I know I can't outright pass on food without offending her, so I scoop tiny spoonfuls of each dish onto my plate and try to look as delighted as I wish I actually were.

But I don't fool Grandma.

"*¡Come!*" she commands. "*¡Eres demasiado flaca!*"

Lucy turns to me, not waiting to finish chewing her mouthful. "She says you need to eat – you're too skinny."

I blush, embarrassed that I'm failing this adorable woman and ashamed that I still can't help but take the phrase as a compliment.

I smile up at her, taking a big bite until she gives me a satisfied smile and turns back toward the stove to stir something simmering in a big pot.

"So what are we doing first?" Sophia asks between bites. "Devil's Cove?"

Everyone squeals.

Grandma turns around and issues something that I can only interpret as a reprimand.

"We'll be fine, *Abuelita*!" Lucy answers back. "We've been a million times!"

Grandma shakes her head as she turns back to the stove.

"What's Devil's Cove?" I ask.

"Oh, you'll see," Millie says with a look I don't like.

I force down as much food as I can, listening to their erratic conversation and laughing along, because with these girls it's impossible not to. I'm swallowing my final bite when Grandma sets a bowl of something white and steamy that smells like warm cinnamon in front of me.

"*Arroz con leche*," she says proudly, setting down five more matching bowls on the table, each of which could easily feed all six of us. "*¡Come, come!*"

**

The drive to Devil's Cove is steep and winding. Lucy parks on a gravel pullout 50 feet from two sheer curtains of granite. There's just enough of a gap between them to see a glassy lake below.

I feel myself relax. Just swimming, then. "How do we get down to the beach?"

Lucy laughs. "You don't come to Devil's Cove for the

beach. You come to *jump*."

I follow them single file through a gap in the chain-link fence, pretending like I'm not freaking out, but inside my brain is going a hundred miles per hour, trying to think of an excuse to bow out and wait for them in the car.

I come up short.

The hike to the cliff is short and steep. Even though I know my eyes are playing tricks on me, it feels like we're 500 feet in the air. No one else seems bothered. They're deep in a four-against-one conversation about some date Sophia had the other night.

"Did you guys kiss?" Millie asks.

"No!" Sophia says.

"Is he your *boyfriend* now?" Millie presses, teasing.

"He's not my *boyfriend*," Sophia says. "I'm telling you, it's not a big deal."

"Not a big deal? It's *Kyle Pelty*," Alma says. "I'll be lucky if a guy like that ever remembers my name."

The name Kyle Pelty sends a jolt of recognition through me. "You went out with *Kyle Pelty*?"

I know Kyle – or know *of* Kyle – because he went to Radcliffe, though he's two grades above me. He's essentially the Paul of that year: jock, perfect hair, killer smile. I'm not *surprised* he asked Sophia out – she's sweet and funny and gorgeous enough to be a model – but it does feel like some clique lines have been crossed here.

I don't know Sophia well enough to be torn up that she has a love interest, but I can relate to how the other freshies feel because of the whole Blythe-and-Tyler thing.

"What if you forget about us?" Alma asks as we stop at an outcropping. My whole body shudders when I look down.

"Don't be crazy," Sophia says, pulling her long hair into a smooth ponytail. "Nothing will ever come before my girls."

"Yeah, yeah," Millie says. "I doubt you'll be thinking of

your girls when Kyle's tongue is down your throat."

"Millie!" Bea scolds. "You're freaking disgusting!" She's the only one who hasn't said much. In fact, she seems a little annoyed with the conversation. "Are we just going to stand around, or are we getting in?" She strips down to her sports bra and running shorts, then leaps over the edge of the cliff without any hesitation.

"How is it?" Millie yells down, but she doesn't wait for a response. Alma jumps next, then Sophia. Which leaves me, Lucy, and a pile of shirts at the top.

"You gonna?" she asks.

I glance over the edge again, balling my sweaty hands into fists. "I mean, it's just so … high."

"It's not so bad once you're down there. The first time is definitely the worst." I feel her watching me as I continue to make mental calculations about the distance between the ledge and the water below. "But no pressure. We'll be climbing back up on those boulders over there. You could just hang out here and wait for us." With that, she disappears over the edge. There's a short scream, followed by a splash and more laughter.

I sit down and hang my legs over the side of the cliff. I know the freshies aren't going to shun me if I sit this out, and I like that about them. They couldn't care less about anyone else's opinion, and don't seem to harbor many about anyone else.

Whatever I have to prove, it isn't to them.

It's to myself.

With a deep breath, I stand up and peel off my shirt. Below me, the freshies cheer.

"She's gonna do it!"

"You got this, Cat!"

I close my eyes and start my countdown, which comes out in a shaky whisper.

Three. Two. One.

What shocks me most isn't the way my stomach seems to have its own out-of-body experience, or how three seconds of falling feels like 30, or even the frigid water that basically paralyzes me on impact. It's the involuntary scream that escapes my throat on the way down.

I'm no expert, but I'd say it sounds just like a banshee.

MILE TWO
CHAPTER 13
CAT

The night is perfect.

Ballpoint pen tattoos and skinny-dipping in the creek. Terrible choreographed dances and more laughing than I've done in a year.

"What do we think, girls?" Millie asks in a rare quiet moment. "Is it time to introduce Cat to Richard?"

The other freshies cheer as Lucy pulls a huge box from the closet and unlatches the lid. A mass of fabric springs from the top: pink chiffon, neon-green spandex, something sequined and shiny. An old VHS tape rests on top.

"There's no backing out now, Cat," Bea says jokingly, popping the tape into an ancient machine on the TV console. "This is it. Initiation."

"What is all this?" I ask.

"*This* is the remnants of my great-aunt Tina's glory days," Lucy says. "She's a middle-aged paralegal now, doesn't have any use for these gems."

She pulls out the green spandex fabric – a full-length bodysuit with sequins on the chest and stirrups at the ankles – and holds it up against her body.

"*Sweatin' to the Oldies* is girls' night tradition," Sophia says, undressing and pulling on a peach leotard and cheetah-print leg warmers. She tosses me something with multicolored geometric shapes. "Here, this is totally you."

Lucy pops in another tape, and the screen lights up with an aggressively happy curly-haired man in a tank-top and short shorts.

"Richard Simmons – a true legend," Millie says in her fuchsia sports bra-legging combo, which almost exactly matches her hair. "Who's ready to sweat?"

We shimmy and flash our jazz hands, shake our hips and grapevine until we're ready to pass out, both from the surprising intensity of Jazzercise and the accompanying fits of laughter. It's in the aftermath of this delirium, sprawled out on the living room floor, that I get brave enough to ask them about Josie.

"Does she ever hang out with you guys?"

Lucy shakes her head. "Jo's great, but she's so focused I don't think she hangs out with *anyone* outside of practice."

I swallow. Let out the real reason I brought her up. "Sometimes, I … I don't know, I get this feeling she doesn't like me."

Alma props herself up on her elbows. "Josie's going through some stuff."

The others nod in agreement.

"Like what?"

"Deadbeat dad. Single mom. Asshole older brother. You know, the usual."

I consider this, feeling a pang of sympathy for her. "You don't think it's me, then?"

"No way," Bea says. "You're basically an answer to her prayers. Coach Davis is quitting after this year, and she's got this idea that the only acceptable goodbye present is for us to win the state championship – which is gonna be impossible, because we'll be up against Aspen Ridge, and we're … well, you know. We're *Plain City*. But she's Josie. You do what she says, can't really challenge her. At the start of the season she kept going on and on about how hard we need to work and how many people we need to recruit if we're gonna pull it off."

This revelation startles me, like finding out someone was just being nice so they could cheat off your homework. "So that's why you wanted me to come to practice so bad that day."

"Maybe that first day," Lucy admits. "But that's not why we keep inviting you to stuff."

"Is it so hard to believe we want to hang out with you?" Millie teases.

A comfortable calm settles over me; the tricked feeling fades. The conversation moves on to other topics, but my mind keeps replaying Bea's comments about their coach leaving and Josie's determination to win the championship. Because I'm suddenly acutely aware that it's not going to land well when the team realizes cross country is just a summer fling for me. A glorified exercise plan.

I'm not *joining* the team. There's no way I can.

**

We don't fall asleep until midnight, so when Lucy's phone alarm squawks us awake at some ungodly hour the next morning, it feels a bit like being brought back from the dead.

"All right, ladies," Lucy says mid-yawn. "Race time."

"Screw the race," Bea says, cocooning herself farther underneath the blankets. Millie, somehow the only one who seems lucid, starts whacking her with a pillow.

"Okay, okay," Bea says, growling. "Take a chill pill, Mill."

"Chill Pill Mill," Millie repeats. "Now *that's* a nickname."

"Yeah, except it's the complete opposite of you," Bea says, punching her arm.

On the drive to the race, I consider faking a stomach ache, which isn't entirely false, but the freshies are acting like we're on our way to my own wedding. I can't back out now.

By the time we arrive, there are already at least a hundred

people gathered, some standing around chatting, some stretching or jogging in place. We park and file out of the car. Even though the sun is just barely peeking up over the horizon, I can feel the heat radiating up from the asphalt.

A few people are dressed in fancy workout clothes and expensive-looking shoes, but there are also saggy grand-mas and pot-bellied dads pushing strollers, small kids – the youngest looks like he's about five – and even an old man dressed in a cowboy hat and Levis.

Lucy notices me gawking. "I remember him from last year. Don't let him fool you. He's damn fast."

Everyone, except for us, has a race number pinned to the front of their shirts. "Are they going to get mad? That we're not, like, registered?"

"Nah," Millie says. "It's a public road. They can't stop us from running."

"Then why would *anyone* pay?" I ask.

Lucy's forehead crinkles up. "You know, it's a legit ques-tion …"

"What the –?" Bea says suddenly. I look up to see Cheeto and Jack approaching.

As if I need another reason to be nervous this morning.

Among the four confused faces, there's a single sheepish one: Alma's.

Everyone glares at her.

"Sheesh, sorry. Jack asked what we were doing today and I told him. I didn't realize he was planning to *stalk* us."

"Whaddup, ladies," Jack says, grinning.

The freshies all glare at him. "You can't tell Josie or Coach or *anyone* we're here," Alma says.

Jack rolls his eyes. "Yeah, duh. We'd get in trouble too, genius."

I laugh, hit with the absurdity of all this – while most teen-agers are revolting with sex and drugs and casual shoplifting, the cross country crowd runs forbidden races in secret.

It's adorable, really.

Could be worse, Mom and Dad, I think to myself.

Jack turns his attention to me. "First real race, huh, new girl? Well, first *fake* real race."

Millie punches his arm. "Her name's KitKat, dweeb."

"Ow," he says, rubbing the spot. "Isn't it you who always says nicknames are dumb?"

"It is when *you* make them up."

He scowls. "Whatever. What I really came over to say is" – he spins around, puts his hands on his hips, and starts twerking – "get used to this view, ladies, 'cause it's what you're going to be looking at the whole race."

The freshies converge on him, swatting him with their water bottles and throwing half-hearted punches. He fights them off, but it's obvious he's enjoying it.

I feel Cheeto's eyes on me. "Good luck," he finally says.

"Thanks. You too."

I feel awkward and unprepared for this conversation, for *any* conversation with him, so I'm grateful when a short balding guy walks by with a megaphone. "Runners, welcome to the Freedom Run! Please make your way to the starting line …"

The butterflies in my stomach become full-blown knots.

I try not to think about how much the time trial hurt. About the shame of falling apart at the end.

Just stick with everyone, I tell myself. *You'll survive.*

The freshies, on the other hand, seem about as far from nervous as you can get. Millie holds a pretend microphone to her mouth and starts singing "Eye of the Tiger" as we walk over to the red, white, and blue balloon arch. She holds her fist out to the rest of us. I laugh and swat her away, but Alma and Sophia indulge her, dancing to the imaginary beat.

Soon all five of them are in on it. They sound terrible – all of them in different keys, more shrieking than singing.

I have the same paralyzing sensation I get whenever Mom does something embarrassing in public, like yelling out at me from the car window after dropping me off at school or cleaning my cheek with her thumb.

But then I realize some of the people around us are clapping along. Millie turns around to face them, as if directing a choir. They're still dancing when the man with the megaphone gets back to the start line and calls us to attention, talking us through the course and reminding us to follow the cones and arrows spray-painted on the pavement.

"Runners, on your marks!"

"Hurry, everyone kiss Olga!" Millie says, reaching over, grabbing the necklace, and giving it a quick peck. Everyone else does the same, either ignoring or not seeing the quizzical look of the lady standing next to us.

When they're finished, I hold the charm up and keep it pinched between my fingers and lips until the gun finally goes off.

Runners spread out across the road. I see Jack and Cheeto up front, amazed at the pace they're able to sustain for three miles. The boys like to mess around, but they can bust it out when they need to.

We're right in the middle. I feel like we should be ahead of most of these people (currently, we're near a stroller dad and a very chesty older woman), but there's no way I'm going to push the pace. Soon we settle into a comfortable rhythm. With all the adrenaline coursing through my body, it actually feels good to finally be running.

It doesn't take me long to figure out the freshies' strategy. The mass of runners who darted ahead at the beginning of the race have now funneled into a long single-file line ahead of us. One by one we start to pass them, three of us on either side, regrouping once we're a few steps ahead. Like we're a 12-legged monster, swallowing them whole.

It feels ruthless and exhilarating.

At the first mile marker, I take a cup of water sitting on a folding table, splashing it on my face instead of drinking it. There are still people ahead, and I feel a sudden compulsion to close the gaps between us and them.

I glance around. Bea, Lucy, and Sophia still look strong, but Alma and Millie are clearly struggling. I want to stay with them, to run in a pack like we did at the time trial.

But incomprehensibly, I know deep down I can go faster. That I *want* to go faster.

Lucy meets my eyes. And like she can see what I'm thinking, she says, "Go!"

I question her with my eyes, either seeking her blessing or simply the reassurance that I'm capable. Maybe both.

She offers me a resolute nod. "Kill it, Cat!"

The other girls offer labored cheers as I move slightly ahead, trying to get a feel for just how hard I can push and sustain for two more miles. It hurts, but the pain is somehow more manageable today than it was at the time trial.

So I push faster.

At some point, my thinking brain seems to shut off. I'm an automaton, a robot. It's a welcome sensation, similar to what I felt at New Horizons during guided meditations. Blissful nothingness. I follow the cones and arrows, go up and down a hill, through the blocked-off city streets, vaguely aware of the sparse cheering crowds lining the course. I know I've passed several people, but I have no idea what place I'm in. Frankly, I don't care. What I feel right now goes beyond winning and losing – a cathartic void that only someone sick in the head can fully appreciate.

I come to my senses when I hear two familiar voices cheering me on.

"Sprint, Cat! Almost there!"

"Come on, Cat! Finish strong!"

Cheeto and Jack are on the sidelines, flushed and sweaty. Which means the end has to be close.

I hear the roar of distant cheers and applause, and as I turn the final corner, I see flags, balloons, and a giant stopwatch flashing red digits. *19:57. 19:58.* The time means nothing to me personally, but from what I remember at the time trial I know it's fast. The freshies and I were somewhere around 22:00 at the time trial. The only person under 20 minutes was Josie.

I scream my banshee cry and sprint through the finish.

I don't truly appreciate how much it hurts until I cross the line. Sweat pours into my eyes as I bend over, chest heaving, hands on my shaky knees.

There's a hand on my shoulder. Cheeto. I know I must really be out of it when I realize I don't even have the energy to feel panicked that he's close by. "C'mon, Cat, you gotta keep moving."

I let him guide me over to where Jack is standing, ready to congratulate me with a hearty slap on the shoulder. "Oh, man, new girl. Coach is going to be *so freaking happy* to meet you next month."

"Water?" Cheeto asks, handing out his half-drunk water bottle.

I take it, smiling my thanks. I take small sips, pacing in a tiny circle as I listen to them relive the race – the boring stretches, the brutal hill. I have to smile at the energy in their play-by-play, as if they're talking about a high-stakes Nuggets game.

Cheeto suddenly points toward the course. "Here they come."

I turn to see the familiar outlines of the freshies, still bound together. It makes me feel a sliver of remorse for leaving them, but I try to remember Lucy urging me on. I'm positive I didn't imagine her sincerity.

I'm feeling weak and slightly queasy, but follow the boys back over to the finish line. We make it over just in time to see them cross.

We high-five and pull each other in for sweaty hugs. As I'm embracing Bea, she pulls back, grasping both of my shoulders. "What was your time?"

I shrug. "I don't know …"

"20:10," Jack says proudly, as if he had something to do with it. "She almost caught me and Cheeto."

They all take turns to congratulate me, even though I know they're still trying to catch their own breaths. I try to enjoy their praise and want to celebrate, too, but the queasiness is getting worse.

And that's when I feel it.

There's no time for me to move out of the way.

I'm pretty sure puking in front of your crush and all your new friends would be humiliating for anyone. But it's even more loaded for me, considering vomit has dictated my entire life for the past year.

When I look up, I expect their faces to reflect the utter horror I feel inside.

Instead, they cheer.

Lucy slaps my back. "Remember that time when you said you weren't really a runner?" she says. "Well, you've officially just become one."

**

The hit-by-a-truck feeling eventually morphs into a pleasant buzz that makes me forget both the pain and the fact that I got exactly four hours of sleep last night. Runner's high, it turns out, is a real thing.

We cool down, stretch, and are back in Plain City by 10 a.m. Lucy drops me off at the high school. I go behind the shed and change into the clothes I brought with me, then walk home, role-playing what I'll say when Mom and Dad ask me their typical questions. I wish I could just tell them the truth – about my night, about the race this morning, about my new friends.

As soon as I open the door, they smile, welcome me home. At least I don't have to lie when they ask me how it was.

"Perfect," I say.

**

The rest of the day is perfect, too. We watch the parade as a family, play games, eat grilled burgers that don't seem like a leviathan to be defeated. Meri even hangs around instead of running off with her friends.

As soon as the sun starts to set, we head to the park to wait for the fireworks. We're searching for a spot near the sidewalk so we don't have to push Penny's chair over the grass when I hear someone call out my name.

I look up to see Blythe walking toward us.

"Well, hello, Miss Blythe," Mom says warmly. "Glad you two had –"

"Mom, we've got to hurry and find a spot before it gets dark," I say, ushering my family away. I look over at Blythe and smile. "I'll come back and find you, 'kay?"

Mom reprimands me with her eyes. "Thank you, Cat, but I'm allowed to say hello." She turns back to Blythe. "Make sure you thank your parents for having Cat over. You'll have to come over to our house next time. You're always welcome."

I think my heart legitimately skips a beat.

Blythe's face falls ever so slightly. To her credit, she looks over at me before she responds. There's just enough daylight for us to see each other's eyes, and I silently plead with her to play along.

She slaps on a fake smile. "Oh, it was fun, Mrs. Shultz. It's so nice to have Cat home so I can finally spend some quality time with her again."

I wonder if anyone else can detect the sarcasm in her voice.

We finally break away. Find a spot to park Penny and lay down our blanket.

"I'll be right back. I just forgot to tell Blythe something," I tell Mom and Dad.

When I find her again, that fake smile is long gone.

"Sure glad we had such a *fun time* last night," she says.

"Okay, seriously, I have *so* much to tell you."

Knowing Blythe, I figure the best way to smooth this over is to skip the apology and just fill her in on cross country, the freshies, the race. If nothing else, I assume she'll be impressed by my sneaking-around skills. I'm usually the one who has to be coerced into breaking rules.

But the look on her face tells me she's not letting this go so easily.

I sigh. "Look, I know I should have told you everything sooner. It's just been ... I don't know, everything's been weird lately. And you've been hanging out with Tyler so much –"

"Don't make this about Tyler."

"So you *weren't* with Tyler last night?" I say pointedly. "You never called, so I assumed the sleepover was off."

"That's not the point, Cat. The point is you've been turn-ing me down left and right, and now I find out you've been sneaking out to go do who-knows-what with other people? How's that supposed to make me feel?"

"It's not a big deal, if you'd just listen –"

"Not a big deal to get lied to? To get *used* by your best friend?"

I scoff. "You want to talk about *using* people? How about dragging me to parties I don't even want to go to and then ditching me for your stupid crush?"

"I already said I was sorry. And anyway, I was just trying to help."

"Well, did it occur to you that maybe I wouldn't *need help* if it wasn't for you?" It feels so satisfying slipping out of my mouth, but leaves behind a bitter aftertaste.

There's a bone-shaking explosion, and a bouquet of light blooms in the night sky behind us. The brilliant red and blue embers reflect off Blythe's glistening eyes.

"Good luck with everything, Cat."

CHAPTER 14

JOSIE

July 16 is the first official day of practice. I get to the school early, eager for Coach to see the fruits of all our hard work. Mixed in with the energy and excitement is relief. When Coach is at practice, I don't have to be the bad guy, at least not so often. He's the one writing the workouts, the one calling out the boys when they're being idiots. Coach is far from a raging dictator, but he doesn't put up with shit, either.

Everyone starts showing up around 6:50. The cars get parked a bit straighter, the daily insult exchange between the boys and the girls drops down to a PG rating. We stand in neat, orderly circles, waiting for him to arrive.

When his red pickup pulls onto Center Street, we erupt into cheers. He waves at us from his window like a soldier returning from war.

The man loves this team.

Which is why him leaving us makes no sense.

He gets out of his truck and we all chat for a bit. He tells us about how his family got marooned in a flash flood during the camping trip they took to Arches National Park; we tell him about the time we got chased by a feral dog on the dirt trail by the railroad tracks a couple of weeks ago.

A good, old-fashioned family reunion.

But when he starts rubbing his hands together, I know he's ready to get started.

"All right, everyone, warm up!" he yells.

We jog our lap and circle up to stretch. He weaves in and out between us, asking us questions about our summers, our families, how training has been going. I beam when I hear people say how great it's been, how strong they feel already.

He makes his way to a spot halfway between the boys and girls and gives three loud claps. "It's good to be back, guys. I'm looking forward to a great season. As I'm sure you've already heard …" He looks at me. I guess he knew I could never have kept his leaving a secret. Or maybe Sergio told him. Either way, it wasn't like he told us not to tell. "… I'm going to be making some pretty big life changes coming up here in a few months. This is going to be my last season here at Plain City."

There are well-intentioned groans, some light-hearted boos. Sergio finds me with his eyes, and I sit up straighter and smile.

Coach continues. "But I don't want this to distract us from having another amazing season. We made some big strides last year, and even though moving up to 5A means we've got our work cut out for us, it would be amazing to see us qualify for the state meet."

I scoff. *Qualify*. I know the competition will be stiffer in our new division, that only the top three teams from each region make it to State. But, come on … *qualify?* Show a little faith here.

"On that note," he says, "let's head to the track." His face takes on a mischievous glint. "Who's ready for intervals?"

**

Most people hate intervals. *Dread* them. I get why – sprinting around the track over and over with just enough of a break between to not fall over and die is no spa day.

But I'm not most people.

At the track, Coach splits us into groups based on pace. Like usual, I'm alone. There have never been any girls close enough to my pace to group me with them, and Coach knows better than to stick me with a bunch of ego-conscious boys.

I walk over to where the freshies are clumped, stretching their quads and shaking out their jitters.

"… and then you just repeat," Millie is saying to Cat. "Over, and over, and over again until you want to slit your eyeballs with razor blades."

Cat looks anxious. Which she *should* be. Early summer training, which up to this point has been exclusively dedicated to building up mileage – minus that one tiny time trial I snuck in – is one thing. Speed work is another.

"This is when things start getting fun," I offer, though inside I'm wondering if she'll survive. Both years I've been on the team, we've had plenty of people come to the June practices who suddenly get "too busy" once Coach starts showing up.

Coach is making his rounds to each group, offering suggestions and encouragement. Finally, it's our turn. "Gutsy new runners stepping up, that's what I like to see," he says to Cat. "I've been noticing your mileage reports, Cat. I'm excited to see what you can do today."

She smiles. I clench my teeth.

He twists the cord of his stopwatch around his fingers, scanning the others' faces. "Girls, let's have you shoot for 1:30s on your 400s. And Jo?" He meets my eyes. "Think you can hit 1:15s?"

"I *know* I can, Coach."

He gives me a thumbs-up, then makes his way to the next group.

"Luce, you should get your inhaler for this one," Alma says to Lucy.

Lucy rolls her eyes, and I narrow mine at her. After a bad

asthma attack last season, she can't mess around. Her mom said she'd pull her off the team if she doesn't manage it this year. Which means it's my responsibility to make sure she does. "Alma's right. No playing with matches this year, Lucy."

She sighs, annoyed. "Okay, okay. Let me grab it from the car."

"Lucy has asthma?" Cat says as Lucy jogs off. "I had no idea."

"The doctor says she shouldn't even be running," Sophia says. "But try telling her that."

As soon as she's back, inhaler in hand, I usher everyone to the starting line. "Let's get this party started."

**

The pace – 1:15 per 400-meter lap – is blistering. Coach wants eight of them.

I hit the first, second, third. By the fourth, I'm really feeling it. I click my watch as I cross the line and feel a surge of frustration as I look down and see 1:17. I lock my hands behind my head and pace in a circle, trying to assess the point where I slowed. Was it the first curve? The last straightaway?

I notice the freshies and Cat making their way around the far curve, locked together in a nice, tight pack. But as I continue to watch them I notice something strange. All their shoulders are sagging, their faces taut with pain and exertion.

All except one.

Cat looks strong. Like she's not pushing herself hard *enough*.

They finish. Alma moves to the grass, collapsing on all fours. Bea and Lucy hunch, white knuckled, over their knees. Sophia wobbles like she might lose her balance. Millie lunges for her water bottle and dumps the contents on top of her head.

Cat, however, is perfectly poised. Hardly seems to be

breathing heavy at all.

Coach claps for them, offers a few encouraging words, then pulls Cat to the side.

He's too far away for me to hear what he says, but I figure it out as soon as they both start walking toward me.

"Well, Jo, think you might have finally met your match," he says to me, grinning like it's a clever joke I'd find amusing. "Let's try having you two work together, see what happens."

I fake a smile.

"Ready?" I say to her, though I know she just finished her last lap a few seconds ago.

But instead of asking for more recovery time, she nods.

We walk to the start line. Her closeness makes me claustrophobic. I don't look over as I get into position. "Ready, set …"

I go.

I'm ahead for a mere second until I see her in my periphery, matching my pace stride for stride.

Let's try having you work together …

Coach's sentence replays over and over in my mind. I know the point is for us to help each other, to run as a pack just like I profess to the team before every workout. But I can't shake the feeling I'm being chased.

We finish interval number five. Then six. Then seven.

The silver lining, I guess, is that the possibility of "meeting my match" gives me extra fuel. We easily clock 1:15 for each lap. When I can tell she's starting to struggle, it feeds the flames even more.

As we start the final interval, lap number eight, I let myself go, losing her after the first curve.

I don't look back.

I click my watch as I cross the finish, feeling a burgeoning thrill when I look down and see 1:05. *One-zero-five.* I look up to find Coach's eyes, expecting to see pride and awe. 1:05s are what the fastest group of *boys* is supposed to be hitting.

But instead of pride and awe, he's glaring at me. "What was that?"

Instantly, I feel defensive. "I don't know, I think they call it *running fast*."

He rolls his eyes, throws his arms up. "Was that the work-out, Jo? To *run fast*?"

I bite my lip. "No."

"No, it was to hit *1:15s*. With your teammate."

Cat is 50 meters from the finish. She's struggling now – head tilted, arms tight, breathing shallow and jagged. I'm not totally sure, but I think she might even be crying.

The sheepishness sets in.

I don't know if I've ever seen him this frustrated, at least not with me. "Don't let me see that again." He breaks his attention from me to cheer Cat in, calling for one of the girls standing nearby to grab her some water. When it's evident she's going to be fine, he turns back to me. "We clear?"

"Yes, Coach," I say. "Crystal."

CHAPTER 15

CAT

Everyone told me things don't really change that much once official practices start – that it's the same thing minus having an adult around. After all I've heard about the coach, I show up to practice feeling like I'm about to meet a celebrity. A deity, maybe. From day one, it's been *Coach this* and *Coach that.*

"Coach says not to drink carbonation, it'll slow you down."

"Coach says to get new shoes early in the summer so you have time to break them in."

"Coach is going to kill the boys when he finds out they broke into the equipment shed and played ping-pong with the groin protectors."

Today, though, is *not* the same thing. Intervals are basically a socially acceptable form of torture.

My body has never hurt so much – not during the time trial, not during the Fourth of July 5K. Like, on the verge of imploding.

I can almost picture Ms. Reid, one hand on her hip, face stern. What my parents would say if they were here, watching me run my guts out, burning calories I don't have the reserves for. This is definitely not "light exercise" by anyone's standard.

Worse, I completely botch the last lap. Midway through the workout, Coach moves me from the freshies group to run with Josie, who's hitting 1:15s. Numbers mean nothing to me, but it feels like a Herculean pace, like we're trying to qualify for the Olympics or something. I stick with her for three, but on the last one my body just … gives out.

I can sense her irritation with me, the tension from Coach. Like I've let them down.

I can't help but think back to early June, how all this started. And I wonder: Is cross country still serving its purpose?

And if not, then what am I still doing here?

**

"What'd you think, KitKat?" Millie asks as we're stretching afterward. "Tell me you don't want to die."

I smile, hoping it masks the hurricane I'm actually feeling inside. "I want to die."

"Well, get used to it. You can basically plan on doing them every Monday."

Every Monday? I think. They might as well meet up to drink gasoline. Push thumbtacks into their fingernails.

Coach stands up in front of everyone, two stacks of paper in one hand and a plastic grocery sack of frozen Otter Pops in the other. "Good work today, crew. I think everyone earned this," he says, handing the bag to Scorcho. "Take one; pass it on. While you're cooling off, I've got a couple things to hand out and go over. One is a meet schedule. The other is this year's parent disclosures. Try to have them turned back in by next week, if possible. District athletics fees are up to $48 this year. I need the money before I can issue you a uniform. Of course, pull me aside if you need help to cover that. We don't want to lose anyone on account of money."

The papers go around. I take one of each. He starts going through the dates on the schedule, but I'm not listening. My focus is glued to the empty parent signature box at the bottom of the disclosure.

Even if I wanted to keep running with the team, I don't see how I'd get around this. If I ask Mom and Dad to sign it, don't I also have to tell them I've been sneaking out every day for over a month? Overlooking the infinitesimal chance that they'd be okay with me being on the team, I'd probably be grounded until the season ends anyway.

And that's all assuming I'd magically find $48 worth of coins in the couch cushions.

Coach finishes his spiel. Most of the team leaves, but the freshies and I stay sprawled out on the grass, finishing our popsicles. Lucy and Alma are debating which course will be hardest when Millie interrupts them.

"So-phi-a," she says in a singsong voice. "I think someone's looking for you."

On the other side of the fence, a tall kid, muscles bulging from his football jersey – Kyle Pelty himself – is looking toward us.

Sophia's already pink cheeks turn even pinker. "Be right back."

She jogs over to him. Millie catcalls as the two of them lace their fingers together through the chain links.

"Gag me with a spoon," Bea says, standing up and brushing grass off her pants. "Let's get out of here. Shotgun, no duels."

"We're leaving you, loser!" Millie calls over her shoulder to Sophia as they start their slow walk to the parking lot.

I stand up to follow. But I'm stopped by someone calling my name.

I turn around. It's Coach Davis.

CHAPTER 16
JOSIE

I'm halfway home when I realize I left the new water bottle Mom found on clearance at CVS on the track, so I turn around and jog back toward the school.

I'm just rounding the bleachers when I hear him.

"Let me put it this way – there's only been a handful of times in the 15 years I've been coaching that I've met an athlete with so much potential. You're a natural. I'm talking months, *years,* of conditioning for most kids to get where you're at after just a few weeks."

I freeze. Coach and the object of his high praise are still out of sight, but I don't need visual evidence to know who he's talking to.

"Yeah, I just … I don't know if I can, like, actually *join* the team, though. Coming to practice was kind of a summer thing for me."

The first sensation that hits me is relief. Amusement, even. *Cat Shultz is not, and never was, planning to join the team.*

But it's quickly followed by alarm.

Because the truth is we need her. I talk a big game with positivity and manifesting your dreams and all that, but if I'm being honest? There's no way we stand a chance against Aspen Ridge without Cat Shultz.

The third and final element in my trifecta of emotions is confusion. If she never planned to join the team, why the hell was she running with us in the first place?

"Is there some sort of conflict with another sport?" Coach responds. I can hear the pleading, the desperation in his voice. "Because I can talk to your coach and we can work around it. Even if you can't make it out to every practice –"

"I don't do any other sports."

"Is it the money? Because we've got reserves for that."

"No, it's … nothing like that."

A pause. "Well, I certainly hope there haven't been any problems with the team."

Warmth rises to my cheeks. I might not particularly *like* Cat Shultz, but other than the stunt I pulled today, I've made a concerted effort not to show it. And if she can't handle getting out-sprinted on *one* interval, at *one* workout, well … she must fit the mold of privileged, entitled white girl even more than I thought.

"Everyone's been amazing. Honestly, it's been great."

It's quiet for a second. I feel the tension in the air even without being directly in their presence.

"Well, Cat. I'd love it if you'd take a couple days to at least think about it. I'm not just being nice here. I'm talking college-scholarship-level potential. And the team could really use you, especially this year with us moving up to 5A. I know the girls are shooting for the moon, seeing how much of a scare they can give their competition."

Not how much of a scare, I correct him in my mind. *How much we can beat them by.*

"That's what I hear," Cat says. "And I'll definitely be cheering everyone on."

A pause. "All right, well … you're welcome to keep training with us this summer, regardless of whether or not you officially join."

"Cool. Thanks, Mr. Davis. See you around."

I hear footsteps on the pavement.

"Hey, Cat?" The footsteps stop. "My door is always open. We've got people on this team who've been through just about everything. I know how tough life can get sometimes. And my job isn't just to help kids run faster; it's to help them get through high school in one piece. That goes for runners who are with us for any amount of time – a week, a month, or four years."

There's a slight pause. "Thanks, Mr. Davis."

"You don't need to call me Mr. Davis. Just call me Coach."

I feel a tear roll down my cheek and hate myself for it.

CHAPTER 17

CAT

"Cat, honey. Have a little more."

My usual trick, spreading my food around in a thin layer all over my plate, doesn't seem to be working.

I don't feel like eating tonight. At New Horizons, Ms. Reid used the term "energy vampire" whenever one of us was being mopey, and I know she'd call me out if she were here. I've been on a steady emotional decline ever since practice this morning, I guess because reality is finally hitting me: My summer escapade is over. It's time to make a clean break from the team. Maybe even come clean to Mom and Dad.

Dinner has been uncomfortable, tense, and I think we're all grateful for the loud knock at the door.

Meri jumps up from the table. "I'll get it."

Chances are it's one of her friends. That, or Paul coming to beg for her back. When the door squeaks open, I see Mom straining to hear the conversation. I almost think she was more devastated about the break-up than Meri was.

There's a muffled voice, but Penny starts making her noises, so I can't tell who it is. When Meri comes back to the table, she flashes me a look I can't quite read.

"It's someone for Cat."

My heart skips.

Blythe.

For the first week after the Fourth of July, I sent her like 20 texts a day and called her every night. Nothing. Then I started trying the landline, but every time I called I got some runaround from her mom: *She's out riding horses. She's taking a nap. She just stepped in the shower.* Eventually I gave up, figuring the best thing to do was steer clear for a while. Let the air settle.

But as I peek out the landing window, I see it isn't Blythe. It's Josie.

I hurry outside, making sure the door shuts tight behind me. "How'd you find out where I live?"

Josie looks at me like I've just asked what year it is. "We live in *Plain City*, Cat. And your sister is *Meri Shultz*. All I had to do was ask the boys."

Thinking of the boys pining for my sister grosses me out, but I don't say anything.

"I just …" She looks all around the porch, everywhere except my eyes. "I just came to apologize about earlier. I wasn't acting like a captain."

My face gets warm. "It's okay."

"The truth is …" She finally meets my gaze, but I can tell it's requiring lots of effort. "The truth is you're an amazing runner. And our team needs you. So I hope today didn't scare you off or anything. Hope *I* didn't scare you off."

Josie has never said so many words to me at one time. Ever. And definitely never anything so *nice*.

I finally find a response, but it comes out awkward and clunky. "No, I didn't … it wasn't you. I just felt bad I let you down. I kind of fell apart on that last one."

Her eyes get big. "Are you kidding? What we did today was no joke. Like, insanely fast times. The goal paces Coach gives us are just that – goals. Missing one out of eight is not a big deal. Better than average, I'd say. I wasn't hitting 1:15s consistently on intervals until the end of last year. And I'm … well, let's just say I'm not slow. I was top 10 at State last year. So, you know … cross country could really lead to something for you."

I take this in. It's essentially what Coach said when he pulled me aside earlier, but it feels different coming from Josie. Something swells inside me.

"So ... we cool?" she asks. "You'll be back tomorrow, right? It'll be a recovery day. Something super easy. He never tortures us two days in a row."

I feel my resolve to quit going to practice – to come clean to my parents – start to waver. Even if I ultimately decide this is it, that I'm not going back, there's no way I could say it to Josie's face right now.

"Yeah. Of course."

A surprising wave of relief washes over me as the words come out of my mouth.

**

"Who was it?" Dad says when I sit back down at the table.

"Oh, um, just someone from the high school." Better a half-truth than a full-blown lie, right? "Recruiting for ... drama club."

Meri glares at me.

Drama club was the first thing that came to mind. But when Mom's eyes light up, I wonder why I couldn't have just said color guard or FFA. Something a little less ... *loaded*.

"Recruiting? Didn't know they did that." I'm kicking myself for my stupidity, certain she can see right through me, but then I realize she's being 100 percent sincere. "What'd you tell them?"

"Oh, you know," I say, avoiding her eyes. "That I'd think about it."

I scarf down three more bites of dinner and escape to my room to avoid any more questions. Not five seconds later, Meri barges in without knocking, shutting the door behind her.

"Drama club?" she says pointedly.

"Yeah. I don't know why you're –"

"Just don't, Cat. Did you know you're actually a terrible liar?"

"How would *you* know she's not from drama club?"

"Remember that time when I *went* to high school? With a bunch of *other people*? Josie Romero is the last person on the planet who would ever be in drama club."

I had figured the two of them would have been in such different social circles there's no way Meri would have even known who Josie is. Clearly, I was wrong.

"Start talking," she says, folding her arms across her chest.

My heart starts to pound. Where would I even begin? "It's a long story."

"Give me the CliffsNotes version."

I sigh. "Okay. I started jogging a few weeks ago."

Her glare gets sharper.

"Coming home has been hard, Meri. Harder than I thought it would be. I started feeling bad again. I'm not, like, purging or anything, but … I've just been anxious and stuff." I swallow. "I didn't want to worry Mom and Dad, but I knew I had to do something. I just thought if I do a little jog every morning, it would help."

Her eyes roll in wide, exasperated circles. She knows my history with running. What Ms. Reid told Mom and Dad. "So how, exactly, does this translate to Josie Romero knocking on our door?"

I take a deep breath. "One of the girls on the team stopped me on the side of the road and basically forced me to come to cross country practice one morning. And it turned out to be fun. So the next day … well, I knew Mom wouldn't let me go, so I … snuck out. And I've been sneaking out every morning since."

I leave out the Frisbee night, going to Colorado Springs with the freshies, and how I have a major crush on a junior boy who drives a moped. Obviously.

I try – unsuccessfully – to read her face, then continue. "I swear, I was only going to go once to check it out, but then I just ..." I pause to let her respond, but she doesn't. "You're going to tell Mom, aren't you?"

"Of *course* I'm going to tell Mom, Cat. Three months ago you were living in a *treatment center.* Which Mom and Dad put you in because they didn't want you to *die.*"

I start to cry, trying to block out the memories trying to infiltrate my mind.

But my remorse quickly morphs into resolve. Because I know myself better than Meri or Mom or Ms. Reid knows me. "But look at me, Mer. I'm eating. I'm happy. I have friends. I don't feel like I want to crawl in a hole every day. For the first time in two years, I'm starting to feel like myself again. Like maybe I'm figuring out how to control this thing."

I can tell she sees my point. I reach for Olga dangling from my neck, formulating my next words carefully. "You have to believe me, Mer. I don't *want* to go back to the person I used to be. Running is the only thing that helps. That makes me feel like things are going to be okay."

"Why can't you just explain all this to Mom and Dad?"

I tell her about the conversation I had with Mom the night before the Fourth. "But she wouldn't feel that way if she understood the whole picture! I'm positive of it. I just need a little more time to figure out how to tell them. Please, Mer ..."

She considers it, then lets out a long drawn-out sigh. "Ugh, Cat ... You can't put me in this position."

I sigh and rake my fingers through my hair. "I just don't know what I'd do if they tell me no."

I'm surprised to realize how true this is. Even though I

was dead set on quitting not even an hour ago, I realize now that running is a necessity. A matter of survival.

We sit quietly for what feels like five minutes, then she turns and looks over at me. "I won't say anything. But I swear, Cat. You're treading in dangerous water here. And if I find out you're relapsing …"

My entire body is flooded with relief. With it comes an idea: a crazy, insane, legitimately stupid idea. But since I've already pushed my luck this far over the line, what's a few more inches?

I open the drawer of my nightstand, pull out the disclosure form I stuffed inside this morning, and hand it to Meri.

She glances over it, then looks up at me. "Are you seriously asking me to sign this?"

"You know how bad my cursive is. Besides, you're 18 – technically old enough to be my guardian anyway, right?"

"No way."

"I'll tell Mom and Dad the truth once the season starts. Invite them to come watch a race or something, introduce them to my friends and the coach. I just … need a little more time to prove to them that I'm better. That I can do this."

Based on the way she's glaring at me and the fact that she doesn't respond for nearly a minute, I figure it's time to cut my losses and retreat. But suddenly she sticks out her empty right hand. "Pen?"

I have to bite the insides of my cheeks to keep from smiling. Any evidence of smugness and she might back out. I rummage through the drawer again and find a loose blue ballpoint missing its lid.

She signs it the way a bitter wife might sign divorce papers. "You have to promise me, Cat," she says, looking me dead in the eyes when she finishes, "and I'm talking pinky-swear-on-our-mother's-grave promise, if you start to feel it coming on again, you'll call me." I nod, and she grabs my shoulders and shakes them a little. "I want to hear you say it *out loud*."

"I promise, Meri. I'll call you."

I can tell she's still mad when she hands the paper back to me. "Says here there's a $48 fee. Have a game plan there? Or were you just going to raid Dad's wallet since you're already lying and sneaking around behind their backs anyway?"

Even if I had a good comeback, I know I just relinquished all my leverage for the next 20 years.

"I'll figure something out. No stealing, I promise."

**

I turn in the disclosure form the next day at practice, holding my breath as Coach glances down at the signature.

"This is great news, Cat," he says. "I was wracking my brain last night trying to think up some way to convince you to stick around."

I smile. "Sorry, I don't have the money yet."

"Don't need it until the first day of school," he says. "Just happy to have you on board."

The workout is a five-mile power run on Stink Dairy. Not the easy Goat Run jog I was hoping for after yesterday's doozy, but with Coach here, I'm beginning to fear those days might be gone forever. Still, I'll take this over intervals. Power runs are about the closest you can get to dead center on the spectrum between jogging and sprinting. Doable.

We're a few hundred meters down the road when Lucy asks, "How are we passing the time today, ladies?"

"Top That?" Bea says.

It's a stupid game. Not even a game really, just a way to fend off boredom on long runs. Someone shoots out a topic – worst dates, most embarrassing moments, et cetera – and everyone tries to come up with the best, juiciest story to go along with it. It's surprisingly anesthetizing.

"Okay, how about craziest idea you've ever had?" Millie says.

Lucy tells us about jumping in Devil's Cove in the middle of November; Sophia and Bea have a shared story – the time they told their parents they were sleeping over at each other's houses when in reality they went to a concert in Denver with Sophia's older brother and his friends.

Suddenly, I have an idea: "New topic. Dumbest thing you've done for cash."

The freshies catch each other's eyes and laugh.

"You tell, Alma," Bea says.

"I've got this neighbor, Al Barker," Alma says. "He hires the neighborhood kids to do manual labor for him. Says it's to build character, but we all know he's just trying to save himself a few bucks since he doesn't have to pay us as much as his usual crews."

"Hey, none of us would have decent running shoes if it wasn't for him, though," Lucy says. "Can't bite the hand that feeds, right?"

When the conversation moves on to someone else's crazy uncle who hired them to hold a sign that said *We Are Apocalypse* in downtown Denver during a Broncos game, I run up alongside Alma. "So this Al guy ... if he ever, you know, needs any more workers, I wouldn't mind helping out."

"Yeah, sure, I'll ask. I'm going over to hoe peppers after practice today, actually. I'll let you know what he says."

I reach up for Olga and smile. I still don't know if I believe in lucky charms, but Olga hasn't failed me yet.

CHAPTER 18

JOSIE

Two weeks before school starts, we have a captains meeting after practice to talk about our progress this summer. It feels good to just be the three of us – me, Coach, and Sergio. The original trio who started this dynasty.

"Feeling strong, Coach," Sergio says, handing him the final mileage reports. "Ten who made the Five-Hundred-Mile Club."

"Thirteen," I say smugly, handing Coach mine.

He shuffles through them, clearly impressed. "Gotta hand it to you two. You worked hard this summer, put together quite the team."

The dust has long since settled after the interval fiasco. One thing I love about Coach is that he doesn't hold grudges, and on my end, I've doubled down on my efforts to reign in whatever weird resentful streak Cat brings out in me. This is bigger than me and her and my vendetta against rich white people.

"Not so ho-hum about our chances now, huh?" I say.

Coach smiles. "Hey, miracles happen; not going to argue with that. No matter what, it'll be a great season." We talk a few more minutes, wrapping up some housekeeping business and nailing down the time for the Five-Hundred-Mile Club dinner. "Sergio, would you mind rounding up the cones? Jo and I will dump the cooler."

Sergio jogs across the soccer field to pick up the orange cones we used for our circuit workout today – 10 laps, slightly faster than race pace, 20 push-ups, squats, and burpees between each one. I currently feel like I've been hit by a dump truck, in the best way.

I follow Coach down to the track where the orange Igloo cooler is sitting on the sideline bench. We each lift a side. "We haven't talked much about this since official practices have started but ... we okay?" he says. "That captains meeting on the last day of school didn't go as well as I'd hoped."

I swallow and force my gaze straight ahead. The cooler is heavy, and we have to take baby steps. "Yeah. We're good."

I'm well practiced at the tone I use. I call it "chilly chill": the way you let people – and by people, I usually mean my dad – know you're fine, but also that they royally screwed up. Mastering the voice is a life skill, in my opinion.

"Dealing with a coach change will be a big deal, I know. I shouldn't have downplayed it the way I did."

"I get it. Trust me," I say, scoffing. "Adults have to make hard decisions sometimes."

I notice him flinch a little out of the corner of my eye and feel instantly bad. He thinks I'm comparing this to my dad leaving, and even if it wasn't completely intentional, there's a hint of truth in it.

"Seriously, though," I say, infusing my voice with all the warmth I can muster. "It's all good. It'll be an awesome season, I can feel it."

Especially when we win, I think.

"You really think we can beat Aspen Ridge," he says as if reading my mind.

I just smile.

"Well," he says, "if *anyone* can pull off an upset like that, it's whatever team you're captain of, kiddo."

We make it to the grass, lift the cooler, and dump. The ice immediately starts crackling under the searing August sun.

"I've been meaning to ask how things are at home, too," he says. "All okay?"

I feel emotion surfacing. Not in a bad way – more in a *get this poison out of me* kind of way. I haven't really had anyone to talk through the most recent Romero family drama with.

"Well, my dad got engaged," I say acerbically.

Coach's eyebrows shoot up. "Whoa. How are you feeling about that? And how's your mom and brother?"

I shrug. "Ziggy and I are fine. I dunno, maybe after this we'll all finally be able to move on."

"But your mom?"

"She's pretty torn up."

He sighs, shakes his head. "That's the hardest thing, isn't it? Watching the people you love get hurt and knowing there's nothing you can do about it. When my parents got divorced, my mom cried every day for a good *decade* before she even took off her wedding ring. The worst part was people telling her, *You've got to move on, Cathy; you need to be strong for your kids*; et cetera. As if she didn't *want* to be strong. As if she was choosing to be heartbroken."

Emotion creeps higher up the back of my throat. "He wants me to come to the wedding the last weekend of September. But I don't want to go. I haven't even met her in person. She's, like, 25 years old, closer to my age than his. Not to mention it's right in the middle of the season."

"We can work it out if –"

"I don't want to go, Coach. I'd rather run intervals for 24 hours straight than go to his stupid wedding."

He gives me a sad smile. "I don't think you should have to do anything that makes you uncomfortable. He chose this life – he has to learn to live with the consequences."

I feel grateful for his validation. Like a load has been lifted off my shoulders.

"Besides, that's the weekend of the Mile High Invitational. There'll be college scouts swarming the place," he says.

"Yeah?"

He nods. "Who knows, you just might land yourself a scholarship before this season's even out. Especially with your high school coach's recommendation."

He winks and whacks me on the shoulder. I feel lighter than I have in weeks.

CHAPTER 19

CAT

When I meet Al Barker on Saturday, the first thing he says to me is that I need to learn to work hard now so I can "keep a good house" someday. I want to be offended, but his frizzy white hair and slight limp remind me of my great-grandpa who died 10 years ago.

A woman's yell from the house interrupts him. "Al? *Albert?*"

"What?" he yells back gruffly.

When she doesn't respond, he sighs and rolls his eyes. "We'll be headed out to the field soon. Don't disappear on me."

As soon as he's out of view, I gape at Alma.

"See?" she says. "The best thing to do is just nod and smile, nod and smile."

Most people in Plain City at least dabble in farming – a garden and a chicken coop, maybe a few barn animals – but Al Barker is a farmer with a capital F. Fields of perfect green rows surround us in all directions. The little house in the center of it all makes me feel like I've somehow stepped back into the 1950s: rocking chairs out front, red gingham curtains peeking through the windows, a white picket fence. There's even a border collie with a bandana sitting on his haunches in the bed of the pickup truck.

Alma leads me to the other side of the house, where a black diesel Chevy is hooked up to a trailer loaded with hot-tub-sized cardboard crates. Gathered around the truck are 10 or so teenage boys in T-shirts and Wranglers.

My stomach lurches. I pull her back around the side of the house. "Why didn't you tell me Cheeto would be here?" I hiss in her ear.

She looks at me quizzically. "You didn't ask. He lives just down the street – he's usually here whenever there's a big project. Al basically thinks he's the golden child ... '*That Charlie Campbell, now he's going to be a catch someday*,'" she says, mimicking Al's voice. "I think he feels responsible for him after ... well, you know ..." Her voice trails off.

"After what?"

"You don't know? Cheeto's dad died last year. Heart attack."

I glance back at Cheeto, who's laughing about something with Jack. It's interesting how people look different after you discover their tragedies.

"Wait a second ... why did you say 'Cheeto' and not 'Cheeto and Jack'?"

I realize my mistake. "No reason. I was just ... I mean, I *meant* to say Cheeto and Jack ..."

Alma's mouth erupts in a wide grin. "You *like* him, don't you?"

I feel myself blushing.

"Well," Alma says, "you obviously weren't around when he and his friends used to terrorize all the girls who live around here. I remember waking up during sleepovers in my backyard with 50 grasshoppers they'd thrown in our tent during the night. Guess he turned out okay, though. Could be worse – you could like Scorcho." She pretends to gag herself.

Al comes around the house, ushering us toward him. "Gather up. Let's go over the plan before we head to the field. We have two mighty fine catchers here today. You boys are to treat them like queens, you hear? Share any food and water you brought with you. Refrain from vulgarities. We're gonna move quickly today, try to clean the field before the sun gets too damn hot. Don't want the police at my house accusing me of breaking child labor laws. Remember, gentlemen – it's snip, toss, snip, toss." He claps his hands in a steady rhythm as he speaks. "And you two," he says, turning to us, "do your best to keep up."

I start to wonder if this was worth the money after all, and Alma must read the concern on my face. "Don't worry, you'll get into a rhythm. Your back will probably be on fire for an hour or so, but after that it just goes numb." We climb up and onto a crate on the edge of the trailer. Jack and Cheeto sit down across from us. "The most important thing is to set the melons down gently," she continues. "If you drop them, they crack."

"You let Alma rope you into this, new girl?" Jack asks as we lurch forward.

"I need money," I say.

"I feel that. Beggars can't be choosers here in PC, it's true." He suddenly looks skeptical. "Wait, hold up. You're a Shultz."

"Just because my sister is popular doesn't mean we're rich." It feels good to finally voice that, as if it has unknowingly been festering inside of me.

He rolls his eyes. "Yeah whatever. You got big shoes to fill, being Meri's kid sister and all."

I'm beginning to realize Jack has two settings: hilarious and annoying. Thankfully, Alma comes to my rescue. "Isn't *your* little sister starting high school, Jack? Wonder what everyone tells her? Just to pretend she's not related to you?"

"Well, there's one thing you can look forward to," Jack says, completely ignoring Alma. "That nickname isn't going to last much longer. You'll be one new girl in a whole sea of them. And as soon as school starts, the boys start fishing." He casts an imaginary line and pretends to reel it in.

Alma groans and rolls her eyes. Beside Jack, Cheeto laughs, but it seems forced.

The truck veers off the main road and drives straight into a field. As soon as we hit the dirt, it's like we're on a raft in choppy water, and I have to hang on so I don't fall off the back.

Suddenly, we jerk to a stop in the middle of an ocean of curlicue leaves. Lime-green- and emerald-striped orbs peek out from behind them like Easter eggs.

Al sticks his head out the tractor window. "All right, enough fraternizing. Jump down, men; let's get picking."

I follow Alma's lead and take my place inside one of the cardboard bins on the back of the trailer while the boys split into two groups behind us. Cheeto's in my line. Normally I'd call that lucky, but since there's a good chance he's about to flatten me with a watermelon, it seems more like a curse.

"Ready?" Al yells out the window.

Before anyone can answer, the truck jolts forward. The boys bend over, searching the leaves with their gloved hands.

When the first watermelon is launched, I'm braced for impact, standing with one foot anchored behind me for stability, but it still takes all my strength not to fall over. I remember what Alma said and set it down in the bin as carefully as possible, while at the same time keeping my eyes glued forward so I don't get blindsided by the next one.

Watermelons fly, one after the other. Unlike running, where in the worst-case scenario you just slow down or stop running altogether, the 20-pound cannons are going to keep coming at me one way or another. I have no choice but to keep catching.

"Hey, Cheeto!" Jack is already sweaty and out of breath. "Did you know there used to be a street named Chuck Norris?"

Cheeto stands up, armed with a melon, his mouth in its usual little half-smile. "Oh, yeah?"

"Yeah," Jack says, deadpan, "but they had to change the name because no one ever crosses Chuck Norris and lives."

Cheeto laughs and tosses me the melon. Thankfully, I'm ready for it. "Well, did you know that Chuck Norris is the reason Waldo is hiding?" he says back.

Maybe it's the heat, but I can't stop laughing.

**

By the time two o'clock rolls around, my face is fried, my arms are ground beef, and I'm positive I've heard every Chuck Norris joke since the beginning of time. Alma and I collapse in the shade of one of the trailer's giant tires. Behind us, the crates are overflowing with hundreds of watermelons.

"Well, what do you think? Worth it?" she asks.

"I guess it depends on if my arms ever work again," I say.

"My feet feel like they're getting bit by piranhas," she says, peeling off her shoes. I take it as permission granted and pull mine off, too. Two huge blisters bulge from the back of my heels. I rub my soles across the grass, which feels inexplicably cool.

"I don't know how you do this every weekend and still have the energy to run. You're tougher than I thought you'd be when we first met." Realizing how that sounds, I add, "You know, because you're so … small."

She gives me a look that tells me she knows what I'm *not* saying – that she's quiet and timid, the one who's usually overlooked – and also that it isn't the first time she's been made aware of this. "Don't worry, you're fine," she says graciously. "I'm fully aware I don't usually strike people as much of a fighter. I do want to point out there's other factors in play, though. My stride is, like, *half* the length of Bea's, which means I have to move my legs twice as fast to keep up. That's the *real* reason I'm slowest."

"What do you mean, the slowest?"

"Of the freshies. I was the only one who didn't get to run at State last year. Varsity's just top seven, and there were two senior girls who edged me out last season. It sucked, big time. Thought I was a shoo-in for varsity this year until you came along." She grins and bumps my shoulder so I know she doesn't resent me for it. Or at least is *trying* not to resent me, anyway. "Now I'm hanging on to the seventh spot for dear life. Not sure why I really care. Six and seven don't even matter anyway. Basically glorified JV."

"What do you mean?"

"Has no one explained cross country scoring to you yet? Only the top five on each team actually place. Whatever spot each runner finishes adds up to the team's total score. So you want the lowest score. Sixth and seventh runners don't officially count, but they can add points to other teams if they finish in front of their top five runners. Make sense?"

I wobble my head from side to side. "Ish."

Even though it seems complicated, I do understand that this means Becca, Gretchen, and the other 20 or so girls behind the freshies – the JV team, as I'm realizing now – are essentially redundancies. That they're running just for themselves, for fun, no chance of even making a dent in the scoring.

I wonder if I would keep going to practice if I were that far back.

Alma sighs. "Sometimes I just wonder what it would be like to, you know, *matter.*"

Before I can respond to this, Jack and Cheeto stagger over from around the side of the house. As hard as it was to catch watermelons, I can't even imagine *throwing* them. "Al says to hold up a minute, he's gotta get some more cash from the house," Jack says to us, pulling himself up on the edge of the trailer bed.

This jostles the trailer just enough to throw off the balance of one of the highest-piled crates. A watermelon falls to the ground, bursting on impact.

"You guys could have died just then," Jack says. "That thing would have snapped your skull clean off your spine."

"Gee, thanks for the visual," Alma says.

I look around. "What should we do?"

"You mean with the melon?" Jack says. "The only logical thing. Eat it."

The three of them crowd around it, scooping up handfuls of pink flesh and shoveling it into their mouths like cavemen. I know Jack is right – there's no other use for it now. In the July sun, it won't last 15 minutes before getting warm and soupy and covered with flies. Still, I glance behind me, checking for Al.

"He doesn't care if we eat the split ones," Jack says. "You've got to learn to chillax, new girl."

I bend down and break off a chunk. It feels impossibly cold in my fingers. They watch for my reaction as I nibble off a bite, then laugh when my eyebrows shoot up.

I've never fully appreciated watermelon until this moment: the texture, the delicate sweetness, the way it seems to melt in your mouth. Ambrosia from the gods. I inhale the rest and reach for more. Soon juice is dripping down my chin.

"That's the spirit," Jack says, wiping his mouth with the back of his hand. "Sometimes on really hot days, my aim mysteriously gets worse."

"I'm telling," Alma says.

"Okay, Miss Innocent," Jack says. "You're telling me that massive one you dropped two weeks ago was a quote-unquote accident, then?"

Alma picks up a fistful of watermelon and chucks it at him.

"Oh, we're going there?" Jack one-ups her with a bigger piece. She squeals as it hits her square in the face.

This starts what I can only describe as the pink, sticky, summertime equivalent of a December snowball fight. Soon, my body feels like I've just showered in maple syrup.

Jack grabs the bowl-shaped end of the melon and chases a still-barefooted Alma around the truck. "Forgot your hat!"

I'm so busy laughing at them that it takes me a few seconds to realize Cheeto is coming after me. I make a half-hearted attempt to get away, but the chase is over in seconds. He pulls back the neck of my T-shirt and drops in a handful of slush, then wraps his arms tightly around me and squishes it against my back with his chest. I wriggle against him, pretending to try to break free.

"Ain't she a mite too young for you, son?"

Cheeto lets go of me so fast I almost lose my balance. A penitent-looking Alma emerges from around the trailer, followed by Jack 10 or so seconds later.

"I better not find the two of you rolling around in the bushes someday," Al continues, giving us the old-person, one-eyebrow-raised scowl.

I feel myself blush but figure between the watermelon juice and the sunburn it's probably not too obvious. I assume Al's going to keep on lecturing, but instead he holds out four white envelopes. "You boys would do well to use this money on a proper outing with the young ladies instead of terrorizing them. Young men don't know how to properly court these days."

"Yes, sir," Jack and Cheeto say in unison.

Al limps back into the house. I peek inside the envelope, counting five crisp $10 bills. Just enough for the cross country fee.

"Well, I guess this is peace out," Jack says, bowing dramatically. Cheeto follows him to the front of the house, offering only a small nod as a goodbye.

As soon as they're out of earshot, Alma does a little squeal.

"Okay, he's *totally* into you," she says.

I shake my head, but can't stop myself from smiling. "You really think?"

"Let's just say never in my whole life have I seen Charlie Campbell so much as *touch* a girl," she says. "Come on, let's head to my house. We can hose off." We walk over to where we left our shoes on the other side of the truck. Alma starts to slip one on. "My mom's going to be pissed about the sticky —"

She screams.

I recoil, thinking there must be a mouse or a rattlesnake curled up inside the toe.

She flips her shoe upside down. Soggy watermelon slush falls into a pile on the ground.

I hear Cheeto's moped start in the front of the house, and soon it pulls into view on the main road. Jack is hanging on the back, his taunting smile visible even from a distance.

"You just got SERVED!" he yells.

They speed off, way out of earshot, but Alma yells back anyway.

"Oh, it's on, boys! It's SO ON!"

CHAPTER 20

JOSIE

Saturday night, I plan to meet everyone at the school for Frisbee, but as I'm running over I realize I don't want to stop. Six miles, seven miles, eight miles; when I hit nine, I force myself to head home. In running, there is such a thing as overdoing it.

As I curve down our street, I notice light coming from our trailer windows and curse to myself. Ziggy was gone when I left, out with friends, and Mom had to work, so I was planning on coming home to a quiet house. I imagined myself taking a bath, maybe doing some research on Mom's computer about the colleges Coach said might be at the invitational in a few weeks. I like my own company. Prefer it to most people, if I'm being honest.

I stop at the base of the driveway, stretching my quads and calves by the mailbox. Two or three days' worth of mail bulges from the opening. I know I'm due for a *Runner's World* soon, so I pull the lid down and sort through the contents. Bills, junk mail, catalogs for stores we could never afford to shop at.

And then I see it. A blue envelope with handwritten lettering. The words "New York City" hang like daggers in the return address.

Dad was pissed when I hung up on him the day he told us about the engagement, so Mom made me call back and apologize. He chewed me out for like five minutes. Something about how his fiancée Marigold was sitting nearby, and it made her so upset when I hung up that she started crying. I didn't even waste my energy trying to argue with him, just pretended to be penitent while I was flipping the bird at the screen with my left hand.

I don't know what possesses me to open the envelope and pull out the contents, but I do.

The invitation is horrendous. Kitsch, but not in a good way, like it was homemade by a second grader. Dad thinks he's still 20 and the shit; didn't even bother washing his disgusting long hair for the photo. Yet radiating from his smug, self-assured face, I see all the fear he's constantly running away from – fear of getting old, fear of irrelevance, fear of no one liking him. And I wish I could see him, right this very moment, just so I could tell him to grow the fuck up.

I feel sorry for Marigold. A few years and her wrinkles will start showing. They'll have a baby together and she'll get all stretched and saggy, and his friends will all stop telling him his girl is hot. Then what?

The last time Zig and I visited, maybe three years ago, he thought he was so cool showing us the subway, the Brooklyn Bridge, the overpriced corner market where he gets his groceries. His apartment was literally falling apart. The shower faucet leaked, there was grime on the walls, and it smelled like burning garbage. Yet every time he looked at us, I could tell he was thinking, *Look how awesome I am.*

The worst part was we had to sleep on his disgusting couches, and his roommates were coming in and out of the apartment the whole night, drunk and laughing like it was the middle of the day. When Mom heard about this, she told him we're not allowed to visit again until he gets his own place.

And I thought to myself, *I hope he never, ever, gets his own place.*

I get why New York City spoke to him. Dad's an artist – or at least a bartender *posing* as an artist. I mean, he has the degree, but only because Mom put him through art school with the understanding that he'd do the same for her afterward. And the only reason she didn't finish earlier was because she got knocked up with his baby. With Zig.

As far as I'm concerned, filthy, overrated New York City can keep him.

I flip the invite over and see a handwritten note scrawled on the back.

Gonna let you two live your lives and make your own choices, but I know you'll regret not coming. Here's the info in case you change your minds.

P.S. I hope you never have to go through what it feels like to be treated this way by your own kids.

No *I understand why you're upset.* No *I know how hard this must be for you.* Classic Dad, putting us on a guilt trip, blaming us for his shitty decisions. Convincing himself – and trying to convince everyone else, too – that he's the victim here.

My rage carries me inside the house, and I'm in the worst possible mindset for what I find.

Some '90s grunge song pulses through the dingy haze in the air. The music is so loud Zig and Vinnie don't look over when I come in, so I have time to assess the situation: Ziggy with a beer in one hand, snickering over some magazine, which I make a concerted effort not to study too closely. Vinnie seated next to him, hovering so close to our scuffed-up coffee table that at first I think he's passed out or something. There's a quick snort, then Vinnie shoots upright, letting out a long, satisfied exhale.

Panic rises as I notice the plastic baggie full of what looks like baking soda, but which I know deep down is not.

The pot boils over.

"Get out of my house!" I shriek, running to the couch and kicking Vinnie's shin so hard I wouldn't be surprised if

I broke it.

He wails, pulling his leg up toward his chest.

Ziggy's bloodshot eyes shoot toward me. "What the hell?"

He's playing tough, but I see the fear in them. That he was not expecting to get caught tonight.

Mom and I both knew he was drinking, occasionally smoking pot. But this? This is something different.

The look in his eyes is terrifying, but I don't break my gaze. He looks a million years old. My amazing brother, star of his Little League baseball team, bug collector, ping-pong partner. He used to do Bob's Burgers impersonations to cheer me up when I was sad, invent a new flavor of homemade hot chocolate every Christmas. And now he's throwing his life away.

"Why are you letting him win, Zig?"

I'm crying now. The tears are stones in my eye sockets, so heavy they feel like they might crack my skull.

"Dad has nothing to do with this!"

"Fucking *hell*, Ziggy, you have so much potential!"

His eyes go wild. "You know who's just like Dad, Jo? You! Thinking your life matters. Thinking anyone cares about you or your fucking dreams –"

"*You're* the one who's like him, why can't you see?! Breaking Mom's heart, just like he –"

Ziggy shoots up from the couch, towering over me. Arm cocked high in the air.

He could kill me with a single punch.

Vinnie knows it, too. High as he is, I see him lurch forward, a look of terror on his face, trying to figure out how to intervene.

Ziggy stays frozen in place, chest heaving, holding my gaze. His eyes go from rabid to bitter to broken, and the tension in my shoulders releases.

I'm shaking so much that I have to steady myself against the wall, letting it guide me all the way to my bedroom. I lock the door then lean my back against it, my lungs fighting for air as if I just finished a race.

The invite is still in my hand. I rip it to pieces and let them fall to the floor.

CHAPTER 21

CAT

Jack names it the Great Prank War.

It's all fun and games to begin with: We steal the shirts they've left in a pile and toss them up a giant pine tree next to the football bleachers; they throw our water bottles on the school roof. Lucy writes VIRGIN LIPS in red lipstick on a bunch of their car windshields after practice; they toilet-paper Alma's yard.

But things escalate quickly. A couple weeks before school starts, the freshies and I go to Millie's house for one last summer hurrah on a night her parents are out of town. At around midnight, we hear something scratching on the front door.

"That's a cat, right?" Alma asks. We've just finished a *Sweatin' to the Oldies* session, and she's still wearing a teal leotard and high side ponytail.

More scratching.

"Probably the wind," Millie offers. "Bea, you go check."

"Why me?"

"Because you're the tallest."

Bea sighs and rolls her eyes, but she goes to the front door anyway, peeking out the eyehole first then slowly turning the doorknob and opening it.

Bea looks back at us. "I think you guys are jus–"

Three figures in horror masks jump from the bushes and onto the front step. I curl myself into a ball on the couch and burrow my head under the same pillow as Alma.

Our screams are eclipsed by a trio of familiar laughs.

I look up just in time to see Bea hit Jack square in the face, knocking his cheap plastic mask to the floor. "Idiots!" she manages to sputter.

Cheeto and Scorcho are laughing their heads off behind Jack. "What are you *wearing*?" Scorcho asks. "We always knew you guys were weird, but –"

"Out!" Millie screams. "Out, or I'm calling the cops!"

It takes us 30 minutes to fully calm down. Now that the threat of us becoming the inspiration for the next slasher movie has passed, I'm most horrified that Cheeto saw me in a shimmery green bodysuit and leg warmers.

"Our next move has to be epic," Millie says matter-of-factly.

"Frozen sardines in Jack's AC vents?" Sophia offers. "Someone did that to my brother once. His car smelled like rotten fish for like six months."

"Bigger," Lucy says.

"Steal Scorcho's retro CD collection?" Millie suggests.

"We don't want to get *murdered*," Bea says. "No, there's only one way to end this madness. It's going to be cruel, it's going to be messy, but they've left us with no other choice."

"What?" I ask.

"The be all and end all of prank wars." Her lips curl up in a sinister smile. "The one thing guaranteed to bring any teenage boy to his knees."

**

Ever since practices officially started, Thursday workouts are reserved for hill training. Josie made a big fuss about us not missing those days, and I didn't fully understand why until my first time running hills. I was sore for three days afterward in muscles I didn't even know existed. Mom even asked why I was walking funny, and I lied and told her I was having cramps. I felt a little bad afterward, because she was all excited since I haven't had a period in over a year.

Coach says Plain City's biggest disadvantage is how flat Plain City is, and he's got a point: The only elevation change is the football bleachers, and you can only run up and down those so many times before losing your mind. More often, we pile into the cars of whoever drove that day and meet at the trails at the base of the hills, 20 minutes northwest of Plain City.

The Thursday before school starts, the freshies and I are chatting in the parking lot, waiting for everyone else to show up, when Sergio says neither Josie nor Coach will be coming to practice today, so he's in charge.

"Where are they?" Lucy asks.

"Coach has a teacher meeting he can't miss this morning. And Jo, I don't know … sick or something. I can't get a hold of her. Coach just passed it on."

As he walks over to tell the next huddle of people, Bea's face gets a mischievous smile.

"What?" Lucy asks.

"Coach *and* Josie gone? It's the perfect opportunity."

It sinks in.

"It all ends here," Bea says, rubbing her hands together, her eyes deadly serious. "Now or never."

**

We arrive at the trailhead and the plan proceeds without any hiccups. We watch the boys disappear up the trail then run to Lucy's car, trying not to laugh as she unloads two plastic bags of tampons and pads she's been keeping in the trunk.

Bea reaches underneath the passenger seat and pulls out a bottle of Heinz ketchup. "The final touch."

I'm practically gagging as we pass the bottle back and forth, soaking the white cotton in bright red goop before attaching it to one of the boys' cars. Soon they're covered – bright-red maxis dot the cars like a bad rash, and tampons hang like ornaments from exhaust pipes and rearview mirrors. As Alma ties the last two tampons to Cheeto's handlebars, we take a step back to admire our work.

It's perfect.

"Let's hit the trails," Bea says.

High on revenge, we do our run, making an executive, Josie-free decision to shorten it by a couple miles so we can make sure to catch the boys' reactions. We time it perfectly, because we're already stretching by the time we spot them coming down the trail on the other side of the parking lot.

They stop running cold turkey. A hush ripples through the line like dominoes.

"What the …?"

"Are those …?"

We all double over laughing. "You just got served!" Alma yells.

"More like *perved*!" one of them yells back.

Jack and Scorcho march over to us.

"You're cleaning this up," Scorcho says.

"Yeah, and you'll be dead meat if it peels off any of the paint," Jack adds.

"Oh, I'm sorry, did we scuff up your '99 *Geo Metro*?" Bea says sarcastically. She stands up, holding her hand out to them. "We'll clean them off. For a truce."

Jack scowls but reaches his hand out to take hers. Before he can grab it, though, Bea retracts hers slightly. "On one condition," she says. "That it will always and forever be known that we won."

"That's not a truce!" Scorcho protests.

136

"Those are the terms. Accept them or clean up your-selves."

Jack sighs and takes Bea's outstretched hand. "You guys are disgusting," he says.

"Trust us," she says with a victorious grin. "The feeling's mutual."

**

The next day is Meri's college send-off.

"Sis, will you take the plates and napkins out to the patio?" Mom asks me in an overly cheery voice.

She's not fooling me. Mom can't sit still when she's stressed. The last time our house was this clean was the day before they dropped me off at New Horizons.

She seems to be taking the college thing harder than Dad. It's not that she doesn't *want* Meri to go to college, I don't think, but rather the uncertainty of having her away. I bet she wishes Paul and Meri had just gotten married. Bought the house next door. They don't really *need* college, those two. Dad would hire Paul, and I'm sure Meri could get a job anywhere. She'd just have to show up to the interview, smile once, and they'd have her sign the paperwork right then and there.

But I think deep down we all knew Plain City was never going to hold Meri in.

"Brats are ready," Dad calls. We gather up outside, and Mom loads potato salad, barbecue chips, watermelon, and buttery corn on the cob onto our plates. My mouth sali-vates. Although I feel the tiniest twinge of alarm at all the food, I'm able to rationalize it away, thinking again how thankful I am for cross country. I tell myself that if I could just skip over the scene where Mom and Dad find out I've been lying, straight to the *real* truth — that I'm learning to manage my problems on my own – they'd be proud of me.

As we eat, we're all careful to steer around the subject of why we're having this meal in the first place. We joke about the time a few years ago when Meri threw her half-eaten corn cob at a neighborhood dog that was crashing our cookout. We laugh when Dad points to the long-unused playset in the corner of the yard and brings up the time Meri and I found a baby raccoon and hid it under the slide for two days, thinking we could raise it as our pet.

But on the inside, I'm having a different conversation. *At least she's not going to some school in New York City or California*, I reason. UCCS is just in Colorado Springs. She'll be able to come home sometimes, and we'll be able to go visit her. Maybe I can even drive myself there when I get my license next year. Honestly, it probably wouldn't be that much different than the amount of time we *usually* see her.

At least, that's what I keep telling myself.

"Earth to Cat?" Meri says.

"Sorry, what?" I say, taking a bite of my brat.

"I was telling Mom and Dad about the activities blitz the student government sponsors during the first week of school. The principal wants everyone to sign up for something – keeps kids out of trouble, he says." She looks at me pointedly. "There are tons of options: clubs, debate team, *cross country* …"

I practically choke. Maybe this was her master plan all along, to out me just before she moves out. We haven't spoken about cross country since I coerced her into signing my disclosure form, but every once in a while when we're sitting at the breakfast table – her groggy eyed and me *pretending* to be groggy eyed – I'll get a disapproving look that says, *You need to tell them.*

"You better think of something to sign up for," she continues. "I doubt Blythe is going to want you over at her house *every day after school*."

I suddenly understand what Meri is hinting at. Once school starts, cross country practice moves to the afternoon. Plus, the races are then, too. I've known about this for a while, but it always seemed so far in the future I figured I'd worry about it later.

But summer is quickly disappearing. And if I don't come up with an excuse for why I'm two hours late getting home from school every day, there are going to be questions.

Mom lights up, clearly missing the tension brewing between us. "Have you given drama club any more thought, honey? I heard from Vicki Delaney that they've already started meeting."

Vicki Delaney's daughter, Monica, is in all Mom's favorite things: drama club, show choir, orchestra. She's basically Mom's dream daughter.

"Not yet. I guess we'll see once school starts," I say.

Meri casts me a disappointed look. I guess she was hoping I'd take the reins and come clean myself. Maybe she thought it was best to drop the bomb tonight, when they are already preoccupied with the college thing. It makes sense.

But I'm not ready to tell them. Not yet.

I look Meri in the eyes and take a big, emphatic bite of potato salad. Just to prove how recovered I am.

We finish just as the sun is starting to make its descent.

There's no more wick to burn.

We wander slowly out to the front yard, Mom pushing Penny, me in step with Meri. Dad disappears into the house and returns with Meri's two suitcases, then loads them in the back of the truck beside the few mismatched pieces of furniture Grandma donated to help furnish her apartment, which are already secured with bungee cables.

A heavy silence settles around us.

"Well ..." Meri says. She touches Penny's cheek, which Penny returns with a sweet coo. Then Meri pulls me into a tight, warm, coconut-scented hug.

I thought I was going to make it through the afternoon unscathed, but my eyes start to water.

"Remember, you can call me anytime," she says in my ear. "You're strong, Cat. Don't let your fire go out again."

Dad gets in his truck. Mom and Meri open the doors on Meri's white Corolla.

"You're sure you're going to be okay watching Penny for this long, Cat?"

Three months ago, there's no way Mom would have let me stay home by myself, let alone be in charge of Penny, for four hours. But today I volunteered, knowing Mom would want the time to focus solely on Meri, and also wanting to prove how responsible I can be. I was surprised when she said yes.

"Of course," I say. "You can trust me."

The look Meri gives me could have fried one of Dad's brats. I return it with one that says, *Watch me prove it.*

CHAPTER 22

CAT

The night before both the first day of school and the first race is the Five-Hundred-Mile Club dinner at Coach's house. Mom thinks I'm at some drama club recruiting event (which, for the record, I *did* go to for like 10 minutes while waiting for Lucy to pick me up in the school parking lot, just in case Monica says anything that then gets passed to my mom). I feel terrible, but the excuse was just too perfect. Mrs. Delaney told Mom about it last week, and I'd already been stressing out about coming up with somewhere I had to be. I try to use Blythe sparingly these days. She hasn't been to our house since the end of June, and even with Mom's myriad of distractions, she was bound to notice there's something fishy about me going to Blythe's and her never coming over to us.

Coach lives in the small 1970s ranch house by the side of the highway on the outskirts of town. You have to drive past it to get to the interstate, so I've seen it literally hundreds of times, always noticing the rusty swing set, the faded blue paint, the unkempt yard and overgrown garden patch. I guess I knew teachers didn't make much money, but I'm still kind of surprised to realize this is where he lives.

His wife is petite and friendly, one of those people who's great at asking questions and even better at faking like they care about the responses. I knew he was married, but didn't know they had four kids. She introduces them as their "feral cats"; the oldest three look like they are in elementary

141

school. The youngest, maybe two years old, is covered in dirt and running around the place in just a diaper.

Coach grills the steaks while Mrs. Davis sets out picnic foods on a long folding table decorated with balloons, streamers, and sparkly foil centerpieces, all in PC High School silver and royal blue. The team is scattered around in mismatched patio chairs, chatting while we wait for the last few stragglers to arrive. I'm sitting in a circle with the freshies, comparing schedules for school tomorrow.

"You got Mrs. Baird for English? That's rough," Alma says, staring at my phone and shaking her head.

"But you got Mr. Richardson for history – that balances it out. Man, if he was 10 years younger ..." Millie says. Bea swats her arm.

I end up having math and computer science with Lucy, chemistry with Millie and Bea, and history with Alma and Bea. I don't know if I'll have any classes with Sophia because she isn't here yet.

I've been playing it cool about starting school, trying to match the freshies' nonchalance. For them, school seems like a box to check to be able to run cross country. But I'm all nerves. It isn't just the fact that I haven't actually done school for basically a year and a half (do I even remember how to multiply and divide?) but I'm also anticipating how it will feel to be a social pariah. Who knows what Blythe has told everyone about me recently? Even though I know I'm happier taking a step back from that world, those are the kids I've hung around with since I was five. To be dropped and forgotten still hurts, and I'm nervous for how it will feel to be stuffed into a building with them. What sort of triggers it will set off.

Coach calls everyone to attention. "Wow. What an elite group. Five hundred miles over three months is no small feat. The first year I started coaching I had two runners reach this goal; this year we have 23. Guess it's a good time to throw in the towel, or next year we'd have to start serving peanut butter and jelly sandwiches." Everyone laughs. "Seriously, though, give yourselves a hand."

We clap, and I feel a surge of pride at the accomplishment. *Five hundred miles*. I think back to where I started. Hardly able to make it to the stop sign and back.

Who would have ever thought? Me, an actual runner?

He says a few more things, then tells us to dig in. I follow the freshies over to the table, where they start loading pasta salad and biscuits and fruit onto their plates. When we get to the end of the table, Coach sets sizzling hunks of steak on each of our plates. There's absolutely no way I can eat the whole thing.

"Best thing about the night before a race? Carb loading," Lucy says to me. "Don't know if it really helps you go any faster, but I'll take any excuse to stuff my face with bread."

School anxiety has taken up so much of my brain space I've hardly even thought about the race tomorrow. The way everyone has been talking about it makes it seem more like a glorified workout than a legitimate competition. I guess most of the other small-town high schools in our district have just a handful or two of kids on their cross country teams, and the Wednesday meets where we'll face off against them are basically a time to work on pacing and pack running to prepare us for the more important races later on.

"Where's Sophia?" I ask when we return to our chairs.

"Oh, forgot to tell you guys," Millie says, jawing a huge mouthful of steak. "She called me just before I came over. Says she's bailing because Kyle invited her to some back-to-school-night party with the football team."

Bea, mid-swallow, nearly spits out her food. "I'm calling her."

"It won't help," Lucy says, blocking her as she tries to scroll to Sophia's number. "Kyle Pelty will lose his novelty eventually. We've just gotta let this run its course. She'll resent us if we get clingy."

This starts a back-and-forth about Sophia and her dating life, a discussion that comes up every time she's not in our presence. Alma, clearly over the debate, rolls her eyes and turns to me. "So who are you lockering with?"

The question catches me off-guard. Blythe and I always planned to locker together, of course. But registration was back in February. Mom filled out all my paperwork, not even sure I'd be back home to start the school year.

I shrug. "I didn't request anyone."

Her face reflects just a hint of surprise. I guess when you're Meri Shultz's little sister, people expect you'd have friends. "They'll assign you someone tomorrow then. Maybe you'll be close to us."

The reminder of all the unknowns hurtling toward me sends my stomach into knots. "Be right back." I set my plate by my chair and walk up to the table to get some water.

Conveniently, at the exact same time as Cheeto.

"Hey," Cheeto says, sweeping his blond hair from his eyes. He's in jeans and a fitted black T-shirt, and he smells like soap.

"Hey."

We haven't really talked much since the watermelon incident. I mean, we've *talked,* but it's always been in a big group, and for some reason that feels 100 percent different than having a one-on-one conversation. It's a pleasant tension, though. Not like my nerves about school tomorrow.

A few seconds pass. His cheeks turn adorably pink.

"So ... what's your goal for tomorrow?" I ask, glad Coach gave us the assignment to ask 10 teammates their race goal. Get two shy kids in a corner together, and they basically need a script.

"Break 17:00," he says.

I try to do the math in my head. Seventeen minutes – less than six minutes per mile. "That's insane."

He scoffs. "If I was a girl, maybe. It's pretty mediocre for a dude."

"Maybe you could sneak into our race. Your hair's long enough, I bet no one on the other team would even notice."

He laughs. "Yeah, but then I'd risk getting whooped by Josie. Or you."

My turn to blush. "Honestly, I'm more worried about surviving the first day of school."

I'm pretty sure Cheeto knows I wasn't at PC last year, but he hasn't ever asked why. I assume the freshies told him I was homeschooled, which I've still never corrected them on.

"Eh, it's not so bad. So long as you enjoy getting shoved into garbage cans and the occasional swirly."

"I mean, who wouldn't?"

"The key is *which* bathroom you hang around," he continues, both of us keeping a straight face. "I'd avoid the one by the gym. The meatheads really stink that one up."

I feel like we're really on a roll here and feel mildly irritated when we're interrupted by Josie and Sergio calling us to attention. I give Cheeto my best wish-we-could-keep-talking smile and go back to sit with the freshies.

"Finally announcing your engagement?" one of the boys shouts. Josie gives him the death stare. Josie clearly hates getting teased about Sergio – not sure if that's because she thinks of Sergio more as a brother, because she *does* like him and doesn't like getting called out, or if she's generally just not into guys – but honestly the two of them do make the perfect captain duo. She's the no-nonsense boss bitch, and he's kind and polite and quietly backs her up. It's a good balance. If Scorcho was the other captain, it would basically be a fascist regime.

"We just wanted to say good luck to everyone," Josie says. "We've had an awesome summer, but tomorrow things get real. We need everyone to be 100 percent in until State is over – not just coming to workouts every day but monitoring what you're eating, going to bed early each night, and staying focused. We're not settling for anything less than a championship this season. Boys *and* girls. Those 5A teams aren't going to know what hit them."

Bea leans in toward the four of us and whispers, "Too bad the only person who needs to hear this is the one person who's missing."

Josie looks at Sergio, cueing him to talk. "Coach always tells us you only need two things to be successful." His voice cracks, and a few people stifle some good-natured laughs. "Hard work and confidence. Simple as it sounds, how many of us really believe it?"

Coach, who is standing nearby next to a metal fire pit, pulls out a lighter from his pocket and holds it to the logs already piled in the metal basin. It takes a few seconds to catch, but soon there's a small blaze crackling in the center.

"We wanted to try something," Josie continues. "We're going to hand out some paper and pencils. Your job is to write down whatever's holding you back: your doubts and fears, the lies you believe about yourself. Could be just one thing, could be a whole list. When you finish, fold it up and hold it up in the air."

The three of them pass out the supplies. Soon everyone quiets down, fully absorbed into the task.

I look around at the furious scribbling, wondering what all these people could be writing. They all seem so confident, so unconcerned by what anyone else thinks of them. It's like together they've built a wall between themselves and the outside world, sheltering them from everything that sucks about being a teenager.

For me, a single thought surfaces. Something that's been lurking in the dark recesses of my mind ever since I got home from New Horizons.

I hesitate, but finally put my pencil to the paper.

I fold it up before anyone can see. Josie walks by and takes it from my outstretched hand, along with Bea's and Millie's.

"Wait, are you guys gonna read these?" Jack asks out loud. "'Cause I might need mine back ..." Everyone laughs as he makes a guilty face. I don't know what, exactly, he's referring to, but I've got some guesses.

As soon as all the papers have been gathered, Josie calls us to join them by the fire.

We circle up, arms woven over shoulders and behind backs until there are no gaps between us. The sun has barely finished setting behind us and the dancing flames cast moody shadows across all our faces.

Sergio holds out the stack, rips it once, and lets it go. Paper scraps flutter down, igniting on impact. The fire brightens momentarily, then settles back into a steady, flickering glow. In seconds, the papers are nothing but a pile of ash.

"Whatever you wrote down, it's gone now – a burnt offering to the running gods," Josie says with a glint in her eyes. "Ever heard the saying, 'Your struggles don't define you?' It's nice, but I like this one better: *You define your struggles*. Whatever you wrote on that paper is your starting line, but it isn't your destination. Things are bound to get tough this season, but take a look around. No matter what, you're not alone. We're not just a bunch of friends. Not just a team. We're a wolfpack. *The* Wolfpack."

My heart swells, the support-group energy reminding me, painfully but also somehow nostalgically, of New Horizons.

"For the strength of the pack is the wolf ..." Scorcho yells.

The response, 25 voices deep, sends chills up my spine. *"... and the strength of the wolf is the pack."*

CHAPTER 23

JOSIE

I don't know why I took it.

It was wrong, I admit. But it was like the paper was calling to me. Begging me to do it. And so, when everyone's focus was momentarily pulled away to feed Jack's attention addiction, I couldn't help but stuff it into my back pocket.

I wanted to know – *had* to know – what Cat could have possibly written down.

I've done my best to set aside my personal prejudices, to rein in my envy, to treat her the same way I treat everyone else on this team.

I just had to know what she considers to be a struggle. Wonder if she can even imagine what it's like to hate your own father, to find your mom mid-panic attack on the kitchen floor, to be terrified of – and for – your only sibling. To know that some days it's either meat on the table or gasoline in the car. To wake up to a thrift-store Christmas and still be grateful for it.

So when I get back home, locked safely behind my bedroom door, I pull the paper from my pocket and unfold it in my hands.

Once broken, always broken.

I laugh out loud.

Broken, huh?

There's no way in hell Cat Shultz could even begin to know the true meaning of that word.

CHAPTER 24
CAT

I'm up the next morning before my alarm goes off. Dress in a new pair of jeans and a beige top Mom bought me the last time we went to Lyman. Straighten my hair for the first time in months. Pack my lunch. The school routine comes back to me, like riding a bike or tying my shoelaces.

But it's different without Meri. No one to share the vanity mirror with me as I put on makeup. No one humming in the bathroom, dancing down the hallway, zapping any bad vibes with her positive energy.

I miss her like crazy. And I'm hit with an overwhelming sense of loss that I forfeited the last year I had left with her.

Breakfast is toast and eggs. Mom always starts the year off by getting up early to make food and see us off, but it usually only lasts a week or two. Penny's been waking up a lot more at night the past few days, so we'll see if she even makes it that long.

Mom's in her fuzzy green bathrobe, taking miniscule sips of coffee from her mug as she leans against the counter. "So you'll be staying after school then? Starting today?"

I take a bite of my toast. My eyes flicker down to the floor, but I force them back to meet her gaze. "Yep."

Her smile elicits a physical pain in my chest. "Well, I'm just so excited for you to meet some new friends. And you're going to love Mr. Edwards. *Oklahoma!* is such a fun production."

In my defense, pretending to join the drama club was the only thing that made sense. If I'd said I'm going to join the debate team, she'd have asked to come to the tournaments; marching band, and she'd expect me to bring home a trombone or something. And both my parents know I'm terrible at sports that require any sort of coordination, so tennis or soccer or swim team were obviously out of the question.

With drama club, there is nothing to bring home, no parental involvement at all until the play actually happens. Which, ironically enough, is the week before State.

Ironic but irrelevant, since I'll have told them the truth long before then.

"So I'll see you at about five? I can't wait to hear about your first day."

I kiss her goodbye and head out the door, breathing in the familiar scent of morning. After the party last night, my first day of school anxiety has leveled off to a minor but sustained case of the butterflies, like a sugar rush after eating too much candy. I repeat a few of Ms. Reid's positive affirmations and try to channel Meri's good energy.

Because really, how bad can it be?

**

Since I missed all of last year, I did a little school tour of Plain City with Mom and one of the school counselors a few weeks ago. Empty, it seemed manageable enough. Now, full of noise and chaos, I might as well be in Times Square. The giant wolf statue in the center of the foyer that seemed so proud and stately is now curtained behind a traffic jam of students all trying to talk over one another.

I'm not sure what I was expecting. A welcoming committee? Someone holding a sign that says, *"You've Got This, Cat"*? I'm hit with a sudden, irrational grudge against Mom and Dad for not having Meri and I one year closer together. As much as I sometimes resent being known as Meri's little sister, I'd give anything to have her here with me now.

I join the current and head toward my locker, pulling my schedule from my back pocket to double-check the combination printed at the top. I long to have Blythe by my side, laughing with me at the absurdity of all this, from the size of the seniors to the packed halls to the fact that the parking lot is full of cars students *drove here themselves*. I scan the crowds for her smile, her high ponytail, not sure if I want to find her or if I'm terrified I will.

I know I can't avoid her forever. There's a decent chance she'll be in at least one of my standard sophomore classes, and an almost-guarantee that I'll see her at some point in the day: the lunchroom, the bathroom, the hallway. Plain City High School is big, but it's not *that* big.

My locker assignment is down by the gym. I squeeze around groups of chatting girls and hip-locked couples until I finally find my number. Someone is already standing in front of it, arranging books on the top shelf.

Josie.

A surge of hopefulness rushes through me. Josie has never been outright unkind, but despite the freshies' reassurances that it's just her personality and/or stuff going on at home, I haven't been able to shake the feeling there's bad energy between us. I've been telling myself to just give it time, that once the season gets going she'll warm up to me. I'm sure it's partially that I'm faster than anyone, myself included, expected me to be. She's never had anyone so close to her pace. But how do I fix that? Run *slower*? Because I know she wants this championship. And from what everyone says, *herself* included, they need me to get there.

But maybe this locker assignment is it. My chance to win her over.

I check the number again, just to be sure, then clear my throat. "Looks like they stuck the two of us together."

Josie spins around, a wild look in her eyes like she's just had the biggest surprise of her life. And not a good one.

My hopefulness evaporates. "Were you supposed to be lockering with someone else?"

It's like I can see her walk herself back from the ledge, force herself to play nice. "My old locker partner graduated last year. They must have assigned us together since we're both on the team." Slowly, she turns back to the open locker, rearranging her stuff to make room for me. "You can take the bottom shelf."

She doesn't look at me again but slides over a little to make room for me. I hang my backpack on the right hook and pull out a notebook and pencil, wracking my brain for something to say. I settle for the lamest question on the planet. "So ... do you like your schedule?"

I glance over just in time to catch the unmistakable flicker of irritation in her eyes.

I'm good at reading subtle social cues. Perceptive, some might call it. Sensitive; aware.

I call it cursed.

Because once a thought like this is put in your head – that you're not as likable or pretty or funny or, yes, *thin* as you should be – it's almost impossible to get it out.

The bell rings, saving me from the degradation of listening to her force an answer. I fight my way past the clog of students, remembering my first class is on the other side of the school. I move as fast as I can but I'm still tardy, and the only seat left in the classroom is next to Matt – my first crush, my first kiss, the one who dropped me like a used Kleenex as soon as he found out I had an eating disorder.

By way of greeting, he gives me an awkward side glance and a forced smile, as if we're strangers meeting in an elevator.

I slump into the seat and look around at the backs of the

heads in front of me. I recognize a few of them as people from middle school, but none of them look back to smile or wave. It's like I've been permanently erased from their memories.

I try to focus on the teacher's first-day-of-school spiel, but my eyes wander out the window, stopping at the edge of the parking lot where the team always meets for practice. The neat lines of parked cars feel like graffiti on some sacred relic. The heaviness of the morning settles in.

Second, third, and fourth period are a bit better, since I have at least one of the freshies in each class, but I can't shake the feeling from this morning. Can't stop asking myself the question that's been repeating ever since in my mind: What is it about me that Josie despises so much?

**

After fourth is my lunch block. The familiar chicken patty/canned mixed vegetable smell wafting through the hallways almost makes me dry-heave, so I bypass the lunchroom and go outside to the courtyard, pulling out the now-squished peanut butter and honey sandwich and apple from my brown paper sack. The freshies all had first lunch, but I don't really mind. I need some time to decompress, to be alone.

I'm just opening my mouth to take a bite when I hear a laugh that sends a shock wave straight through me.

And there she is. Blythe, standing next to another table, surrounded by people – some I recognize, some I don't – laughing at inside jokes, asserting their social status with their clothes and shoes and vocal inflections.

She's in her cheer uniform. But that's not the only thing about her that throws me: It's the second piercing in her ears. The bleach-blond streaks in her hair. The way she moves her hands when she's talking.

It's Blythe, but it's not. She's a whole different person.

She must feel me staring because she looks over at me, right into my eyes. But instead of looking panicked or wistful or even vindictive, her gaze is empty. Devoid of any emotion at all.

Deep down, I truly believed that if we could just lock eyes, our fight would be as good as over. I'd apologize for the hundredth time about what I said at the fireworks; she'd tell me she's sorry for ignoring me all summer.

The reality is that she simply turns away from me, slipping back into her conversation as if she'd never looked my way at all.

Mom told me that when I was a toddler, I had this little red blanket I'd carry around, like Linus from Charlie Brown. Whenever I had it with me, I was a super chill baby, hardly ever cried. If they couldn't find it, though, it might as well have been the end of the world.

Blythe, I realize, has always been my human version of a safety blanket. I never had to worry about being lonely at recess or not having anyone show up at my birthday party. Later on, that translated to tampon security and never facing the terror of sitting alone at a middle school lunch table. An automatic, unconditional constant. And I always equated that security with friendship. With *best* friendship.

But truthfully? I've never felt freer, more alive, than I have these past few months I've spent without her.

Mostly, that realization is liberating. But underneath it lies an involuntary thought that makes me feel disloyal and shallow and petty.

Blythe is clearly moving up the ranks of the social pyramid, the one my sister sat comfortably at the top of for four years. But somehow, the only place I fit in is with a bunch of outcasts.

And even then, I think as Josie's face materializes behind my eyelids, *belonging isn't quite it.*

CHAPTER 25

JOSIE

The locker room is buzzing with excitement, but I'm still kicking myself for letting my emotions show this morning. I just wasn't prepared for the surprise. That last look Cat gave me before the first bell rang was like a wounded animal, enough to crack even my stone heart.

I didn't see her back at the locker all day.

Millie is blasting hip-hop on a portable boombox and half the girls are dancing around in their sports bras, singing into deodorant microphones. I'm happy they're having fun and would join in, just for the camaraderie, if I weren't stressed about the Cat thing. I mean, what if she bailed? I don't know if I have it in me to beg on her doorstep again.

I'm pulling my blue singlet over my head when she walks in.

I finally let myself exhale, but as I study her for a few seconds, I realize she's clearly not herself. The slumped shoulders, the deep-set frown. She looks like she's trying not to cry, and I can't help but wonder how big a part I played in that. Millie must notice her mood because she puts her arm around her, shoving her deodorant stick in her face, essentially forcing her to sing along, and I'm grateful because it does seem to cheer her up a bit.

I finish getting dressed and head outside. It's a hot day, mid-90s. Cloudless sky. The fields surrounding the school, sparsely marked with orange cones and white chalk arrows, seem to ripple through waves of heat.

A bus pulls up alongside the curb on the other side of the fence, spitting out a team in yellow jerseys. Sandridge. I count the girls as they step off. Three, six, eight …

And that's it. Eight. Eight to our 25. I know I should feel bad for them, but it's validating to see how much deeper we are than all these other small-town schools.

It seems like most of our girls are out of the locker room, so I announce the warm-up.

The pre-race routine isn't much different from practice. We jog and stretch, laugh while Millie does a painfully accurate impersonation of the principal. All the while I've got my eye on Cat, trying to read her. There's still a deer-in-the-headlights look in her eyes, but at least she's responding when people talk to her, even smiling a little.

Finally, Coach's voice booms through the track's PA system, calling all the girls to the start line.

We walk over together, a blue wave overtaking the soccer pitch. Coach appears at midfield, holding a starter pistol – when we host the meets, he has to be both coach and race official because there's no one else to do it.

After delivering a brief rundown of the course for Sandridge's sake, he lifts the pistol over his head, freezes for a few dramatic seconds, then fires it into the air.

Even though Sandridge is no competition, there's still an intoxicating energy surrounding the first official race of the season. I feel a switch flip inside me and let myself fly.

Within 100 meters, I've taken the lead.

We hug the fence surrounding the football field. A quarter mile down.

Loop around the quad. Half a mile.

Follow the sidewalk to the edge of the city park. Three quarters.

Coach is waiting at the turnaround point, the first mile marker, to make sure everyone stays honest and actually goes around the cone. Since I'm the only runner around, I get him all to myself. He claps and cheers then yells out my time – 6:09, which is dead-on with my target pace. If I can keep this up, I'll PR, for sure.

Back on school grounds, I make my way up the berm and around the school's perimeter. When I reach the other side, I'll be two-thirds of the way through the course. One mile from the end.

I'm plotting my finish line strategy when I hear something behind me.

Faint footsteps. Labored breathing.

I don't look back, figuring it must be a parent hurrying to cheer on their kid at the second mile marker, which is notorious for being the spot most runners hit a wall.

But the sounds are persistent, cadenced.

And getting closer.

When I turn right and down the berm, my field of vision broadens. A quick glance, and I see that the approaching footsteps aren't a coddling parent, but Cat.

She's gaining on me.

And just like that, all the charity I was feeling earlier evaporates into the blazing sun.

CHAPTER 26
CAT

I didn't even want to run today. In fact, I was seconds away from heading home after the bell rang. Between my interaction this morning with Josie, seeing Blythe 2.0, and the general reminder of how utterly sucky public-school life is, I wanted nothing more than to lock myself in my bedroom and drown myself in TV. What stopped me was imagining Mom, who thinks I'm well on my way to high school bliss at drama club. And I just couldn't stand to see the disappointment in her eyes.

So I showed up. Kissed Olga for good luck, just hoping to make it through the race in one piece.

But a mile in, I realize this is exactly what I needed.

Ironically enough, what's propelling me forward is something I overheard Josie say once: *"Bottle it up, burn it like fuel."* She was talking to one of the other girls on the team who was explaining some humiliating interaction she had with a bunch of frat-bound seniors at the gas station.

I wonder if Josie knows how much fuel she put in my tank today.

It's hard to describe, this resentment I suddenly feel toward her. A tipping point, of sorts. Blythe's obvious dislike of me is painful but understandable; Josie's makes no logical sense. I've done all I can to prove my loyalty to the team, met her expectations. I've analyzed and reanalyzed our every interaction.

But I'm done trying to please her.

She's been in the lead the whole race, followed by one of the few Sandridge girls. I left the freshies pretty early on and have been sitting comfortably in third. But here, at the first mile marker, I feel something primal enter my body – a ravenous hunger that consumes my entire being.

I close in on the Sandridge girl. There's a noticeable change in her posture as I overtake her, like a flower wilting.

I speed up. It's like the first mile was just a warm-up, a chance to work out my tension. My limbs feel fluid and mechanical. The sun, bearing down like an oven, doesn't even bother me.

I'm making my way around the perimeter, 100 meters from the second mile marker, when I realize Josie is within striking distance.

Coach sprints toward us from across the soccer field, shouting out the time on the race clock. *"12:20…12:25…"*

I'm flying.

Coach's encouragement is focused on Josie first, of course. I see her posture straighten, her pace quicken.

Then he turns to me. Finds my eyes.

"Get up and run with her, Cat! How much do you want it?"

The question sinks deep. How much *do* I want it?

Summer flashes before my eyes like a deathbed vision. Sneaking out for jogs. Lucy nearly plowing me down with her car. My first morning practice, snowballing into 50 more. Dirt roads at sunrise. Unexpected friendships. Feeling alive again, like I'm waking up from a long, deep, nightmare-plagued sleep.

And somewhere along the way, running stopped being the escape and became the destination.

Cross country, I realize, is no longer a personal revolt or a new way to mask my body issues. It's who I *am*.

And maybe I was never born to be a Meri or a Blythe, but that doesn't mean I have to be invisible.

With Josie locked in my line of sight, I try to match her lengthening stride. We round the tennis courts, the final stretch before entering the track for the finish.

Less than a half mile to go.

My legs, my lungs, my *everything* burns, but I drive my arms forward as we enter the gate, offering up my banshee cry as I turn the corner. Logically, I know it's me making my body move, but it's like I'm operating completely outside of conscious thought – my vision is blurred, the cheering around me distant and tinny like it's being played through an old 1940s radio.

But I do notice that the gap between us is starting to shrink.

My brain conjures an image of Josie deflating like all those people I passed in the Fourth of July 5K. Just like the Sandridge girl. The resulting endorphin rush could carry me a whole other mile.

I push harder.

150 meters … 100 … 50 …

I'm just lucid enough to know I've stolen her lead from her just a few strides from the finish line.

And I don't feel an ounce of regret for it.

CHAPTER 27

JOSIE

The door is locked when I get home. Figures.

I growl and pull out my keys, immediately seeing that Ziggy is on the couch playing some loud, hyper-realistic shooter game as I push open the door. He glances over at me, his eyes steely, but I don't even care tonight. Let him come after me. I'm pissed enough that I'm 99 percent sure I could take him.

I toss my duffel with my race uniform and flats hard on the floor, as if today was their fault somehow. My brain has been trying all afternoon to blame this on something – the heat, Cat's dramatics, my fucking period – but I don't let the thoughts stay. I have to take ownership of this.

That, and make sure it never happens again.

I get out a pot and fill it with water, then rummage through the cupboards for a box of pasta. I stick the pot on the stove and stare at the water until bubbles start to surface. It's like I'm watching a simulation of what's happening inside of me: tiny beads of rage multiplying uncontrollably, headed soon for a full boil.

Ziggy's silence isn't helping. He knows today was my first race, and even though we're not on talking terms, he could at least acknowledge that I'm alive.

"You'll be happy to know I got my ass kicked today," I say, willing to be self-deprecating for a little human interaction.

"Didn't ask," is all he replies. His eyes don't even flicker away from the screen.

**

Saturday is my chance for redemption: the Aurora Invitational. Just like the Mile High Invitational in a few weeks – my excuse for missing Dad's wedding – Coach says there will be college scouts here, too, though not quite as many. If I can do well at both races, my chances of landing a scholarship skyrocket.

But for me, the biggest draw of the invitationals is the chance to race against Aspen Ridge. Since we're not in the same region, invitationals are the only opportunity we'll get to match up against them before State. If we can beat them today, we'll shake up the high school cross country world. Their national ranking will be at stake, and probably their Nike sponsorship too. And even if we *don't* beat them, I'm positive we'll get close enough to at least freak them out.

The best part is they likely have no idea what's coming.

To the 5A world, we're nobodies. Invisibles. Small-town hicks who got into the division on formality. A macro-representation of my micro-existence.

But not for long.

We've just filed off the bus. Coach is last, shaking his head as he tosses Jack's racing flats toward him. "Honestly, Wilson, you'd forget your legs if they weren't attached."

"Sorry, Coach."

There's a ripple of muffled laughter. Coach always checks the seats after we get off. Two years back, one of our top guy runners left his racing jersey on the bus, and because it was so close to race time, he had to borrow one from the girls. He never lived it down.

Of course, this wouldn't be a problem at district meets, where there's only one or two buses in the parking lot. But at invitationals, finding your bus after drop-off is like searching for a specific Twinkie in a Twinkie factory.

Last year at this race, there were more than 2,000 runners split between four races: a varsity and JV heat each for the boys and girls. Invitationals don't mean a thing in terms of ranking, but because so many teams from around Colorado enter, they showcase the best of the best. For a team as dominant as us, they're the only September races that really matter.

With so many runners, anything can happen. If you've got a lightning-fast number one and number two, but your three, four, and five are just mediocre, you'll get buried in the scorecard. On the flip side, if you don't have a single standout runner, but your six and seven are decent, you might be able to add enough points to the other teams' scores to put you over the top.

They're also the only indicator of how you might stack up in the championships in October. Sure, you can track other teams' race results. Compare their times with yours on similar courses. But there are too many variables: the weather, the direction of the wind, how deep you are into the season – and maybe most importantly, the intensity of the competition. Running is a lot more like wrestling or boxing than most people think: Put two comparable runners together on a course, and it's always a cockfight.

I scan the field for the Aspen Ridge baby blue, but don't spot it.

"Serge and Jo, why don't you take the team and go find a spot," Coach says, pulling back my attention. "I'll go grab the bibs."

As Coach walks toward the registration tent, Serge and I cut through the park, searching for a pavilion that hasn't already been claimed. The team follows behind us, laughing and joking and generally not paying attention. Like usual.

Serge hasn't said much to me since the race Wednesday. He knows me well enough to wait for me to instigate the conversation when I'm on edge.

"It won't happen again," I say, responding to a question he hasn't asked.

I can tell he's choosing his words carefully. "You were close to last year's PR, and it was only the first race of the season." He glances over his shoulder, checking to see who's in earshot. "Her success doesn't make you a failure, you know."

I know he's right, and more importantly that he's being genuine, but the triteness of the phrase still irks me. I roll my eyes. "There can only be one first place, Serge. Sure, I expected to have to work for the individual state title, but not against my own teammate."

"Since when have you cared about the individual title?"

"What, can I not have a goal to be first overall?"

"You can, it's just ... winning State as a team is the only thing I've ever heard you talk about."

"And it still is the most important thing."

His eyes shift back and forth. "Okay, well ... having her around definitely boosts your –"

"I know, Serge!" I snap. "I know. I don't need you to lecture me on why we need her. I'm fully aware of it already."

He stares at me with his typical patient, even-keeled gaze. "Just be careful is all I'm saying. That stuff's contagious."

We've arrived at an empty pavilion. Without another word, he rejoins the boys. Everyone starts unloading earbuds and pillows and boxes of Wheat Thins for a day of racing and chilling out, fully oblivious to our conversation.

I don't have to ask to know what he means by "that stuff." Competitiveness. Rivalry. Jealousy. For three years, we've had no animosity on the team whatsoever, and as captain, I'm the one who's supposed to be setting the highest standard. If I turn this into a feud between me and Cat, do we really deserve to win any more than Aspen Ridge?

I start unloading my own bag and look up to see Coach approaching, his brow furrowed.

"Bad news, kiddo," he says, handing me the stack of racing bibs and safety pins so I can pass them out. "Aspen Ridge didn't show."

"What?"

He shrugs, apologetic. "Apparently there was some national invitational in North Carolina they ended up flying to last minute."

I want to scream. It isn't fair – how can we prove ourselves against them if they never even show up? If they never give any other Colorado teams a *chance* to challenge them? I tell myself they're avoiding us, that they're scared, but inside I know the truth is that they still haven't even heard of Plain City.

"Coach Horton from Roosevelt assured me they'd be at the next invitational," Coach continues. "Says their school district caps interstate sports travel to one event per month."

A bitter laugh escapes my throat. *One interstate event per month.* We'd be lucky to get funding to attend one national race like that in an entire *year.* Even then, we'd probably have to sell our souls to some door-to-door candy bar fundraising company.

I take a deep breath. Try to shelve my anger for when the race starts.

"The scouts are still here, though, right?" I ask.

Coach smiles. "Just talked to one myself. Show 'em what you can do today, Jo. Aspen Ridge or not, today's a big one for you."

**

We're stretching when the announcer calls the varsity girls to the start line. I'm grateful the freshies are there to lighten the mood, to conceal the silent tension between me and Cat. The two of us haven't acknowledged anything with words

since the race on Wednesday – just the occasional intercepted glances and a palpable chill to the air whenever we're
near each other. She also hasn't used our assigned locker at
all since the first day of school. I think she's just using her
cross country locker to store her backpack and carrying all
her supplies from class to class. Which I'm not complaining
about.

We're just about there when the freshies start making a
scene after spotting Sophia's football player boyfriend on the
sidelines. I'm hurrying them toward the start line, spouting
off some captainly spiel about staying focused, when I notice
the shell-shocked look on Cat's face.

I remember my first invitational and all the emotions
that came with it. It's a lot, seeing 350 runners all lined
up together. A 50-color rainbow. Energy so thick you could
almost reach out and grab a handful.

But if she can't handle this, there's no way she'll survive
the intensity of State.

We take our places. I tune everything else out – Cat, the
announcer delivering his rehearsed speech, even the cheering crowds – until the gun goes off. The Pavlovian signal for
my legs to break their shackles.

I swim through the sea of runners, elbows sculling, throwing a shoulder at anyone who tries to cut me off. You can
easily end up with spiked shins or bruised ribs in a race like
this. My freshman year, someone tripped and got trampled
by at least a dozen runners before the official blew the whistle, calling everyone back to the line for a restart.

The chaos is one of the reasons invitationals are some of
my favorite races.

The other reason is that there's actually some competition.

The first mile I'm not even in the top 10. Rabbits, we call
them – people who treat the start like a 400-meter sprint

and then basically have to crawl to the finish line. I sometimes wonder if it's a strategy teams use to throw off the elite runners, to see if they can bait them with the fear of not being able to catch the leaders.

But I've run enough races to know not to fall for it.

I keep a steady pace, careful not to lose sight of the girls in front but waiting for signs to make my move. And sure enough, up ahead I start to see the runners tightening up, elbows hugged to their chest, heads slightly cocked. I kick it up a notch until the gap between me and the next runner starts to close. It feels good to attach all my rage to some nameless, faceless person, keeping myself focused on their backs until I've passed them.

I don't worry about Cat and whether or not she's lurking behind me, waiting to pounce. I just focus on the runners ahead.

By mile three, I've moved up to third place. I know the two girls in front of me from last year – Caitlyn Roberts and Cici Thomlinson. Both seniors, and both in 4A, so I've never had to race against them at State, and because we're moving directly from 3A to 5A, probably never will. I have tons of respect for them both, even consider them pseudo-friends, but I wonder how much of that is situational. It's a lot easier to respect other athletes when they aren't your real competition.

Caitlyn has a mean kick, so I know I need to pass her soon to give myself a big enough lead that she won't catch up at the finish. Luckily, this part of the course takes us right by our pavilion, and I'm instantly buoyed by my teammates going wild as I pass. It's just the boost I need.

I give Caitlyn a nod of solidarity as I pass. *No hard feelings.*

Now in second, I lock eyes on Cici's jersey. She's a monster. All lean muscle, a tattoo peeking out from her shoulder strap. I've raced against her at every invitational and never beat her before. The thought of passing her almost scares me, like I need someone to give me permission first.

But she's within reach. And I feel amazing.

I shake off my self-doubt and push forward. My splits from the first two miles were hovering right around six minutes, and I won't be surprised if this third mile is in the five-minute range. Which is crazy. Easily a career PR, faster than I hoped, but certainly not faster than I deserve. I know I've earned this.

I pass her with a quarter mile left. Sprint with every last ounce of my strength. Break the finish line tape with both hands up, already celebrating my victory.

I'm lighter than air, the breath filling my lungs sweet and satisfying. Strangers hurl congratulations at me, and I do nothing to suppress the smile on my face.

But I still have a job to do. Instead of reveling in the praise, I backtrack along the sidelines toward the final stretch, eager to see how my teammates are faring, to cheer them into the finish.

I don't have to wait long. Bea comes in fourth, right after Caitlyn, then Lucy and Sophia are seven and eight. There's a blur of color, then I spot Cat, our fifth runner. She looks beat but perks up as she spots the finish line. I lost count of her place, but she's definitely in the top 20, which means our team score is going to be insanely low.

Exhilaration rips through me. I'm not sure if it's because the team will undoubtedly win the invitational, or if it's because of the comfortable distance between me and Cat. I don't overanalyze it.

"Let's go, Cat!" I yell, feeling much more generous toward her than I have for weeks.

I cheer for Millie then Alma, our six and seven. With everyone safely across, our victory secured, I search for the water table. I'm taking my first sip when a tall, angular woman in an expensive-looking tracksuit approaches.

"Josie Romero?" she says brightly. "My name is Diane Colter. I'm with the University of Colorado ..."

**

Four hours, 12 individual medals, and one first place team trophy later, we find our bus and reboard. I'm fully aware that I've got an hour of bad singing and ear-splitting laughter ahead of me, but today I don't even mind. We deserve to celebrate.

The Wolfpack showed up today. Four in the top 10 in the varsity race. Clean sweep of first, second, and third place medals for JV – Gretchen, Becca, and Elise – highlighting just how deep our team is this year.

State-champion-level domination.

The boys did all right, too, coming in third. On any other year, third would be amazing for the girls, too, but we're on a whole different plane this year.

I'd call it magic if I didn't know how hard we've worked to get here.

The next invitational, three weeks away, can't get here fast enough. We're ready to give Aspen Ridge that good scare Coach has been referring to.

A good scare, or maybe just beat them altogether.

CHAPTER 28

CAT

The bus hums like a dance party. I go through the motions, smile and laugh on cue, but I can't shake off my disappointment about the race. The whole thing was so fast paced, so overwhelming, I hardly realized what was happening until it was all over.

The worst part of all was Josie's smugness disguised as consolation.

I don't understand how no one else seems to notice. The way she's only nice to me when I don't do well, when she thinks she's got me pinned under her thumb. I'll take her outright contempt over self-gratifying pity.

I guess it's never too early to start stockpiling fuel for the next race.

I thought I was hiding my emotions well, but Lucy, who was sitting beside Alma in the seat in front of me, gets up and slides next to me and Bea when the bus driver isn't paying attention.

"This was your first invitational; you can't be so hard on yourself. We all have bad races. And you didn't even do *bad*."

"I'm not upset," I lie.

Yeah, right, she says with her eyes. "You *just* started running. I think you forget how new you are since you've been killing it." She puts her arm around my shoulders, gives them a little shake. "No one can be 100 percent all the time."

"Yeah, *chillax, new girl*," Alma teases, jokingly using Jack's favorite catchphrase.

As if beckoned, Jack bounds next to Alma in the seat in front of us, eliciting a sharp rebuke from the now-attentive bus driver and a glare from Coach.

"Sorry!" Jack yells, clearly not. He spins around to face us. "So, who's y'all's dates for homecoming?"

I've seen the hand-painted signs advertising the upcoming dance around the hallways at school, and I'd be lying if I said I hadn't spent any time daydreaming about Cheeto asking me to go.

"You asking us on a date?" Bea says. "'Cause I speak for all of us when I say that's a hard pass."

"Gross, no," he says.

"What, are you going?" Millie says. "You trick some poor, unsuspecting freshman into thinking you're cool?" She and Sophia, who are sitting behind us, lean forward and rest their chins on the vinyl seat to get in on the conversation.

He laughs sarcastically. "Funny. No, dummies. We're gonna crash it."

"*Crash* it?" Bea says.

"Yeah. A bunch of us are going stag. We got old-school suits and everything. We're even gonna –" He stops himself. "Well, I can't give away *all* the surprises. But it's gonna be epic."

For the first time in maybe ever, Bea and Lucy actually seem impressed by Jack's idea.

"We could use some ladies," he continues. "Not as like, you know, *dates*. As co-conspirators. That is, if you can find something to wear that would fit the occasion."

Lucy and Bea both crane their heads over me, joining their gazes. "You thinking what I'm thinking?" Lucy asks.

"Tina's clothes!" Bea's not usually one to get giddy, but right now I half expect confetti to burst out of her ears. "Oh, I'm so in. Cat? Alma? Mill and Soph?"

Meri went to every single dance in high school, and every time I watched her get all dressed up and sparkly, I couldn't help but fantasize about playing princess for a night. I'm fully aware this isn't exactly the same thing, but with the dance a couple weeks away, my options are to stay home and endure Mom's attempts to overcompensate for my lack of a date or join Jack's revolution.

Kind of a no-brainer.

Besides, if this is Jack's idea, there's a good chance Cheeto will be coming, too.

"Yeah, sure. I'm in," I say.

Millie nods furiously. Alma holds up both thumbs.

We all turn to look at Sophia. "So, um, Kyle asked me to go a couple weeks ago."

From the look on Bea's face, Sophia might as well have said the two of them are engaged.

"Your first dance, Soph!" Lucy interjects before Bea can say anything. "Do you have your dress picked out?"

Not going to lie, it's hard not to be jealous as Sophia describes it – beadwork on top, lace overlay. She's going to look absolutely gorgeous.

"Just curious when, exactly, you were going to tell us about this?" Bea says.

"Hmm, wonder why I didn't?" Sophia responds pointedly.

There's a moment of awkward tension, but Millie diffuses it by announcing she has a hair crimper. Alma offers up a collection of old high heels. I volunteer Mom's old stage makeup, sure that she won't mind contributing to the cause.

"I don't know, girls, this might be the best idea we've ever had," Millie says.

"Hey, it was *my* idea," Jack says.

Millie glares at him and rolls her eyes. "Whatever."

**

That night, as I head into the kitchen for dinner, Mom's eyes linger on me. "You look a little sunburnt, honey. What is it you were doing this morning?"

It was obviously too early to get sunburnt back when practice occurred in the morning, but ever since school started, I've noticed my shoulders getting freckles and a tan starting to form around my neckline. But the worst part of having afternoon practices is that I have to get ready again before I can go home. Most of the team just heads home sweaty, still dressed in their uniforms or workout clothes, but I have to shower, redo my hair, and change back into my school clothes before I can show up on my front door. Which means I'm always dead last out of the locker room.

I grab a plate, avoiding her eyes. "We decided to do improv group in the courtyard since it was nice out." I'm not sure improv group's even a thing, but she bought it this morning as my excuse for being gone all of Saturday.

No response. I dish up a plate of her sausage potato casserole and sit down. Dad's working late, so it's just me, Mom, and Penny at home.

"I ran into Blythe's mom at the bank today," she says, spooning something mushy into Penny's mouth.

I nearly drop my fork.

"She said Blythe has a pretty serious boyfriend she's going to homecoming with," she continues, giving me the cautious, what's-this-going-to-trigger eyes. "Is this why we haven't seen much of her the last couple months?"

I let myself breathe.

That was a close call. *Too* close.

I nod, frowning, figuring I may as well hitch a ride on the "poor me" bus.

"Why didn't you tell me?" she asks.

"I don't know ... I guess because I don't really like him that much." Not a lie.

"Well, have you met anyone in drama club you might want to go to the dance with?"

I can't believe my luck. The Blythe alibi handed to me on a silver platter, then this gem of a lead-in. "Oh, a few of us are going to go together. Stag. We just decided today."

Her eyes light up. "Oh, that's perfect, honey. We'll have to start looking for a dress."

"Actually, we're not dressing up. Nice, I mean. One of the girls has a bunch of old '80s clothes, and we're gonna crimp our hair and stuff," I say, really trying to sell it with my smile. "Do you think I could borrow that tub of your old stage makeup?"

She looks at me quizzically. "If you're set on borrowing, why not just borrow one of Meri's nice dresses?"

Luckily, dressing up in '80s stuff seems like just the kind of thing drama club would do, so I try to capitalize on that. "It's *drama club*, Mom. The point is to be ironic."

"Who's coming to pick you up, then?"

"The dresses belong to one of the girl's aunts, so we're getting ready at her house then meeting up with the boys at the dance."

"We won't even get to meet your new friends, then?"

I shake my head apologetically. Mom sighs, disappointed, then slips another spoonful into Penny's mouth. "Well, we'll just have to have them over another time then. Movie night, maybe?"

I nod but can't see that ever happening. Not because I don't trust the freshies not to blow my cover, but because they don't know there's any cover to *blow*. Everyone thinks Mom and Dad can't make it to the meets because of work. And if the truth ever gets around to Coach, he'll know my disclosure was forged. That I don't actually have permission to be on the team at all.

I genuinely thought coming clean would be easier once the season started, once I had a race to invite them to, tangible proof of my growth and success. But I was wrong.

There's just more to lose.

**

Saturday afternoon, the day of the dance, I have Mom drop me off at Lucy's house. It's sad watching her eyes dart around, trying to catch a glimpse of my new friends, probably hoping they aren't imaginary. Lucy doesn't live in the best area, either, and I can tell she's trying to pretend that doesn't make her anxious.

Everyone's already there, sorting through the huge box of clothes Lucy brought down from her grandma's house in Springs. Both times we've had *Sweatin' to the Oldies* nights, we've just worn the workout clothes – bodysuits, leg warmers, leotards – so I've never really had a good look at the fancy dresses before, but man, are they something: a fuchsia ball gown with puff sleeves the size of watermelons, a fitted gray and pink polka-dot halter neck, a solid gold long-sleeved tunic with a diamond-shaped hole in the chest. I choose a baby-blue silk gown with a scalloped neck, fanned sleeves, and a bow that spans my entire waist.

We each pick out a pair of the high heels Alma brought, then start on the makeup, which, thankfully, Mom let me borrow. There are palettes of eye shadow in every shade imaginable, bright-pink lipstick, and blush as red as cherry pie filling. We cake the stuff on until we're hardly recognizable.

Then we move on to hair. We curl, we fluff, we crimp, and we rat until we've achieved maximum poof, then douse ourselves in Aquanet until we're basically glued in place. Just when I think things can't get any more hilarious, Millie pulls out a pair of scissors. Before anyone can stop her, she has bangs. It makes me think of Blythe, the friendship I lost or gave away, and I'm sad for a fraction of a second until everyone's laugh-screams draw me into the hilarity of the situation. The angle of the bangs is so severe it almost looks intentional.

Lucy's mom knocks on the door to make sure we're okay.

"Fine, *Mamá!*" Lucy manages to yell between laughing convulsions.

"We better head over soon," Bea says, smirking as she punches Millie's arm. "Before we have any more casualties."

**

The boys are waiting for us outside the front entrance of the school. My heart skips in panicked relief when I spot Cheeto among them.

I didn't think it was possible that anyone could match our epic transformations, but the boys have proved me wrong. All of them are decked out in old suits and cowboy hats and a few have giant, gaudy belt buckles reflecting off the sunset behind us.

But the real kicker comes when they take off their hats.

Their long hair is gone, replaced with the most disgusting mullets you could ever imagine. Steps in their sideburns. Little rat tails in the back, curling up grotesquely. I'd cry – for a certain head of blond locks, specifically – if I weren't laughing so hard.

"Ladies, you're looking fine this evening," Jack says with mock chivalry. I can tell he's impressed with the effort we put into this. He holds his elbow out to Millie, who takes his arm. "Shall we?"

The rest of the boys follow suit. I link up with Kyle, a quiet sophomore I don't think I've ever had a one-on-one conversation with before, and try not to be bothered when Lucy takes Cheeto's arm.

The crowd parts for us as we make our way onto the dance floor. It's like a movie scene – everyone freezes and stares; the music fades. The moment is suspended in air, the fate of our crusade hinging on what will happen next.

What *happens* is a plot twist I never expected.

The music starts playing again, some bouncy song I've heard on Lucy's radio a few times. A few people laugh and clap, a few others flash us what can only be described as courtesy smiles. And then, everyone turns back to their own little circles, chatting and dancing awkwardly in prototypical school dance fashion. No longer paying us any attention at all.

We haven't started a revolution. Aren't going to be deified in Plain City High School lore, martyrs in the war against oppressive teenage norms.

No one cares.

I look nervously back at Jack, expecting his face to reflect the disappointment of a failed coup attempt. This was his baby, after all.

But he's already dancing. They *all* are – terribly, like they've got ants crawling up their legs, but it's dancing nonetheless. And the looks on their faces reveal an unmistakable message: *Mission accomplished.*

It hits me that maybe the point never was to make a statement. Maybe they just thought dressing up in old clothes and dancing like lunatics sounded fun.

Which I guess, in a way, is its own kind of revolution.

*

When the first slow dance comes on, I head to the refreshments table to get some water. I'm just about there when I spot Blythe and Tyler. He's turned toward his friends, laughing in that typical dirtbag way, while she and the other girls stand silently around. She looks beautiful – all curls and dewy skin and pink gauze – but she has a bored, empty look in her eyes.

I have the sudden urge to approach her – with an olive branch or a lightning rod, I'm not sure which – when I feel a tap on my shoulder.

It's Cheeto. Even *trying* to be ridiculous in that blue polyester suit, ironically the same shade as my dress, and the mullet peeking out from his wide-brimmed black cowboy hat, he looks amazing. My breath catches at his proximity.

"Do you want to …?" He motions to the middle of the dance floor.

"Sure," I say, attempting, though probably failing, nonchalance.

I follow him to an empty spot on the dance floor and lift my arms up around his neck. He touches my waist gently, his hands barely making contact with my dress.

We sway for a while, the gymnasium quiet except for Adele crooning through the speakers.

I analyze his every movement. Every twitch.

"A hundred bucks her mom made her say yes," he finally says in a low whisper, inches from my ear.

He slowly spins us until I can see a junior or senior couple a few yards away. The bored-looking girl has her elbows locked and barely touches the boy's shoulders with the tips of her fingers, as if afraid he has some communicable disease. He looks pained, like he's trying to think of something to say.

It's tragic, really, but I'm grateful for the icebreaker. "They're totally hitting it off," I say.

"Someone's gonna have to pry them off each other."

"Yeah, come on, people. Keep it PG-13."

We laugh. He turns his attention to my dress. "That's a really big bow."

"That's a really blue suit," I say. "Whose attic did you raid to find that gem?"

He hesitates just long enough for me to realize my mistake. I'm pretty sure I'd sell my soul for a rewind button.

"It was my dad's," he says. "From his high school prom, actually."

"Alma told me. About him. I'm really sorry."

"Thanks. Yeah. It sucks."

"What was he like?" I say, immediately second-guessing myself. "I mean … sorry … you probably don't want to talk about it."

But he smiles. "No one ever asks. Too worried about making me sad or whatever." His face crinkles up like he's thinking. "Let's see, in some ways he was a pretty typical farm guy. Couldn't be lazy if he tried. Fixed everything himself, never threw anything away." He tugs on a lapel. "Case in point."

I smile.

"But he could get, like, real philosophical too. He read Whitman and Steinbeck for fun. And he was an artist. Taught me how to whittle." He lets go of my waist with one hand, reaches into his suit coat pocket, and pulls out his moped keys. A small carving of a wooden fish dangles from the ring.

"It's beautiful," I say. "Why a fish?"

When he puts the keys back in his pocket and his hand returns to waist, his grip is a little tighter. "Fishing was kinda our thing. There's a spot we'd always go, close by where we run hills. At sunset the light would hit it just right, and the whole pond looked like it was on fire." He seems lost in some memory until the music stops. It's the first time I've ever wished a slow song were longer.

Somehow separating feels even more awkward than starting to dance. He scratches his head. "Shit. Dancing with a girl and talking about himself the whole time is something my dad definitely *wouldn't* have done."

"It's fine," I say truthfully. "*More* than fine. I loved hearing about him. Seems like he was a really cool guy."

He smiles proudly, as if the compliment were meant for him. There's something sad about it, I guess because it's a look a dad should be able to give his son, not the other way around. A smile Cheeto will never have waiting for him at the end of a race or when he's graduating from high school. Walking down the aisle or holding his first child.

I clear my throat. "Anytime you want to, you know, talk about it ..."

He meets my eyes, and a palpable energy passes between us. All my nerve endings fire.

"You might regret saying that before tonight's over."

"Doubt that," I say.

Taylor Swift blasts through the speakers, and the whole gym erupts into cheers as Millie materializes beside me. "There you are!" she says, pulling my arm toward the center of the dance floor. My eyes stay locked with Cheeto's as she drags me away.

"Just look for the big blue bow," I say, and he flashes me that impossible half-smile.

MILE THREE
CHAPTER 29
JOSIE

I'm sitting in US history, staring at the still-pristine test packet on my desk Mrs. Buttars handed out 10 minutes ago. The questions make no sense. I'm pretty sure she hasn't taught us any of this stuff, and even if she had, it seems a little cruel to be having a test already, just three weeks into the school year. History was my favorite subject last year when I took it from Coach, but she speaks in such a dry, drawly monotone that it's a major accomplishment not to fall asleep every day.

I give up trying to eke out answers to the test questions – clearly a lost cause – and instead let my thoughts wander to where they want to go. To running.

Too soon, they end up in a place I don't want them.

Cat.

Our third meet, an inconsequential Wednesday race in Lyman, I won easily. I had the thought that perhaps her insane kick during our first race was just a fluke, a combination of beginner's luck and veteran's folly.

But at our fourth meet last Wednesday, another home race, she caught me again at the final stretch.

Which, if I'm keeping score – and I *shouldn't* be – means we're 2-2. Neck and neck for the top spot on the team.

Never in a million years did I think my position on the team would be threatened, and likewise, I never realized how possessive I actually am of being first. The thing is, I can tell she knows how much it bothers me. I'd bet money that half the reason she's pushing so hard is out of revenge. But I haven't *wronged* her; I mean, doesn't a person have the right to not particularly like someone else? Is it a crime to not want to be her friend?

In all honesty, having established our mutual dislike makes everything easier. No more facades, no more pretending. Our relationship is strictly business – we train together when we need to, speak to each other only when something absolutely has to be said. Coach either genuinely doesn't notice – bitchy *is* my default, after all – or he's chosen to ignore it, in which case he probably figures the rivalry is serving us both well at this point.

It's not all gloom and doom, though. On a team level, we're absolutely steamrolling everyone. It's the season of my dreams, really. There are even a handful of JV girls closing in on the freshies' tails, which is great because it gives us a contingency plan, and it also pushes everyone up front because no one wants to lose their varsity spot. Win-win.

And it's not like I'm hurting for the competition with Cat, either. I've already beat my end-of-season goal time and have been emailing a few college scouts back and forth, though I've told myself I can't focus on all that until the season's over.

Still, Cat's a side ache I can't seem to ignore. But this week's invitational – our last chance to meet Aspen Ridge before State – is a race I'm determined to win, both as a team and individually.

I'm deep in a visualization of passing Jenna Woods and Brit Carlson – Aspen Ridge's number one and two, both still edging out my times based on recent race results – at the finish line when the intercom beeps on and the principal's voice reverberates through the speakers.

"Lockdown. I repeat, lockdown."

I figure this is a drill no one told us about, and can't believe my luck. Mrs. Buttars will *have* to give us another day for the test now.

We've been doing these drills since elementary school, so the motions come easy: pencils down, lights off, move to the inside wall below the hallway windows. I don't particularly want to be crouched on the floor, shoulder to shoulder with classmates I barely know, but if it means we get out of the test today, I'll take it.

Mrs. Buttars turns off the light, shuts the door as we drag ourselves into place. A few girls whisper and laugh next to me and immediately get shushed; people pull out their phones and start playing games or texting. The official lockdown drill rules say to keep devices off and out of sight, but I guess Mrs. Buttars is picking her battles today.

My mind wanders back to running. I let it take me out of this classroom, away from the discomfort of the present moment, until I can almost feel the grass beneath my feet, the breeze in my hair; can almost smell the intoxicating scent of sun-warmed rubber emanating from the track. I'm calm, tranquil even, until a warning light flashes in my brain, pulling me back to reality.

Drills don't last this long.

Ten minutes pass. Fifteen. Twenty.

By the half-hour mark, my entire left leg is asleep. I feel sorry for Mrs. Buttars, who is probably 70 years old and not cut out for this – who *is*, really? – and even in the darkness I can see the fear flickering in her eyes.

Every noise – the natural creaks and groans of this ancient building, the whir of the AC vents, my fellow students readjusting on the stone-hard tile floor – sends goosebumps up my arms.

The time when the bell should have rung comes and goes; I'm supposed to be at lunch right now, but I'm certain the sour gnawing in my stomach isn't hunger.

People around me are texting manically now, maybe with their parents, maybe with friends in other classes, trying to figure out what is happening, what is taking so long. I try to read their faces for clues but get nothing.

There is no warning when the single shot, at once distant and deafening, echoes through the dark classroom.

CHAPTER 30

CAT

The evacuation goes smoothly. We've practiced. We know the drill.

The lines in the teachers' faces are more pronounced in the sunlight. Like they've aged in an hour's time. I, too, feel older, but definitely not wiser. I want to crawl into my bed, pull the covers over my head, hide there forever.

I've been texting Mom so at least she knows I'm safe. Those of us who had our phones with us have been passing them around so everyone can contact their loved ones. No one knows what happened yet, but 20 police cars are parked haphazardly in the bus lane, and an ambulance has pulled right up to the school, the back nearly touching the front doors.

I want to run home, but they're making us stay until everyone is accounted for. It's strange, I think – all these procedures and routines they've implemented to create a sense of order, safety, control. But at the end of the day they don't prevent the bad things from happening. Don't fix the problem.

A lot of people are crying. I feel too shocked to cry, like I'm in a movie scene, living someone else's reality. I think part of what makes it so surreal is that it almost feels normal in a way, and deep down I know it *shouldn't*. You hear about these things so often that you get to this point where you can't help but assume it's only a matter of time before it happens here.

And then it *does*.

I can tell some people are mad, too – not at anyone in particular, just the situation. Two boys next to me are talking about it in hushed whispers, their comments infused with a gutting sense of hopelessness.

"We're in fucking America. One shot probably won't even make national news."

**

They finally release us to our parents, and I find Dad among the crowd. He walked, probably to avoid the traffic chaos, and as we make our way home he keeps a hand on me the whole time, like he's worried if he's not touching me I might just disappear.

At home, Mom helps me take off my backpack and pulls me in for a hug. Dad kisses the top of my head and goes outside. Whenever he's upset he likes to work in the back-yard, rearranging the woodpile or pretending to fix some-thing. His way of coping, I guess.

Mom asks if I want to talk but I'm not sure what to say, so instead I help her clean the kitchen while we listen to a playlist of music from her childhood, familiar songs that I'd never claim as "my music" but that are comforting, nonethe-less. I'm wiping down the counters when the front door opens and shuts. I assume it's Dad coming back in from inside until Meri appears in the entryway.

"Thought I should be home tonight," Meri says.

Mom and I rush toward her, the three of us holding on to one another like we haven't been together in years. Dad's suddenly right there – he must have seen Meri's car pull in – and he puts his arms around all of us.

It's here, cocooned in their warm, safe embraces, that I finally crack. Mom wipes my tears with her thumb. "It's okay, hon. Let it out."

I let her comfort me until the tears subside, then join Meri and Dad on the couches while she goes to check on Penny, who's been asleep but must be waking up based on the noises coming from her room.

"There isn't much online," Meri says, scrolling through her phone. "Just two paragraphs on the 1211 app that says there are unverified reports that a single shot was fired. They've gotta have something on channel four by now."

She flips on the TV as I pull out my phone, reading my missed texts from the group chat I'm on with the freshies.

Alma: u all okay??

(Four thumbs-up.)

Sophia: Anyone know what happened? Anyone get hurt?

Lucy: (Shrug emoji)

Millie: No practice right?? I NEED to run rn

Bea: Practice def canceled

Lucy: God I'm still shaking

Sophia: KitKat u there?

I text back my own thumbs-up with a "glad everyone's safe" as Mom wheels Penny into the living room. On TV, a mustached reporter from the local station in Lyman stands in front of the school, stating facts I already know: A shot was reportedly fired, the school has been evacuated, police are on the scene.

My eyes settle on Penny, whose chair is now parked by Dad's recliner. She's babbling to herself, a story only she can understand, her loose arm waving in the air as her eyes wander across the ceiling. I realize I'm almost envious that she gets to live in her own head, completely oblivious to what's going on around her. That she'll never have to process the world unraveling.

We sit like that, hearing the same thing repeated over and over, until they break for a commercial. When the livestream returns, the reporter announces they finally have information.

"I've just spoken with authorities about today's lockdown incident at Plain City High School. The Surrey County sheriff did verify that, yes, a shot was fired on the premises, but the bullet discharged into the floor as it was being wrestled from the 17-year-old suspect. Thankfully, no one was injured. He's been taken into custody at the Surrey County Correction Facility, where he will await sentencing. We will continue to update you on the situation as more information becomes available …"

It's a measure of relief. But someone still felt low enough to bring a gun to school – someone I might have passed in the hallway this morning. I can't help but wonder what drove them to that choice, whether I could have done anything to prevent it. A smile, a hello, a simple *How's it going?*

It's a brink I don't understand fully, but more than I'd like to.

Finally, after a half hour of the reporter hashing and rehashing the same few details, Mom calls us over to load up our plates for dinner. I've never been so grateful for an excuse to shut off the TV.

We sit around the table, quietly load our plates with piles of spaghetti.

Finally, Dad asks, "How's college life, Mer? Ready to move back home yet?"

Our forks twist around, around, around. It's like none of us can bring ourselves to take a bite.

"Good." She doesn't sound very convincing, but it's hard to tell if the lack of excitement in her voice is about college or the day's events.

"How about your roommates?" Mom prods. "Remind us of their names again?"

"Risa and Nicole. Yeah, they're nice." We chew in silence for a minute or two. "I want to hear how school's going for Cat. You know, other than this."

"Fine," I say.

"Does Mr. Stevens still wear that tie with rubber ducks on it every Friday?"

I smile. "Yep."

"And how's drama club? Mom tells me you spend a *lot* of time at play practice. Can't wait to come see it in a few weeks. *Oklahoma!*, right? Imagine that."

I don't respond.

"Which part will you be playing? Ado Annie?"

I glare at her. "An extra."

Mom smiles sympathetically, probably assuming my glare is due to the already discussed (and, yes, completely fabricated) fact that I didn't land a character role. She's not even pretending to eat; she's pulled up close to Penny's chair, stroking the underside of Penny's forearm like a worry stone. "It's your first year doing the play, honey. You can't expect to be a lead right off the bat. Just need to work on your singing a bit. I haven't heard you practicing much."

The tiniest smidgeon of irritation creeps in. If Mom paid more attention, she'd know she hasn't heard me practicing at *all*. That I don't, and haven't ever, sung a note from *Oklahoma!* or any other Broadway production.

None of this is Mom's fault, I remind myself.

Meri's reprimanding gaze reminds me of this fact, too. In all honesty, I feel terrible that I've let it go this far, not to mention *terrified* every time Mom runs to Walmart in Lyman. The truth – that I'm not in Mr. Edwards's play at all, that I've never even *met* the man – is a ticking time bomb.

The question isn't *if* Mom and Dad will find out, but *how, when,* and *from whom.* Every day, I go home knowing full well there's a possibility that Mom has run into Vicki Delaney at the bank or something.

I keep my eyes locked with Meri's, trying to silently communicate that I'm working on it, that I have things under control. That signing her name on my form was 100 percent worth it.

She's the first to break our gaze.

**

I'm tossing and turning in bed later that night when my bedroom door creaks open.

"You asleep?" Meri whispers through the darkness.

"I wish." I pull the covers down, and together we go to the window and slide it open. A cold breeze takes my breath away. The last few September afternoons have been beautiful, as close to perfection as it gets, but as soon as the sun goes down the temperature takes a nosedive.

I go back to my bed and pull off the comforter. Meri helps me shove the goose down through the window, then we climb outside and huddle together with the blanket wrapped around our shoulders.

"How's school *really*, Cat?" she says.

"I wasn't lying," I say. "I mean, there are good days and bad days, sure, but cross country kind of balances out the hard stuff." I want to tell her about how I've never laughed as hard as I do with the freshies. About challenging Josie for first position on the team and the massiveness of the invitational. About crashing the homecoming dance. About Cheeto.

But the details of my life seem pretty petty right now.

"You still need to tell Mom and Dad, Cat. You can't just keep putting it off because things seem okay right now."

"I will. I promise." Now it's *my* turn to change the subject. "How's *college* really?"

She looks out toward the road. "Honestly? Not what I thought it would be. I was so excited for a change, I didn't realize all the stuff I'd miss about ol' PC."

Selfishly, I feel vindicated. "Are you going to keep going?"

"I'm not going to *drop out* just 'cause I feel a little homesick. Who do you think I am?" she says, bumping my shoulder with hers. "It's just, I don't know ... My whole life I've been waiting for my chance to get out of here, to see what life's like out there in the great big world, but I guess I'm starting to wonder if ..." Her voice trails off. She sniffs, and I'm not sure if she's crying or just cold. "Anyway. I'm sure I just need to give it time."

It seems all wrong, hearing her talk like this. I'm not used to playing the "supportive listener" role, and I feel myself floundering for what to say next. "Do you ever talk to Paul?"

In hindsight, not a great question for the moment. I feel her body stiffen beside me. "No. But I know he's already dating someone else."

"What? How do you know that?"

"Celeste Ryland lives in the dorms across from him. I guess she went to a party and saw the two of them together. Says she looks like a quote-unquote *sluttier version of me*," she says with a bitter edge to her voice. "Seems like breaking up was the right decision after all."

I get what Meri's saying, but I also can't help but wonder if this is a self-fulfilling prophecy – a real-life manifestation of the whole *which came first, the chicken or the egg* thing. Because if there's one thing I'm sure of, it's that Paul genuinely loves Meri. It's not like he'd just forget about her the second they're apart. If anything, he's just trying to make her jealous.

I wait for her to say more, but she just closes her eyes, breathes in deep as a gust of wind whips around us. She seems comfortable in the silence.

She'll be leaving us for school again tomorrow morning. This moment is all I have with her, and I can't afford to waste it on silence.

"Do you think life ever gets to the point where it makes sense?"

She puts her arm over my shoulder and pulls me in. "Shit's always going to happen, Cat. So long as you've got people to love, I'd say you're one of the lucky ones."

CHAPTER 31

CAT

School is canceled Thursday and Friday, and all sporting events are canceled for the rest of the week, including our participation in the invitational on Saturday. After my experience at the last invitational, I can't say I'm incredibly disappointed. I wonder how Josie's feeling though, since it means we won't get to race against Aspen Ridge at all until State.

Things mostly go back to "normal" the following week. Practices resume, races are back on. Everything still feels weird though, like the world was knocked off orbit and we're all holding our breaths, waiting to see what happens next.

I don't know the boy who brought the gun to school. It doesn't seem like anyone really did. He was a junior who had just moved here from another state and hadn't made any friends yet. Apparently the gun was his dad's, though no one's sure how he got the combination to the safe. They also aren't sure why he brought it, who his intended target was. If he even had a target at all.

So many questions we'll probably never get the answer to.

I think about his family several times a day, wonder what they're doing, what they must be feeling. Even though I didn't know him personally, I'm still jarred, and my anxiety – heady and obnoxious even at the best of times – takes full advantage of the situation. I feel myself constantly on edge, my mind racing with what-ifs and dark daydreams. I guess it's the realization that you're never as safe as you think you are. The not-so-gentle reminder that in the blink of an eye, life can change forever.

All the adults seem distracted, too, which, if I'm being honest, makes my current personal situation easier. Mom and Dad seem to be caught in a stupor, analyzing and reanalyzing what the school could have done differently, how this will change the community. Like most small towns in America, the political situation here in Plain City was already tense; this just seems to have added more fuel to the flame on both sides of the aisle. The television is constantly on. Conversation, no matter the topic, somehow always finds its way back to the almost shooting.

Running is my escape. Not that cross country isn't stressful; it is. But I guess that's the point – running gives my mind something else to worry about. In the whole scheme of things, who wins or loses a high school cross country race won't even make the footnotes.

So I figure if I've got to be worrying about something, it might as well be about beating Josie.

It's not her as a person but what she represents. I've come to realize there's nothing I could do to make Josie like me. And in the same way, I can't change who I am. But I have this feeling that if I beat Josie, it's proof I can conquer my own demons. That even though I'm stuck with myself, I can at least break free from the things I don't *like* about myself. Show my weaknesses who's boss.

At the invitational a few weeks ago I saw someone with a shirt that said, "Pain is weakness leaving the body." That sentence, cheesy as it may be, has been on repeat in my mind ever since. When your lungs are on fire and your head pounds and your legs feel like they're about to fall off, there's no room in your mind for fear. It's drowned out by the pain.

So I keep pushing myself harder.

Two more district races come and go. I win one; Josie wins the second. It's like we can't quit this game of back and forth.

At the seventh race, Josie edges me out. Coach pulls me aside as I catch my breath at the finish, and I can only hope my flushed, sweaty skin masks the frustrated tears pooling in my eyes. He tells me good job, reminds me that I'm doing amazing for my sophomore year. Says there will be plenty of races for me to shine over the next two and a half seasons. That my turn will come.

I know he means well, but I can't help but think how easy it is for him to say all this. How to him, none of this even matters. They're just words.

Just like how easy it was for Ms. Reid to recite all those positive affirmations. Or for Blythe to say, "Just be yourself." Or for Meri to think that telling Mom and Dad the truth won't be that big of a deal.

You can try walking in someone else's shoes, but chances are they're not going to fit.

**

The last Thursday in September is our final hill workout. With the sun setting earlier and earlier, Coach says he's starting to worry someone's going to get lost up in the hills in the dark.

I ride up in Lucy's car with Bea and Millie, laughing at their pointless and way-too-heated argument about whether Batman or Superman is the better superhero.

"No no no. Batman is better," Lucy says. "He's just a regular guy turned badass, so it's more authentic. Of *course* Superman has more powers; he's an alien."

"Yeah, but Superman can *fly*," Bea says. "Flying trumps

everything."

Millie cuts in. "The real question is who would you rather make out with?"

We're the last ones to pull into the parking lot at the trailhead, and I can tell Coach isn't happy we're a few minutes late. Even though it's not surprising – who hasn't been more on edge lately? – his irritation still shakes me up a little. You wouldn't want to get on his bad side.

We warm up and stretch, then hit the trail for the sevenmiler. I'm fourth in line, just behind Lucy. I try to focus on the gorgeous changing leaves, the refreshing autumn breeze, but the breakneck pace commands all my attention. I can barely get enough air into my lungs, and after just a few minutes, I'm already lightheaded and have a killer side ache.

We've made it maybe two miles up when I notice how hard Lucy seems to be breathing, the way she's wobbling from side to side as if she can't keep a straight line.

"Can we stop?" I call up to the front. I'm not usually one to petition Josie for breaks, but after all Lucy has done for me, I'm willing to sacrifice a little of my pride for her sake.

No answer. If anything, Josie pushes harder.

A couple more minutes pass. Lucy's shoulders slump, and her head starts to look like a marionette with a loose string. A gap is beginning to form between her and Millie in front of her.

Bea, behind me, yells assertively, "Josie, hold up!"

That does the trick. Josie stops, irritation written all over her face as she turns around. But the look disappears as soon as she sees Lucy. "Do you have your inhaler, Luce?"

Lucy shakes her head. She looks even worse from the front – the terrified expression on her face, the gray tint of her complexion.

Alma starts pacing on the trail. "This is all my fault."

I don't get what she means until I remember that it's

always Alma reminding Lucy to get her inhaler. Usually the freshies are all packed together in Lucy's car, but Sophia got her permit over the weekend, and Alma rode up with her. It was nice not being smashed, window to window, in the back seat, but I missed the two of them. I also can't help but wonder if the car ride divide had anything to do with the weird energy between Sophia and Bea lately.

"Don't blame yourself," Bea says, leaning over her knees to catch her breath. "It's mine, if anyone's. I should have grabbed it from the glove box."

Even though we've been stopped for at least two minutes now, Lucy's breathing doesn't seem to be slowing down. Her entire body is shaking like it's the middle of January and she's stuck outside with no coat on.

"We have to get her down," Josie says. "I'm going to run back, grab her inhaler, and tell Coach to call her mom. Sophia, you and Cat help her walk down. No running; just take it nice and slow. Got it?" The two of us nod. I'm not sure why she picks me out of everyone, but now's not the time to analyze it. "The rest of you keep heading up. Bea, it's your job to make sure everyone's back down before the sun sets. The last thing we need right now is someone getting stranded on the mountain with a sprained ankle because they couldn't see the trail."

As Josie disappears down the trail, the "why" finally sinks in: If I help Lucy down, I miss most of the workout. Josie's using this to gain an advantage over me. Infuriating as this realization is, this is Lucy's health on the line.

I lift her arm over my shoulder. Her skin is cold and clammy against mine, her muscles tense.

"All right, Luce. Slow and steady," Sophia says soothingly. "Let's just take this one step at a time. Big deep breaths."

I've never been around a woman in labor, but if I had to guess it would be something like what's happening to Lucy right now. Her face is contorted in pain, and somehow each breath seems both deep and shallow at the same time. We've made it down the first bend when I notice her fingers are flexed and curling like she's been injected with some sort of poison. It's freaky.

"What's wrong with her hands?" I ask.

"It's her body's response to not getting enough oxygen. This happened once last year." On the surface Sophia seems calm, but I get the sense she's trying not to panic. "We have to hurry."

Minutes pass – 10, maybe 15 – and Lucy seems to get paler with each one. Just when I'm starting to wonder if she's going to make it, I see Josie bounding back up the trail, inhaler in hand.

"Her mom's on the way. She says to have her lie down as soon as possible."

Josie shakes the inhaler, then holds it up to Lucy's mouth and gives it a pump. Lucy breathes as deeply as she can, but it doesn't seem like she gets much in. The three of us watch on helplessly.

"That's it," Josie coaches. "Big breaths. You're going to be okay, Luce."

After a minute or so, she does seem to relax a little. The gaps between her breaths stretch, if only by a few milliseconds.

"Let's make a three-man carry," Josie says, but Lucy shakes her head and takes a wobbly step forward. Josie doesn't argue with her, just motions for me to grab her other arm for support.

We start moving down, one baby step at a time. It seems like we'll never make it down, but suddenly I spot the parking lot peeking through between the gaps in the trees.

Coach meets us at the trailhead, taking over the job as Lucy's crutch and leading her to a grassy patch near one of those old-fashioned water pumps by the bathrooms. My shoulder and arm are completely numb from supporting Lucy's weight, but my relief that we made it down is stronger.

The boys appear seemingly out of nowhere, congregating like moths around a lantern. Based on the beads of sweat glistening off their chests and faces, they just finished their run.

"Give her space," Coach says to them, motioning for them to back up. "In fact, Serge, why don't you take them over and start stretching?"

The boys slowly retreat and Lucy lies down, knees up and hands covering her eyes. She's not shivering violently or the color of oatmeal anymore, which I figure have to be good signs.

"Well, kiddo, you picked the hardest possible way to get out of a seven-miler," Coach jokes, kneeling next to her. When she laughs, I feel a sudden release of tension in my shoulders. "You're going to be okay," he says. "Your mom's on her way now."

I only get to enjoy the post-rescue mission endorphins for a few minutes before I start worrying about how *I'm* going to get home. It's a 20-minute drive back to Plain City, and even if I leave now – which I can't, since my ride is out of commission for the foreseeable future – I'll still be home later than usual. I know the other girls should be getting back down the mountain soon, but so far there's no sign of them.

I pull out my phone from my zippered shorts pocket and see that Dad has called twice. I start a text to tell him I'll be home a bit late tonight, but the screen suddenly goes black. Battery dead.

Great, I think.

I'm walking over to the parking lot to grab my water from Lucy's car when I pass Cheeto fiddling with his moped.

"She okay?" he says.

"I think so. Freaked me out, though."

"Yeah, for sure." His hand reaches up as if he's going to sweep the hair from his face, but it must be a muscle memory thing because there's nothing there to sweep away. I can't say I approve of the boys deciding to leave their mullets in place until after State, but I have to give them props for their complete disregard of public opinion.

"Didn't you ride up with her?" he asks.

I nod.

"I could give you a ride home if you need. It usually takes, like, an hour for her to get back to normal."

An hour. I definitely can't wait that long. But I know the boys usually stick around and play Frisbee in the field until after dark. "You're not staying for Frisbee?"

He shakes his head. "Can't. Math homework. I got a D on my last test and my mom's breathing down my neck about it."

"Okay. Sure. I mean, if you've got time." I consider asking Cheeto if I can text home on his phone, but the thought of mixing my cross country and home life, even in this minuscule way, still makes me panicky. Mom is just the kind of person who would save the random number in her phone and invite him over for Sunday dinner. "Let me just go make sure Lucy's okay and tell her I've got a ride."

When I run back over, he's already sitting on the moped. He hands me his helmet, one of those turtle shell ones with no visor, and I buckle it under my chin and use his arm to steady myself as I climb on behind him.

A few of the boys whistle and catcall as we're heading toward the entrance of the parking lot. He laughs and waves them off. Even though we danced together way more than anyone else did at homecoming, the fact that he's willing to endure getting teased by his friends over this feels more significant.

Whatever "this" is.

"You might want to hold on," he says over his shoulder as we're about to pull onto the main road. I wrap my arms around his waist as the engine revs, almost giddy at the sensation of weightlessness. It reminds me of the times my grandpa would hook a sleigh on the back of his tractor after a big snowstorm and pull us through his fields.

It's almost just as cold, too. I don't know whether it's the post-workout chills or just the effect of the air whipping around us, but the temperature seems to drop by about 50 degrees. I hold on tighter and turn my face sideways, using Cheeto's back for a shield. I don't even know how he can see with the wind blowing in his eyes.

When we get halfway down, he brakes and lets the moped idle in front of a dirt path veering off the main road. "Do you have to get home, like, *right* now?"

I know I should say yes.

Instead, I say, "You're the one with math homework."

He smirks, then pivots the handlebars to the right, taking us slowly down the path, which dead-ends at a pond. The sun setting behind us makes the water look like molten gold.

All at once, I know exactly where we are.

He parks on the dirt under a large oak tree and kills the engine. Other than birds singing in the distance, the evening is perfectly quiet and still. I take off the helmet, hang it on one of the handlebars, and follow him to the edge of the pond. "I can see why you love it here. It's beautiful."

I'm not just saying it. The autumn backdrop makes it particularly lovely, with patches of orange and red and yellow splashed across the rolling hills. A real-life Bob Ross painting.

He twists his thumbs up into the hem of his T-shirt. "We were up here the night before he died. It was a heart attack, so it wasn't like he knew it was going to happen. But I sometimes wonder if he did. He kept telling me all these stories – how he met my mom, how he felt seeing me as a baby for the first time. And I just brushed him off, thought he was being weird, too sentimental, you know? Now, every day, I wish I could go back. Look in his eyes, really listen. Ask him a million questions."

I feel like now would be a good time to reach out and touch his arm or something, but I can't make myself do it. There's a nagging worry in the back of my mind that I'm misreading the cues here: Maybe I'm just easy to talk to. Or maybe he can somehow sense that I'd understand, that I know what it's like to feel broken.

"You're shivering," he says suddenly, and it isn't until that moment that I realize how cold I am.

"I'm fine," I lie.

He looks momentarily unsure of himself, like he knows he's about to cross a line he can never uncross, then wraps his arms around me and pulls me into his chest. My face fits into the crook of his neck like a puzzle piece, his skin warm against my cheek. We stand like that for I don't know how long – him occasionally rubbing the sides of my arms, me standing perfectly still, silently begging the universe to stop time.

Safe. It's the best way to describe the moment. Yes, I have butterflies; yes, I feel a warmth radiating from my core clear down into my fingers and toes. But the most intoxicating sensation is the security of his arms, the soothing rise and fall of his chest.

I close my eyes and let my full weight rest against him.

A minute passes, and he pulls back slightly. Our chins brush as he meets my eyes, and there's a fullness about them that tells me exactly what he wants. Instinctively, my hand reaches up to my chest, feeling for my necklace.

But it isn't there.

"What's wrong?" he says, clearly seeing the alarm on my face.

"Nothing, it's just … my necklace is gone." I feel irrationally panicked as I scan the ground around us, but the sun has completely set by now, and everything is filtered through the gray lens of twilight.

"The wolf one?"

I nod, surprised he's noticed it before. Even though we're standing on gravel, he gets on his hands and knees and starts searching. I crouch down next to him and run my hands over the pebbles, feeling nothing but the occasional twig. I'm frustrated I've let this kill the mood, knowing deep down it's just a cheap, mass-produced piece of metal Meri's cheer coach probably bought at Claire's. Luck isn't *real*. Based on what's happened in the world these past few weeks, there's no way it can be.

The last time I'm absolutely positive I had the necklace was in the shower last night, which means it could be anywhere – at school, on the trail, in the middle of the road somewhere between here and the trailhead. Barring some miracle, it'll be impossible to find.

"It's really okay," I say, touching his arm. "Thanks, though."

He keeps trying for a few more seconds then stands back up, brushing dirt off his knees. "Was it a gift or something?"

"No, not really. It was my sister's." I decide against including the detail *Millie named the wolf 'Olga' and now I kiss it before every race*.

"Meri?"

I nod, feeling suddenly self-conscious. I wonder if he's comparing the two of us, thinking how unfortunate it is that I didn't land in the same gene pool she did.

"You guys pretty close?" he asks.

"Yeah. Well, we used to be, anyway. The past couple years she's been … you know, busy. And she moved out last month to go to college."

He nods. "Must be something to have Merideth Shultz as

a big sister."

I have the sudden, horrifying thought that maybe his interest in me is purely related to the fact that Meri is my big sister. Like, maybe he thinks getting close to me will boost his social status somehow. Or worse, he has a thing for her, and I seemed like the next best option.

I suddenly feel cold again. But instead of reaching out for his arms, I hug my elbows to my chest. "Yeah. It's *something*." I hear the spite in my voice and feel instantly guilty for it – it isn't Meri's fault she's perfect. "I should probably get home."

He looks like he's going to say something but stops himself, turning his gaze out toward the pond. The air is suddenly thick between us, the silence drawn out and heavy. I feel like a kid who finally talked their parents into buying an ice cream only to knock it off the cone after just one taste.

"Meri seems nice and all, but she's not really my type." He picks up a stone and skips it across the pond. "In case you were wondering."

It takes a concerted effort to swallow down my pride, but slowly, the warm feeling inside me starts to return. "Yeah?" I say, playing along. "What *is* your type then?"

He turns to face me, then reaches out and takes both my hands in his. His fingers graze my palms, sending shock-waves through my body.

"My dad said you shouldn't have a type. That you should save that for beer and livestock."

I smirk. "Your dad was wise."

He meets my eyes and smiles. "There's something else he said, too."

He pulls me closer. I see his cheeks flush, feel the heat radiating off of them.

"What?" I say softly.

"He said you should always ask a girl before you kiss her."

Al Barker is right. Charlie Campbell is a catch.

Slowly, I move my lips toward his. I'm slightly worried I've forgotten how to kiss, and anyway, this feels 100 percent different from whatever happened with Matt. This is sacred, holy; something pristine and magical. I don't want to screw it up.

But it doesn't take long to come back to me. And then some.

**

It's officially dark by the time we leave the pond. Cheeto seems confused when I ask him to drop me off at the school, but I tell him I forgot something in my locker. Not a lie. Changing back into my school clothes is always worth the extra few minutes.

Luckily, there are still lights on in the school and a few cars in the parking lot. Cheeto turns around and kisses me as I'm unbuckling the helmet and it takes all my self-control to actually get off the moped.

"'Night," he says, wrapping an arm around my waist.

I kiss him one more time for good measure.

Not until he's completely out of sight do I sprint back into the school. My hair, tangled from the wind, is not quite in school-day shape by the time I walk out of the locker room, but it's going to have to work.

I try to think of a good explanation for my lateness as I speed-walk home. As perfect as tonight was, I have a gnawing feeling in my stomach that I'll be paying for it.

And I'm not wrong.

As soon as I open the door, Mom and Dad are both right there, as if they've been camped out on the landing. Mom lets out a dramatic sigh.

"Where have you been?" she asks.

"We were working on the dance for one of the scenes." I glance at the clock on the wall. It's already 8:30 – I'm a full three hours later than usual. "And then we went to some-one's house after."

"Why didn't you answer your phone?"

"I tried to text you but it died," I say, pulling it from my pocket and holding it out for proof. "The battery doesn't last that long. It's old, remember?"

"You couldn't borrow someone else's?" Mom says. "Send a quick *I'm running late?*"

I huff, exasperated, even though deep down I'm kicking myself for not following my first instinct. I know I'm the one in the wrong here. "I didn't think it was a big deal. Meri came home late every night. *Way* later than this."

"Yes, well, last time I checked, you aren't Meri."

The pleasant buzz lingering from tonight fully evapo-rates. "Gee, thanks for the reminder, Mom."

A pained look crosses her face, but she doesn't apologize. "What's gotten into you lately?"

"Isn't this what you *wanted*, Mom? For me to get friends so I'd get out of your hair?" I say spitefully.

"Don't talk to your mother that way," Dad snaps. "You owe her an apology."

Mom looks at me like I've just spit on her face. It makes me feel even more terrible, especially considering tonight's deception is just the tip of a very big iceberg.

"We just worry about you, Sis. Want to make sure you're okay."

A heavy sensation settles in my chest. It's suddenly hard to breathe.

This is my chance. The perfect opening to purge myself of my secret, to cough up the lie that has been stuck in the back of my throat for the past three months.

But somehow all I can manage to say is, "Why does Meri get to be Meri, and Penny get to be Penny, and *I* have to be Sis?"

CHAPTER 32

JOSIE

Lucy's asthma attack shakes me up. While no one would ever say this out loud, I know it was my fault for pushing them too hard on the hills. She seemed almost back to normal when I hopped in Serge's car to come back home, was holding her own in an argument with her mom, who was chewing her out for not taking the inhaler on the run. I just hope she doesn't nosedive again. We're already walking on thin ice with her parents, who I know wish she would just quit.

Mom is off on Thursdays, so I always look forward to a good meal that night. She's an amazing cook and loves to try out new recipes. Says she might even try culinary school once she gets enough money saved up. During the season she tries to make sure our meals are high complex carb/high protein, then doubles or triples the recipe, so we have leftovers for a few days. I think food is her love language. She's never been great at any of the others, quality time or words of affirmation or whatever, but I try not to judge her too harshly. She's had it rough.

I smell the spices all the way outside the door. Definitely something Italian.

Thankfully, it's just Mom inside. No Ziggy in sight. She smiles at me as I walk in, but I can tell she's been crying. When she's cooking it can be tricky to know if they're real tears or onion tears, but something about her face tells me it's not a chemical reaction.

"Everything okay?" I say, setting my backpack on the couch.

She moves her head back and forth, halfway between a nod and a shake. "They will be."

I sit on an aluminum barstool, stealing a pasta noodle from the colander. "Wanna talk about it?" I say.

I assume she's going to say something about her job, or some news report, or some Ziggy assholery.

What she says instead takes my breath away. "Vinnie hit a little girl on her bike today. He'd been drinking."

I feel the blood drain from my face. "Is she okay?"

Mom nods, clearly grateful for this footnote. "Broke both her legs, but she was wearing a helmet and doesn't seem to have any internal injuries."

I shake my head, run my fingers through my scalp. "*God*. And Vinnie?"

Mom gets a bit teary again. "He's shaken up, from what Carol tells me. They've got him at the detention center in Lyman."

What she doesn't say – but what I know she's *thinking* – is how easily this could have been Ziggy. How it could be him sitting in a detention cell right now, contemplating how he might have just ruined his whole life.

And no doubt, she would have blamed herself.

When Mom first found out Ziggy drinks and smokes weed, she tried to put her foot down, but he threatened to run away. And then there was Dad, of course, backing him up with some bullshit like, *"It's just what teenagers do,"* clearly trying to earn brownie points and be the "fun dad." But, too bad for him, there's no amount of schmoozing that would ever get Ziggy back on his side.

Then there was the cocaine thing a few weeks ago, though he still claims it was only Vinnie messing with that stuff. Even so, he's been grounded ever since. Which was probably the only reason he wasn't *with* Vinnie when he hit the girl. Granted, you could go down a million what-if rabbit holes here, so I guess I'll just stick with being grateful he wasn't involved.

"Is he home?" I ask.

She nods. "Hasn't come out of his bedroom since we heard the news." She glances toward the door, lowers her voice. "If I'm honest, this is about as good of a scenario as we could have hoped for. God knows he needed a wakeup call." And then, more to herself than to me, she adds, "Been getting our fair share of those lately, haven't we?"

I know she's referring to the incident with one of the students bringing a gun to school. That day sparked something in her – lit a fire I haven't seen in her eyes since Dad left. The best way to describe it is that she just seems … awake. I guess it was just a reminder of how fragile life is. How quickly things can change.

It's been just over two weeks since then, but I've relived the moment I heard that gunshot hundreds of times. *Thousands*.

And I can't help but wonder if things would have been different if one of us had invited him to come run with us.

It's a thought that makes me sick to my stomach. Makes me want to reach out to every awkward kid in the hallway, every person sitting alone at the lunch table.

We'll take you.

"I heard the wedding got postponed," Mom says seemingly out of the blue, interrupting my thoughts. "I wonder if Marigold is getting cold feet."

Usually, a comment like this would make me suspicious Mom is plotting ways to win Dad back. But something in her face tells me this isn't the case right now.

"I *hope* they just call it off," I say. "Otherwise, the season will be over and I'll have to think of another excuse why I can't go." We catch each other's eyes. She gives me her typical *be nice to your father* smile, but there's less scolding in it than usual.

"I wasn't going to tell you this, but when I first got the news, I called him. Your dad. And you know what he said?"

"What?"

"Said he wasn't surprised that something like that would happen in this shitty town. Asked me what kind of a mother I was keeping you here. Then he changed the subject and started complaining about how his landlord raised his rent again."

I'm not surprised to hear all this, but I can tell that Mom truly was.

And I realize why she's telling me this story: That was it. *Her* wakeup call.

"I called him an asshole and hung up," she says proudly, and I laugh, walking around the counter and wrapping my arms around her. "Dad served his purpose – he gave me you and Zig. But I think I'm finally ready to let him go."

I've been waiting *years* to hear those words.

I think about how complicated life is – how horrible things can spark hope. Not always. I assume the family of the kid who brought the gun to school will never be the same. That the whole "beauty from ashes" thing might seem impossible, or at least a long way off.

But sometimes, as anyone from a Podunk farm town would be able to tell you, shit does make a pretty good fertilizer.

CHAPTER 33

CAT

The easiest workouts are always the day before a race: three miles or less at a nice comfortable jog, no sprints or surges. Their sole purpose is to loosen us up and make sure our legs are fresh for the meet the next day. Josie usually even lightens up a bit and lets us do Goat Run or maybe a little harmless trespassing through some farmer's cornfields. We laugh a lot. Mess around. It's like for one day of the week, we get summer back.

But the day before City County, two weeks before State, the usual Tuesday magic is missing. In general, magic has been harder to come by lately. Everyone's tired. On top of races and training that still seems to be getting progressively more intense, we've got droning teachers to endure, math homework, and midterms to study for.

Of course, I have a distraction.

It's been a week since Cheeto and I kissed, and I haven't felt this light in weeks. This hopeful in more than a year. There's a strange, unfamiliar feeling inside me that things are going to be okay, that I can make it through anything.

Even the silent abuse of a team captain who for some unknown reason has a personal vendetta against me.

And right now, my mission to beat her is fed by the desire to show her it doesn't have to be this way. That you can be fast *and* a nice person.

She's especially despotic today, vetoing Goat Run because of the potential for rolled ankles. I sense a collective deflation, but no one challenges her. The freshies have warned me she gets increasingly edgy the closer we get to State, and I get it – she's a competitor, and she really wants us to win. Still, I feel like there are better ways to channel state champion energy than tyranny.

We're on our way to the train tracks, the most boring run in all of Plain City, when the tension finally cracks.

Millie starts teasing Josie about Serge, and instead of her usual eye roll and sarcastic comeback, Josie responds with a five-minute chew-out about how immature and irresponsible Millie is, and by default, the rest of the freshies.

But the afternoon manages to get worse.

Sophia starts limping. It's barely noticeable at first – in fact, the only reason I'm clued in at all is because Lucy asks if she's okay.

"It's my shin," she says, grimacing. "I don't know what's wrong."

By the time we're back at the school, Sophia can barely stand on it. She doesn't complain, but Coach must notice because he calls her over to talk to him while we're stretching.

They're too far away for us to hear what they're saying, but we all watch as Coach kneels down to check her leg.

"Probably just shin splints," Josie says. "Happens to everyone."

Coach helps Sophia up, but she yelps as soon as she tries to put weight on it. He lowers her back down and hands her his cell phone, then disappears around the equipment shed. She calls someone, intermittently wiping her eyes as she talks, and when he reemerges around the corner, he's holding a pair of crutches.

"I don't know, Jo," Alma says, tense. "Doesn't look like shin splints to me."

I'm not sure what shin splints are – or the obviously worse alternative – but I don't ask. I don't want to give Josie any reason to unload her wrath on me.

Sophia hobbles toward us on the crutches and picks up her water bottle and the long-sleeve shirt she left in the stretching circle.

"What's going on?" Josie asks with more accusation in her voice than I think is necessary.

"My mom's picking me up to take me in for an X-ray in Lyman."

The low chatter stops. Everyone gets stone-faced.

The noise that finally breaks the silence is Bea's scoff, her head moving in a slow back-and-forth as she leans across her leg for a stretch.

"Sorry, is this *funny* to you?" Sophia says, clicking her long red nails against her water bottle.

"Not funny, no," Bea says. "But it *is* ironic that the rest of us have been sacrificing for the team while you've been off doing who-knows-what with your Ken Barbie. And now *because* of you, our chances for State are on the line."

Sophia's already puffy eyes flash with anger. "Are you saying I'm *hurt* because I'm *dating Kyle?*"

Bea shrugs without looking at her face. "You know what Coach always says. If the boot fits …"

"That's not fair, Bea," Millie interjects. "This is *high school*, not some Olympic training program."

Josie cuts in. "No, Bea's right. If more of you took this seriously –"

"Maybe not all of us joined cross country because we want to be world champions," Millie interrupts. "Cross country used to be fun, Josie. You turned it into fucking boot camp."

I'm stunned. This is the first time I've ever felt any sort of tension at practice, and definitely the first time I've ever heard anyone openly challenge Josie. At first I feel vindi-

cated, like maybe I'll finally have a platform to air my griev-
ances and expose her secret Machiavellian plot against me.

But when everyone starts arguing, I recognize the cost.

"What's going on?" Coach says, jogging over.

"They're ganging up on Sophia because she's hurt. Like
what's happening to her leg is *her* fault," Millie says, motioning to Bea and Josie. "It's not fair, Coach."

I can tell that he, too, isn't sure how to handle the situation.

Josie holds firm. "What's *fair*, Millie? All of us made a
commitment when the season started, and when just one
person doesn't hold up their end –"

Coach shakes his head, disappointment radiating from
his eyes. "Nope. This isn't who we are, girls. If you had a
magic crystal ball, Jo, maybe you could make these kinds of
claims, determine the causes and effects of everyone's problems. But you don't. And we don't even know what's wrong
with her leg yet. What the team needs right now is a *leader*."

Finally, I think to myself. *A little justice.*

Josie grits her teeth and stands up. Jogs toward the school.

Coach pinches the bridge of his nose and shakes his head,
then walks off. Millie and Alma help Sophia to the parking
lot to wait for her mom.

One by one, everyone else disperses, dry leaves scattering
in a gust of wind.

**

Cheeto is waiting for me outside the door by the locker
rooms. That's been our thing lately, him walking me home,
or at least to Mr. Dawson's hedges to make sure no one spies
on us from the window. Mom would probably love to meet
him, but I don't feel like asking him to pretend to be into
musical theater, or explaining to him why I'd *need* him to.

We walk slowly. I'm in no rush to get there. Gratefully, Mom and Dad didn't ground me for my lateness the other day, but things have been tense. I've been spending most of my time in my room, pretending to be busy with homework.

"What happened with Sophia?" he asks.

"Something's wrong with her leg," I say, shrugging. "I guess she had to go get it x-rayed."

"Sheesh. That sucks, right before State. Josie didn't seem too happy about it, either."

"What *is* Josie happy about?"

He laughs, which feels validating, and we move on to lighter topics. He tells me that he finally passed the math test; I tell him about the kid who threw up all over his desk and had to get escorted to the nurse's office while we were watching *The Miracle of Life* in human biology.

"I mean, I'd have made myself barf if I'd known it would get me out of watching the whole thing."

I laugh, but the casual way he mentions making himself throw up sinks deep. Not in a way that offends me, but simply as a reminder that at some point, if this whole thing keeps on going, he'll find out that I used to do that very thing.

And what will he think of me then?

I think of the way Matt looked at me when I told him I had an eating disorder. We were at a party, hidden in some dark corner he'd led me to, and from the way he'd just kissed me, I felt like he was someone I could confide in.

He never kissed me again. Never even *touched* me again.

I try to shake the memory off. "Agreed. It was straight-up disgusting. How are there so many humans on earth?"

We both know the answer, of course. It feels like the two of us are magnetized.

He finds my hand. His are perfectly calloused, and there's something about running my thumb along the bumps on the underside of his knuckles that calms me.

And that's when the dizziness hits.

I stop walking. Close my eyes. Impulsively squeeze his hand tighter.

"You okay?"

I force myself to nod, but my breath comes out ragged and shallow, not unlike Lucy's mid-asthma attack. I have no way to know if it's related to the dizziness, or just me panicking.

I channel Ms. Reid, allow her mental visage to guide me through a few deep lungfuls of air. I feel my body start to settle down.

When I open my eyes, I can tell I've legitimately freaked Cheeto out.

"Sorry. I'm fine. I don't know what happened. Just felt a little dizzy."

It's true, and it's not. At my lowest point, I was having dizzy spells daily. *Multiple* times daily, ultimately culminating in me passing out in the bathroom, where I hit my head on the back of the vanity and almost bled out. My hand reaches up to the back of my head, finding the jagged scar hidden beneath my hair.

This was just a fluke, I tell myself. *Everyone gets dizzy sometimes.*

He pulls me close to him. I smile, reaching up on my tiptoes to give him a quick peck on his lower lip.

But inside, I'm a little freaked out myself.

CHAPTER 34

JOSIE

It's not unusual for injuries to start cropping up at this point in the season. After months of intense training with no real breaks, aches and pains are inevitable – tendinitis and runner's knee, shin splints and IT band strains. I've nursed a few running injuries in my day, but nothing that required anything more than rest and a little ibuprofen.

But stress fractures are a whole different beast.

Doctors usually recommend a full six to eight weeks of rest after a stress fracture diagnosis. Which, this close to State, would be a season-ender. A death knell.

What was that thing I said about shit being good fertilizer?

I guess sometimes shit's just shit.

**

Sophia shows up to school the next day in a boot and crutches, confirming what everyone was too scared to say out loud at practice yesterday: Our fifth runner is officially out for the rest of the season.

The fissure from yesterday's practice widens into a full-blown fault line. When it's time to get ready for the race, the locker room is eerily quiet. No French braiding one another's hair. No jokes about the boys. No deodorant lip-syncing.

And I know it's partially my fault, but I'm too upset to fix it.

There are three races left. *Three*. And not just *any* races, but the three most important races of the season. City County is essentially the championship of our district, a matchup of all the high schools we've already pulverized during the Wednesday meets – a race we should win handily. Then next week is Region, the state qualifier. And we have to be in the top three 5A teams at Region if we want to advance to State.

In other words, there couldn't be a worse time to fall apart.

Two days ago, I wouldn't have even thought twice about our chances for qualifying. But losing your fifth runner is a big deal. We're deep enough that we should still be okay, but it doesn't bode well. Any other pop-up injuries or kinks to our roster, and we could find ourselves in serious trouble.

**

The bus ride to City County is agonizing. The girls usually all sit in a clump near the front, sometimes squishing three to a seat just to be close together, but today, everyone spreads out throughout the bus, watching quietly out the window or leaning back on the seats with their eyes closed, headphones on and scowling as if daring anyone to bother them.

If Coach notices the tension, he doesn't say anything. I haven't talked to him since I stormed off yesterday, but I don't feel like apologizing. I meant what I said – it isn't fair that some people on the team are more dedicated than others. Like Sergio, Coach is too soft sometimes. And if you're expecting to win a state championship against a team like Aspen Ridge, you can't relax your standards just to avoid conflict. People need to be held accountable for their actions.

I sit a few rows behind Sophia, still dressed in her school clothes. She sits sideways in the seat, her crutches resting on the window. The black plastic boot she's wearing for the stress fracture juts out into the aisle, reminding me of a gorilla foot. She's clearly devastated. I feel sorry for her, sure, but that's life. What's that thing Coach always says? You have to sleep in the bed you make.

We arrive at Taylor Park and go through the motions: course walk-through, warm-up, stretch. When they make the call for the varsity race, the seven of us – me and Cat, the freshies sans Sophia, and Gretchen, who I can tell is excited to finally be on varsity but is trying hard not to look *too* excited, considering the situation – head over without even doing the team cheer.

A gruff-looking woman in the center of the field raises her megaphone to her mouth and spouts off the rules and course directions. Finally, the gun is raised, and a shot rings through the air.

My pace immediately feels off – too quick, uneven – but still I take the lead. Taylor Park is one of those courses that weaves you in and out of thickets so you can't really see your position until the end of the race. It's beautiful this time of year, all the gold leaves and drying prairie grass, and I don't mind the seclusion. In fact, I wouldn't have it any other way right now.

I just hope everyone behind me is pulling their weight, too.

That's the hardest thing about being the fastest on the team as well as the captain. I have no idea what's going on behind me, no way to encourage everyone else until we're at the finish line.

The trail leads me around the perimeter of the park before spitting me out by the sports complex, my first real chance to see more than 20 feet in front of me. People are gathered around the baseball diamond, cheering and waving signs. Coach emerges from the throng, clipboard in hand, yelling out my time and pace. I'm off-target by 10 or 15 seconds, so I try to kick it up a notch.

"Let's go, Jo!" he yells. "Push it, push it!"

And then, not two seconds later: "Come on, Cat! Get up and run with her!"

Shit.

We're halfway through the race, maybe slightly more. I'm not quite myself today, so I know holding her off is going to require straight-up grit. I reach down inside and channel my inner G.I. Jane, tuning out the aches and pains starting to vie for my attention.

I drive my knees higher, lengthen my stride. But despite my best efforts, I soon realize the sound of the leaves crunching isn't only coming from my feet on the trail.

She doesn't tailgate me. Doesn't sprint ahead.

No. Cat Shultz has the audacity to pull up right beside me.

CHAPTER 35

CAT

I do as Coach says. I get up and run with her.

And when I do, I feel her whole body tense.

I think about the first of the season, back when I wondered how a team could be both close-knit and competitive. Supportive and ambitious.

But the truth is out now: It *can't*. At best, the whole Wolfpack dogma is idealistic. At worst, it's a flat-out lie.

She surges; I do the same. We play tug-of-war for a few hundred meters, trading the lead position back and forth until we've finished our loop around the complex and are back in the trees. The dirt trail, sandwiched between two rows of small orange cones, narrows into a single-track path that feeds into a thin wooden bridge spanning a creek.

We're several feet away from the bridge when she steps in front of me. Not *merges*. Not *gradually slides over*. No – Josie Romero abruptly, deliberately, veers in front of me, and I have no time to react or adjust my trajectory, so I fall into the brush beside the trail.

For several seconds, I'm too stunned to move. My eyes land on the small beads of blood pooling inside a scrape that runs from my knee to the back of my calf. What finally pulls me out of the trance is the hollow pounding of her footsteps on the bridge, which fades into a dull thud as she reconnects with the dirt trail on the other side.

I jump back to my feet. Accelerate to a full-on sprint, faster than my finish-line kick. I'm surprised at how fast I catch up to her, and even more surprised that I have enough air in my lungs to deliver the only form of retaliation I'm lucid enough to come up with at the moment.

"What the *hell*?"

She doesn't respond. Doesn't even look over at me.

"*Why?*" I yell, frustration rising like bile in my throat. "Why do you hate me?"

Again, she says nothing. We run like that, shoulder to shoulder, neck and neck, until we turn a corner and both of us can see the finish line on the horizon. I feel her tugging on the pace as the world starts to get dark and blurry, like someone is turning down a dimmer switch.

And at that moment, I know she is going to win.

But just before she leaves me in her wake, words punctuated by jagged breaths, she says this: "I don't care enough about you to hate you, Cat."

CHAPTER 36

JOSIE

The cheap plastic trophy slams against the window as the bus hits a pothole, the dull thud of the winged shoes against glass betraying the fake silver. A big enough jolt, and the fixture just might break clean off.

It's slipping away.

In all of my worrying about Coach leaving, it never occurred to me that the team could implode on its own.

I try to pinpoint when the momentum shifted: Sophia's stress fracture diagnosis? Lucy's asthma attack? The shooting?

Perhaps we peaked too soon. Maybe I pushed them too hard, too fast.

Whatever it was, it all came to a head today.

It would be one thing if it were just the run-off between me and Cat. Yes, I cut her off. But that's part of the game. No different from a premeditated fourth-quarter foul, or a little well-acted flopping during extra time. If she wants to be a runner, she needs to learn the tricks of the trade.

And as far as what I said? I wish I could say I feel bad about it.

Unfortunately, this isn't just about me and Cat. It's about the whole damn team.

None of the freshies raced well. They all ran alone, spread out all over the course, getting passed by people they were lapping in earlier Wednesday races. When the emcee read out the results, I couldn't believe what I was hearing. We were still first place, yes – but only by two measly points.

I never knew it was possible to win and lose at the same time.

I could make excuses and blame it on the fact that we were missing Sophia, but we should have easily clinched the City County title without her. We've already *destroyed* all these teams.

Barely scraping by here means that winning Region will be a stretch.

And State?

The bus stops; we silently file off. Coach is last, following us to the patch of grass near the parking lot where we've gathered hundreds of times for post-race wrap-up team meetings – a time for Coach to recognize stand-out performances, read out the list of people who PR'd, and remind us of our end goal.

Today, though, all he says is, "See you tomorrow."

CHAPTER 37

CAT

I'm shaken. *Shaky.* From the encounter with Josie, yes, but more pressingly from nearly passing out at the finish line, the world spinning around me like a carousel. What I can't figure out is if the trembling that followed is biological or just an emotional trigger – PTSD from the absolute worst memories of my life. But whatever's causing it, it's *real.* I can hardly tie my shoelaces or grasp the strap of my duffel bag as we're loading back onto the bus.

On any normal day, the freshies would be a welcome distraction. But today, they're a black hole of their own. Nothing has been resolved – no apologies made, no attempts to make up. I'm annoyed, actually, that they're being such typical teenage girls. They always seemed above cattiness, caring way too much about each other to allow a disagreement to wedge itself between them.

We get back to the school, unload the bus. Everyone is upset, including Coach.

It's miserable. *I'm* miserable.

So miserable, in fact, that I'd consider quitting right here and now – the whole *point* of this was joy – if it weren't for that niggling itch deep down inside of me. I *have* to beat Josie. It's no longer about shaking off demons or standing my ground but an act of self-preservation.

She started this war, and I'm willing to do just about anything to make sure she doesn't win it.

I change back into my school clothes and head to the

bathroom to try and tame my hair. I'm just finishing the last few plaits of my braid when I overhear two voices coming from the open door connecting the adjacent locker room.

I crane my neck to hear.

"… and it's not even about me anymore, I just … I don't want to see her get hurt. Radcliffe bros are all the same."

Bea and Lucy. Talking, no doubt, about Sophia and Kyle.

I'm not a "Radcliffe kid" in that sense, and I know deep down Bea wasn't referring to me.

But in my current state, all frayed nerves and gunpowder, watching as my friend group deteriorates before my very eyes, it strikes me as an injustice.

As I pass by them to get to my locker, I say, "What do you guys say about *me* when I'm not around?"

I regret it as soon as it comes out of my mouth, realizing I've just built an unnecessary wall between us. Declared myself inherently different from them.

I *also* realize that Bea has been crying. That I don't understand the context of the conversation. Of the *situation*.

I feel myself shrink.

And then Bea, with a pointedness that feels rehearsed, mentally or otherwise, says, "Not everything's about *you*, Cat."

It hits home in a way few other phrases could.

Shell-shocked, cheeks burning, I grab my stuff from my locker and walk out.

Outside, Cheeto is leaning on the side of the brick wall, backpack slung over one shoulder. Tears spring to my eyes. I turn toward home, not ready for him to see me as my true self: the girl whose greatest talent is falling apart.

He jogs to catch up. "Hold up. What happened?"

I walk faster. There are so many emotions tangled up inside me, I don't know how to sort them out quickly enough to come up with a coherent answer. Do I start with how Josie

226

tripped me during the race? How I just made a jackass of myself in front of my only friends? How I just heard my greatest fear spoken aloud – that maybe the root of all my problems is simply selfishness?

"I doubt you'd understand," I say.

"Try me."

"Okay, well … how about Josie trying to sabotage me?"

He's quiet for a few seconds. "I know Josie's tough, but I can't see her –"

"See, I told you." I clench my teeth. Walk faster.

"I want to be on your side, Cat. I'm trying to understand, but –"

"How *could* you understand?" I snap, angrily wiping the tears from my cheeks with the back of my sleeves. "You're *one* of them. And I'm a nobody. Just Meri Shultz's little sister."

There's a noticeable shift in his gait. A deflation. We cross the street to the opposite sidewalk, just out of view of the school parking lot, five blocks from home.

"Look, I like you. You *know* that I do," he finally says. "And I get that it must be hard to feel like you're living in someone else's shadow sometimes. But, like, everyone's going through stuff."

My insides twist in a macabre, acrobatic sort of dance. It's like I can see the cracks forming in the ice, and I'm backpedaling, trying to get back to land before …

It's too late.

I didn't used to believe panic attacks were a real thing. Would laugh right along with everyone else at the kid at the lunch table breathing in and out of their lunch sack as they pretended to freak out about something.

Until I had one myself.

The sound that comes out of my mouth is closer to a dying animal than anything human. My tears fall harder, faster, and suddenly I can't walk any farther, the numbness creep-

227

ing up my arms and legs eclipsing every other sensation.

I press my palms into my eyes so hard that it hurts, then feel a vague, disembodied sensation of a hand on my shoulder.

"Cat –"

"Just go," I croak between sobs. "I want to be alone."

I sense him linger momentarily, then hear the slow, quiet retreat of footsteps on the cement.

I cry harder. Because as much as I *want* to be alone, I *need* to be with someone. *Anyone.*

I hold myself upright until I'm absolutely sure he's gone, then drop to the curb, burying my face in my knees and hugging my legs tight to my chest. I try to coach myself to breathe, but the other voice inside my head is louder.

You're weak. Pathetic. Narcissistic.

Desperate, I pull my backpack from my shoulders and open the front zipper. My hands fumble through pencils and scrunchies and chapstick tubes until I finally feel the smooth edges of my phone.

I pull it out. Find Meri's number in the contacts.

It rings twice before she answers. The first thing I hear is the sound of happy voices in the background, which, not surprisingly, is extremely unhelpful.

"Cat? Are you crying? Hang on, let me get outside." The voices get quieter. A door opens and shuts. "You told Mom and Dad, didn't you?"

"No." My voice quivers with emotion.

"God, Cat. Tell me you aren't relapsing."

"No, I'm …" The dizzy spells, the fading out – they can't be related to my disorder. This isn't a relapse. I've been eating. Haven't purged once since my first month at New Horizons. "… I'm fine."

"Well obviously you aren't *fine*. Why are you crying?"

My body feels like an empty shell. My mind is barely functioning. I try to think of a way to explain the firestorm inside me, to thread together the whole story, when I suddenly realize the problem isn't Josie or the freshies or Cheeto or even my own self-loathing.

It's something deeper. Something I don't have the words for.

Meri sighs. But instead of sympathy, all I hear is exasperation. "I should have told Mom and Dad a long time ago."

The residual anger inside me starts to bubble up. "Cross country's not the problem, Meri!"

"Then *tell* me what *is*!"

Two heaving sobs escape. "I didn't call you to lecture me!"

"No one's *lecturing* you, Cat. But you're clearly not in a good place right now, and I want to help."

My sobs sound maniacal. Completely out of control.

"'Kay, I'm hanging up and calling Mom and Dad."

"No!" I beg. "Please, Meri! There are two races left – you can't do that to me."

"Can't do that to you? Can't *do that to you*? No, Cat, you don't get to use that line on me, because none of us had a say in what *you* did to all of *us*. Do you know how much we've worried about you this year? That Mom and Dad would just randomly start crying at the dinner table? Did you know they gave up the trip to Hawaii they had planned for their 20th anniversary to pay for your treatment? I screwed up by signing that disclosure, Cat, but you have to start taking some responsibility for yourself. We can't baby you forever."

It's like all the air is knocked out of me. Like I'm drowning on land.

I manage to pull myself together enough to say, "You're right, Meri. I won't bother you again."

"Cat, don't."

I'm suddenly calm. *Too* calm, like my body is devoid of

any sensation at all. "No, I get it. I'm dead weight. You know what would be the most helpful thing you could do, Meri? Stop pretending to care. Let the facade go. You'll be doing us both a favor. And you know what? I'm actually glad you're finally being honest with me. So I'll return the favor: I always thought I hated being known as your little sister. But maybe I just hate *you*."

"You don't mean that, Cat." I can tell that she's crying now, too, but I don't care.

"I do," I lie.

The line goes dead.

And just like that, I've managed to snip my final lifeline. Ruined three perfectly good relationships in less than 15 minutes.

Has to be some sort of record.

**

When I get home, I fully expect Mom and Dad to confront me. To sit me down and tell me I'm on house arrest for the next year, maybe sent off to some boarding school for troubled teenagers.

But the night passes without incident.

And the next day. And the next.

I'm stuck in a miserable, endless loop, an alternate universe consisting of all the things that could have possibly gone wrong. I often catch myself daydreaming about what I would change if I had a do-over: Be honest with Cheeto and the freshies? Follow Meri's advice and come clean to Mom and Dad about cross country? Tell them I was struggling way back in June and accept any kind of help they'd have been able to offer?

But there are no do-overs.

Wednesday is the day of Region. A thick blanket of

clouds settles over the sky around lunchtime and is the color of a bruise by the time we're released from fifth period. We have to leave school earlier in the day than usual to account for our longer bus ride since the race is almost all the way to Springs. A two-hour drive, which – based on the recent camaraderie – is sure to be a heartwarming experience.

We get dressed and load the bus. "You'll all have to move up front," Coach announces once we're all on. "The cheer squad is coming to support us today."

As if things could get any worse.

Alma scoots next to me. We exchange a sad smile, both of us mostly on the sidelines of the freshies' main argument but still feeling the ripples. I watch out of the corner of my eyes as the cheerleaders begin to file on, hating everything about every girl that passes: the over-poofed hairdos, the gaudy makeup, the scent of their Victoria's Secret body spray.

And then I see Blythe.

She looks less than thrilled to be there, a sentiment clearly shared by most of the squad. It makes me irrationally angry to know they are only here as an obligation. There's no doubt in my mind that this is an outreach effort, probably instigated by the mouth-breathing principal, who clearly doesn't see reality, either by choice or because he really is an idiot.

We meet each other's eyes, and both of us immediately look away.

For an hour or so of the ride, I distract myself with homework. When I finally look out the window, I realize it's started to rain. The droplets hit the windows like bullets, each one splitting into a thousand tiny shards on impact.

This is the first time we've had to deal with any kind of bad weather. It *is* October, so I guess it was bound to happen at some point, but it seems a little cruel for Mother Nature to hit us with a rainstorm now when we're already drowning.

We arrive at the park and set up. The cheerleaders stand in a clump under the pavilion, trying to stay dry, fully engrossed in their meaningless gossip about clothes and boys and weekend plans.

I head to the bathroom. Raindrops pelt the top of my head, but I don't try to shield myself. As soon as the race starts I'll be soaked to the bone anyway.

I've had plenty of time this week – *too* much time, really – to focus on this race. It's pretty much been my only distraction from the shitshow that has become the rest of my life. Beating Josie feels like my last bastion of hope. And in all that time spent thinking about it, I've realized something: It isn't just revenge I'm after. It's *validation*. Being the top runner on the team would mean all this has been justified, that my secret was worth it because I truly had something to lose.

If I don't win, it's like it was all for nothing.

I once overheard Jack say, "Second place is just first loser," and I'm starting to believe he's right.

The bathroom is one of those cinderblock facilities with no door, just an open entrance to the left for the boys and to the right for the girls. I walk in and find a stall. When I open it back up to go wash my hands, I see Blythe standing near the sinks. Alone. Facing me like she's prepping for a showdown.

"What are you doing?" I say.

"How are you, Cat?"

"Like you care."

"Just answer the question."

I walk past her and start washing my hands. "I'm *great*. Never better."

"That's not what Meri says."

I glance around the bathroom, check under the stalls for

feet. "What did she say? Did she *call* you?"

"She's worried about you, and she asked me to check on you. Were you purging in there?"

Of all the infuriating, demoralizing, knife-to-the-chest moments that have happened this week, the revelation that Meri and Blythe have been talking to each other about me behind my back tops the list. It's like *they're* the ones who are sisters, best friends, and I'm just a problem to be dealt with.

"Meri thinks you might be relapsing," she continues.

"*I'm. Not. Relapsing.*"

"Then you're going to have to find a way to prove it real quick."

I freeze. "Why? What are you –"

"I told her where the park is and what time the race starts. She should be here any minute. Thought it would be better to tell Mr. Davis in person that you forged your disclosure. Your parents, too." She shakes her head like I'm the despicable one. Like I'm the one who sold my soul. "I can't believe you'd do this to them."

I feel the blood drain from my face. Grab the sides of the sink to keep myself from lunging at her.

"Believe me, Cat. We're doing this for your own good."

CHAPTER 38

JOSIE

I have two choices: Tell Coach or don't.

I didn't mean to hear Cat's conversation. In fact, I'd *un*hear it if I possibly could. Nothing like feeling sorry for your enemies to throw a wrench in things.

The only reason I walked into the bathroom in the first place was to find her after the announcer made the first call for the race. The rest of us were waiting to go warm up, so I went in roaring, ready to tear her apart, but there was such an intensity in the two voices coming from the other side of the brick partition that something stopped me. With the rain drumming on the tin roof I had to strain to hear, but I'm absolutely certain I caught the words "relapse," "purging," and "forged disclosure" before retreating back outside, trying to hide the shock on my face.

I'm good at reading between the lines, though.

At the very least, I know this: Cat shouldn't be running today.

From what the other voice in the bathroom said – some cheerleader, I think – Meri was supposed to be here before the race started, relieving me of the responsibility to make this my problem.

But here we are, all lined up, and the starter is already making his way to the center of the field. Cat hasn't said a word since she emerged from the bathroom. Has hardly even

234

looked at anyone.

I scan the crowds for Meri's curly red hair, but I don't see her.

There's still time for me to run over to Coach. It would cause a scene, no doubt, but I'm sure they'd hold the race.

The competitor in me realizes this is basically my wish come true: an opportunity to sack Cat forever, to get her out of my hair. Restore order to the universe.

But if I do that, I'm only increasing the odds we won't make it to State.

It isn't just that, though. There's something else stirring inside me, something jarring and unexpected.

What if Cat truly needs help?

I think of her note from the Five-Hundred-Mile Club dinner, the one that left me seething. *Once broken, always broken.* I feel a twinge of guilt remembering how hard I judged her, the fury that it sent pumping through my veins.

I glance over at her on the start line, and I see it now in the expression on her face. Wonder how I could have possibly missed it.

I've heard of runners developing eating disorders, have even read articles about it in *Runner's World,* but this is the first time I've ever heard of someone *trading* an eating disorder for running.

"Runners, on your marks!"

I take a deep breath. Crouch into place.

I guess I've made my choice.

CHAPTER 39

CAT

The gun fires, and my whole body floods with relief.

No getting pulled aside by Coach. No Meri.

This was the best-case scenario, really: Meri showing up after the race started, too late to pull me off the course but not too late to see me running. To see how passionate I am about this sport, how *good* I am at it.

And I know, just *know*, that if she can see me win this thing, she'll finally understand.

**

The first few hundred yards are wet and muddy and chaotic.

Running in the rain is a whole new beast. I can hardly hear or see anything, and it takes a significant amount of energy just to keep from going down on the slippery grass. Then there's the wind. I try comforting myself with the fact that it'll be at our backs for the finish, but I curse under my breath every time a gust hits.

I find Josie's back and imagine I'm tethering myself to her. Every race I've won, my victory has come at the very end, passing her on the kick, so my strategy today is to stay right behind and save just enough energy to outsprint her. With the roar of the rain, I'm not sure if she realizes how close I am. If so, she doesn't show any signs of it.

There are a few rabbits, but we pick them off, one by

one, until it's just us. One and two. This fact alone should be enough to qualify Plain City for State. It's pretty tough to beat any team whose top two of five scoring runners have a cumulative score of three.

Coach is at the first mile marker yelling out times. I'm way slower than usual, but I decide not to worry about splits and my PR. Time is relative in a race like this, meaningless even, and I'm doing what I set out to do.

So far, so good.

We keep a steady pace for the next mile. I find myself searching for Meri among the pockets of people huddled under umbrellas and trees. But between the blurring rain and the fact that everyone is burrowed under scarves, hats, and raincoats, it's too hard to identify faces. She could be anywhere.

With three quarters of a mile to go, we come to the only hill on the course. It feels like I'm ice-skating on an incline. I make it to the top, but my relief quickly turns to panic when I start to slip as the ground angles downward. I barely catch myself before totally wiping out and do some mixture of surfing and shuffling all the way down.

Thankfully – *miraculously* – I'm still on my feet when I get to the bottom. I'm so shaken up that it takes me a minute to realize I'm closing in on Josie. Her shoulders are sagging, her arms tight. A surge of heat flows through me, some alchemic reaction of anger and vindication.

I don't think about Blythe or Meri or Mom and Dad. Don't think about my burning lungs, the way my limbs are now numb from being pummeled with freezing rain. I don't think about *anything*, just let myself succumb to whatever force is carrying me forward. My legs fly. My arms swing in perfect synchronization.

If I can maintain my position, keep her in sight, this race is mine.

I zone out. By the time I snap back into conscious thought, the finish line is in view. I let out my banshee cry, hoping it leaves Josie's ears ringing.

"Fight, Cat!"

I glance over at the cheering crowds on the sidelines. It's Cheeto. I meet his gaze and feel grateful tears spring to my eyes.

"This is yours!" he says.

The last minute of a race is never fully in focus: dreamlike and foggy, simultaneously sped up and slowed down. Your senses play tricks on you. Because of this, I'm not completely sure what happens when I finally break the plane of the two flagged cones marking the finish.

But when someone pulls my tag from my bib and yells, "One!" I realize I've done it.

I've won the race.

I stagger out of the way and collapse to my knees. My head feels heavy, my vision swimmy. Tears pour out of me, mixing with my sweat and the rain.

I turn to see Coach walking over to me. Grim-faced, phone in hand. I realize at that moment that the tears pouring down my cheeks aren't happy tears. I'm crying because I know this is it. My last race.

I brace myself for what's coming. For the disappointment. The shame.

But I'm totally unprepared for the words that come out of his mouth: "There's been an accident."

CHAPTER 40
CAT

I'm in the passenger seat of Coach's wife's big white van, the vehicle version of an orthopedic shoe. Two of the kids in the back are screaming, and one is asking five million times for a snack. Inexplicably, the baby is fast asleep.

Four is a lot of kids.

As Coach pulled me off to the side after the race, he told me he got the call from the school secretary, who said two frantic parents showed up in the office asking where drama club was. He didn't continue, but I can finish the story on my own: the secretary radioing down to Mr. Edwards, him telling her there is no Cat Shultz on the play roster, the four of them being utterly confused until the secretary says, "I think I saw a Cat Shultz on the excuse list for the cross country race this afternoon …"

The look of shock on my parents' faces as they realize that what at first seemed like a misunderstanding is actually something quite different.

When I asked Coach if Meri was okay, he said the only news the secretary gave him about Meri was that she was being taken to a hospital just outside of Springs.

It's strange. Falling apart is so easy with the stupid, trivial stuff, but I'm able to keep it together during earth-shattering moments. I nod my head. I jog to the pavilion and get my duffel bag. I get in the car with a near stranger, because having Coach's wife drop me off at the hospital was the best solution anyone could come up with. Coach couldn't leave the team alone, and if I rode back on the bus, there'd be no way for me to get back to Springs.

So here I am. Riding shotgun with Mrs. Davis.

She doesn't try to get me to talk, which I appreciate. Just tells me stuff that doesn't need a response, like pointless stories about her kids, how she forgot to bring raincoats because she didn't realize it was going to storm until they were already halfway to the race, how she and Coach met. She refers to him as "Frankie," which in other circumstances would probably make me laugh.

While she's talking, I stare at my phone. There are 25 missed calls and 14 voicemails. All from my parents.

And a single text message from Meri.

It takes me 10 minutes to work up the courage to open it.

I'm coming to meet you at the park. We're going to work through this together. Love you sis.

The thing about earth-shattering moments is they always catch up with you.

**

It's still raining buckets when we take the exit. Mrs. Davis pulls into the parking lot of a tall yellow-brick building. The letters *SFMC* loom over a cross.

She takes the roundabout in front of the main entrance. "Here, we'll walk you in and make sure you find them okay," she says, unbuckling her seat belt.

I glance back at the still-screaming kids. The sleeping baby.

I've already inconvenienced them enough. Inconvenienced *everyone* enough.

"No, it's okay, I'll find them. Thanks for the ride, Mrs. Davis," I say, already opening the door. My heart thrums in my chest.

"Are you sure?"

I nod. Force a smile and shut the door before she can argue.

My jersey is still damp, and the chill in the air goes straight to my bones. I jog inside and am greeted by a woman at the front desk.

"I – I'm looking for my sister," I say.

"What's her name, hon?"

My voice catches in my throat, the reality of this nightmare finally sinking in. "Merideth Shultz."

She types something on her computer. A shadow seems to fall over her face, and my chest pounds even harder. "I'm going to have you wait right there for a minute, all right?" Her voice is saccharine. Frighteningly so.

She disappears through a doorway to the right of the desk, leaving me alone in the entryway to memorize the finite details of the room: the fake flower arrangements, the teal vinyl chairs, the cheap watercolor paintings. And the smell – bathroom cleaner mixed with old people – makes me feel like I'm going to be sick.

The woman is gone for an eternity.

Another doorway on the left clicks and starts to open. It's one of those automatic doors that seem to move in slow motion, and I hold my breath as I watch it swing, expecting the receptionist or even my family to emerge from the other side. Instead, it's a random nurse who doesn't even look my way before disappearing around the opposite corner.

I can't wait any longer.

The door is on its mechanized retreat back into place, but I jog over and catch the handle before it shuts, ignoring the *Authorized Personnel Only* sign posted on the front.

I slip through the gap. On the other side I hear distant voices, but all I see is a hallway of closed doors, empty stretchers, and machines pushed up against the walls.

And then: the sound of squeaking wheels on tile floors. The patter of footsteps.

The distant voices get louder, clearer, until I see a gurney emerge from an intersecting hallway.

Six indistinguishable figures in aprons and masks surround it, rushing, *racing*, to an unknown destination. My view of the patient is mostly blocked, but I do make out one thing: a mess of curly red hair.

An invisible rope coils around my gut, my chest, my throat, then drags me back into the lobby and out the revolving glass doors at the front of the hospital.

Back into the rain, where the gray sky is quickly being swallowed up by night.

I do the only thing that makes sense.

I run.

CHAPTER 41

JOSIE

The bus ride home is agonizing, silent.

We won Region outright. Our ticket to State, punched.

But somehow none of it matters.

All I can think about is how I've been feeding off this stupid, unspoken rivalry between me and Cat, the role I might have played in her struggle.

I did to *her* what has been done to *me* my whole life – refused to give her a chance.

And what did I gain? Absolutely nothing. I lost my top position anyway.

The downpour has morphed into a blurry sleet. The bus skids several times, making us swerve in a stomach-lurching weave on the slippery road. I think we all sigh in relief when we arrive back at the school, still upright.

Before everyone unloads, we have a quick meeting on the bus so we don't have to stand in the cold. I can tell Coach isn't upset with our performance this week, but it's still tense. Just like everyone else, he's clearly worried about Meri.

Everyone else leaves, but I stick around to help unload the coolers in the back. We're carrying them to the equipment shed when Coach says, "Cat's parents didn't know she was running cross country. Which tells me something else was going on with her."

Guilt rises up in my chest as the weight of this sinks in.

I don't want to tell him what I heard in the bathroom.

That I knew she shouldn't be running, that all wasn't as it seemed.

But I know I have to.

His eyes go wide as I relay the details of Cat's conversation. There is no condemnation in his eyes, but he doesn't try to absolve me, either. We both know I should have told him before the race started.

He looks like he's trying to find the right words to say when he gets another call.

"You're kidding me," he says to whoever it is on the other line, closing his eyes and pinching the bridge of his nose. He starts pacing in a circle. "Yes … yeah, she dropped her off an hour ago. Said she watched her walk inside. All right, thank you."

"What?" I ask as he hangs up.

"That was the school secretary. Cat's gone. She's not at the hospital."

"Gone?"

"I don't know. She must have left."

The uneasy feeling I've had since the end of the race burgeons into full-blown panic.

**

When I get home I throw my bag on the floor, open the phone, Google the address of the hospital. It'll take an hour and a half to drive back there. In this weather, probably even longer.

The other problem? I don't have a car.

But there's no way I can sit around and wait for news.

I go to Ziggy's door and pound. "Zig, I need your help!"

He's been even more reclusive than usual lately. After Vinnie's accident he shut down, and I still haven't figured out if that's a good thing or a bad thing. Everyone says that you have to hit rock bottom before you can start moving up, but I don't think that's always necessarily true. Sometimes the stones are too jagged, the ascent too steep. And that's when people give up.

"Zig?"

I wait as patiently as I can as the seconds tick past. His car is out front, so I know he's home. He must either be ignoring me or asleep.

Or something's wrong. And after all that's happened today …

Fear settles in my gut and I back up, ready to kick down his door, when it opens a crack.

"What do you want?" he barks.

I take a deep breath, my fear eased by the alertness of his eyes, and explain the situation as quickly and succinctly as possible. From the look on his face, I'm certain he's going to say no.

Instead, he grabs his keys from his dresser. "Let's go."

CHAPTER 42

CAT

Ever since I started running I've wondered what comes after the pain. If you push yourself past your limits and still don't stop. Pull a Forrest Gump for real.

Tonight, I've finally figured it out.

After pain comes numbness. And lucky for me, that's exactly what I'm going for.

I have no idea how far I've gone. Five miles? Ten? Twenty? I'm soaked through – my clothes, my skin, my hair. I might as well be swimming in ice water. A third-class passenger of the Titanic, treading against the inevitable.

I have no plan. No destination.

A tiny voice in my mind tells me to stop, to think of my parents. But a louder voice reminds me that they know the truth by now: that Meri was driving in a rainstorm because of me. That I'm a selfish liar, too cowardly to face my own demons, instead just dressing them up in new clothes and sweeping them under the rug for later.

And I'm certain they must be wishing it were me in that hospital bed instead of her.

There's this idea people feed you that life always corrects itself. *"Everything will be okay in the end, and if it's not okay, it's not the end."* I think it's supposed to mean that the universe has some master plan, and if things aren't going your way, you just have to wait it out because the giant teeter-totter of life will eventually send you back up to the top again.

But it's a lie. And a cruel one.

Kind of like the lie I've been living. Not the cross country cover-up lie, but the deeper, more sinister one – that I've overcome everything. I remember Ms. Reid saying eating disorders are rarely just eating disorders; that they're a symptom, a manifestation of something deeper. Which is a terrifying prospect, because it means it's not the disorder that's the problem.

It's *me*.

Instead of confronting the truth, I figured out how to seem as "fixed" as possible. What to do and say to generate the gold stars and discharge papers, how to hide the parts of me I didn't want others to see and certainly didn't want to acknowledge myself.

And that's the crux: I haven't just been lying to my parents. I've been lying to myself, too.

But if there's one thing I'm absolutely sure is true, deep down to the very core of my being, it's this: I'd never be able to live with myself if Meri dies.

CHAPTER 43

JOSIE

Two hours later, I call Coach and he confirms the worst – that Cat is still missing. He's now in direct contact with her parents, who've also called the police. They say they are "out looking," but I highly doubt it. They're probably just treating this as a normal runaway situation, assuming she's at a friend's house or hiding out in a mall somewhere. That she'll eventually turn up.

And as much as I wish that were true, I have a nagging feeling in the pit of my stomach that it isn't.

"I mean, how far could she have gotten?" I say. Ziggy's been surprisingly chill about this – I'm still in shock that he even agreed in the first place – but I can tell he's at the tail end of his patience. We've been on what feels like every road within a 20-mile radius of the hospital, hardly able to see and sliding around on the road like a wet fish.

"Just one more," I say, searching the map on the phone and spotting a winding black county road on what looks like the outskirts of civilization. We had to bring Mom's laptop so we could keep the phone charged; I'll ask for forgiveness later.

"I promise I'll pay you for the gas. And then some."

He sighs and drives out of the parking lot. I direct him where to go then sit quietly back in the seat, not wanting to aggravate him by pointless chatter.

"I thought you hated this chick," he says.

He must have heard me talking to Mom about her. I *did*

once say she was ruining my life, which seems so stupid now.

"I never *hated* her," I respond, recoiling when I remember what I said to her just before I surged past her at City County. How could I have been so cruel? "I just … well, she's Meri Shultz's little sister, you know?"

It sounds so petty now. So childish.

Since he was first to engage, I take it as a sign he's open for talking. "Have you talked to Dad lately?"

He shakes his head. "You?"

I shake my head too.

"Do you think you hate Dad?" I ask. "Like, *really* hate him?"

He's quiet for a minute. We've said the word "hate" and "dad" in the same sentence so many times, but the word is starting to leave a bad taste in my mouth.

"Yeah. I fucking hate him. But it doesn't really change anything either way, does it?"

I think about Cat, and Dad, and the girls' soccer team, and everyone else I've spent so much time and energy holding hostage against themselves.

"No," I say. "I guess it doesn't."

CHAPTER 44

CAT

Thirteen months ago, Mom found me in the bathroom in a pool of blood.

I don't remember anything. Not the falling or Mom's screams or being carted off in an ambulance. I *do* remember being glad when I found out it was an accident. That I hadn't *tried* to kill myself, that the truth was that I just passed out and hit my head on the edge of the vanity.

The scariest part? Realizing I'd gotten to the point where doing it on purpose was actually a possibility.

**

My cross country jersey is still soaking wet, suctioned against my body. I don't know what *city* I'm in, let alone which road I'm on: some deserted route with no lights or houses, devoid of any evidence of civilization at all. The starless, moonless sky gives away nothing. I haven't been passed by a car for miles.

My body is starting to shut down. I know this because not only is my vision blurry and my limbs numb, but I'm burning up. I'm hot, *so hot,* while fat cotton-ball snowflakes fall delicately around me. The kind that made me giddy as a kid, that I would spend hours trying to catch on my tongue.

My tearless sobs echo in the silent darkness. There are no birds singing or insects chirping, all of them burrowed away in some safe place, out of danger.

Of course, just hours ago I didn't care about *safe*. Punishing myself was the point. Shame and fear and the prospect of losing Meri had pushed all logical thought from my mind.

But maybe clarity is a side effect of slowly fading away, too. Because right now, terrified out of my mind, I know without a doubt that as angry and hurt and betrayed as my parents must feel, I'm only contributing to it.

That their love is just as real as my self-loathing.

The road curves into a bend. I drag myself around it, hoping, *praying*, for a gas station or a house on the other side. A barn I could hide away in until morning.

But when the curve straightens out, I see nothing but a black, endless void. No signs of life.

My heart sinks. I feel nauseated, disoriented.

I need to lay down. Need to sleep. I have the sickening thought that I should probably stay near the middle of the road because it's the only way anyone will ever find me.

I look around – one last, desperate attempt to climb out of the hole I've dug for myself. And when I do, I notice a pinprick of light in the distance. A car? A flashlight? The light at the end of that proverbial, one-way tunnel?

Regardless, it gets closer.

It takes every ounce of self-control to hold my body still, to keep my legs upright beneath me. The glare grows brighter until I see that it's not one light but two.

Headlights.

I stick one hand weakly in the air.

The car must have its brights on, because it very nearly blinds me as it approaches. I shield my eyes but sense it slowing. Stopping.

The passenger side door opens.

Someone is saying my name, speaking words that don't fully register.

The only thing I truly comprehend are warm arms enveloping me.

CHAPTER 45

JOSIE

Last night's storm ushered in a cold front. A shock-to-the-system cold, the kind that feels like a cruel joke after months of warmth and sunshine.

No matter how many Colorado winters you've been through, you're never ready for it.

I'm standing in front of the team gathered in the corner – *our* corner – of the empty parking lot, waiting for the last few stragglers to arrive. Evidence of how much has changed since the summer months surrounds us. The once lush, green fields are now brown and dry and dusted with snow. Icicles hang from the lampposts. Even the darkness holds significance – it's just before 7 a.m., our usual summer practice time, and it might as well be midnight.

Between the darkness and cinched sweatshirt hoods, I can't see anyone's faces, but that's for the best. I pick up what I need to know from the way they've congealed into a solid mass, how tightly their arms are linked – not just holding on to each other, but holding on like they're afraid to let go. Like this alone is what's keeping them all upright.

I don't know where this team's been for the past two weeks, but I'm sure as hell glad to have them back.

Scratch that – I *do* know. Because the splintering was my fault.

It's why I called this meeting in the first place.

"Thanks for waking up early to be here. I know it's been a long night for most of us. In case you haven't heard, Cat is awake and talking, and her sister's stable. They're both going to be okay."

There's a ripple of relieved murmurs.

I pause to collect myself, to make sure that what comes out of my mouth next is what I really want to say. "Man, you guys. What a season. We've had our share of highs – dominating our district meet schedule, winning our first ever invitational. But we've hit some lows, too, especially these last few weeks. And I want to apologize for the role I played in that. I haven't been the leader you guys deserve."

No one challenges that assessment.

I take a deep breath, releasing it in wispy white tufts. "But I'm sure I speak for everyone when I say the fear we all felt last night when we learned one of our own was in trouble was the lowest point of all. You might start hearing things about Cat. Maybe you already have. I don't know the whole story – don't even *need* to know the whole story – but one thing I *do* know is that she needs us now, more than ever. My challenge for all of you is to defend her. Refuse to gossip. Treat her the same, like the amazing runner and friend we know she is. Every single one of us is broken in some way."

Behind us, light begins to creep up the sky, the horizon slowly materializing like a Polaroid picture.

Their faces get clearer. My stomach tightens.

"There's one more thing I need to say. I started out this season thinking we have to win at all costs. I had this thought that …"

I catch Sergio's eyes, and he offers a supportive smile. I think of myself five months ago, imagining I could sway Coach's decision with a win. It seems so stupid now – immature at best, but delusional is probably more accurate. And I can't pinpoint the exact moment when I figured out my master plan wasn't going to pan out because there *was* no lightning strike. No aha moment, no eureka.

It was the small, steady reminders throughout this season that sometimes strength isn't about your grip but about your ability to let go.

"Actually ... it doesn't matter. What I really want to say is let's finish out this season the way we started. Running because we love to run. Because we love running *together*. And you know what? No matter what happens, that's enough. That's always been enough."

CHAPTER 46
CAT

I wake up in a hospital bed. Mom is sitting in a chair next to me.

It all floods back: The race. Blythe. The accident –

"Meri?" I gasp, sitting up.

"She's okay. A few broken ribs, some bruises and scratches." She strokes my arm, which is hooked up to an IV. There are cords and wires attaching my body to a beige machine I'm assuming must be a heart monitor based on its steady beeping.

Mom's eyes are swollen with exhaustion, and her face is creased with worry lines.

Put there by me.

I start to cry. Bury my face in my sheets to catch my tears.

She doesn't tell me it's okay, and I'm grateful. She just keeps stroking my arm like that, letting me cry for a few minutes before gently tugging down on the sheets so she can meet my eyes.

"So no drama club, huh?" she says with a wry smile. "Is being in the school play really *that* embarrassing?"

"No more embarrassing than running cross country," I say. My lower lip trembles. "Mom, I'm so sorry. I was –"

"There will be time for explanations, Cat. For *consequences*. But right now, the only thing that matters is that you're safe." She leans forward and cradles my chin. "I love you. And nothing will ever change that."

I nod and feel her warmth wash over me. "I love you too, Mom."

We hold each other's gaze for a few seconds. "That was a brave thing your friend and her brother did, searching for you in the snowstorm like that. Because I don't know what I would have done if ..." She stifles her own sob.

I realize I don't remember the details of being found. How I went from running out of the hospital to lying in a bed inside it.

"Josie, I think she said her name was? Seems like such a nice girl."

My jaw goes slack, and tears spring once again to my eyes as the memory materializes: the headlights, the warmth of her arms, the fact that I was minutes away, *seconds,* from giving up.

Mom looks at me quizzically, but I just smile. "It's a long story," I say.

"We'll have to have her over for dinner," she says.

I nod. "Definitely."

**

The next few hours are painful, in more ways than one. I have a few more checkups, they take out the IV and unhook me from the machines, then we meet with the doctor from Springs who first treated me for my disorder last September. He tells me I'm manifesting many of the physical symptoms I had last year – low bone density, hypoglycemia, and brady-cardia, which is an extremely low heart rate. I tell him I don't understand; I've been eating. And up until a few weeks ago, I felt better than I ever have.

He swallows. "Your parents tell me you've been running? In secret?"

I nod, feeling my cheeks redden.

"Running is an intense sport, Cat. It can take a long time – months, even years – for body systems to be restored to full functionality once their processes have been disrupted by an eating disorder."

I'm embarrassed, ashamed. He's telling me what I already know – or what I *knew*, rather, and allowed myself to conveniently forget. That I should never have been running like that. I think back to the promises I made with myself at the beginning, and how completely I failed at keeping them.

It was so easy to forget because of how good I felt. Because my life suddenly seemed worth living again.

But I guess it's like the whole thing with the frog and the boiling water. It's just a nice, warm bath until … it's not.

I take a deep breath, terrified to ask the question on the tip of my tongue – both because I'm scared of his answer, and because of the potential reaction from my parents.

But I have to.

"Will it … *ever* be safe for me to run again?"

Mom and Dad look over at me. Their expressions are strained, but not upset.

He clears his throat. "Many athletes with eating disorders go on to have very successful careers with professional guidance and regular monitoring. And, most importantly, honesty with the people who care about them."

I nod. It's a jab I know I deserve.

He continues. "With those considerations, I don't see why that can't be true of you."

I smile, grateful for any sliver of hope I can get.

**

As soon as the doctor is out the door, I look over at Mom. "Can I go see her now?"

Mom told me earlier that watching Meri be rushed down the hall by the doctors was the worst possible moment I could have walked in. That if I would have found my parents in the ICU waiting room, they could have reassured me she was going to be okay. As bad as the accident was – a texting driver who hydroplaned and crossed the median into oncoming traffic – her injuries were never life-threatening. They were initially worried about internal bleeding or a ruptured spleen, but her worst injury ended up being a few broken ribs. Nothing that won't completely heal.

Mom nods and helps me out of bed. I still feel weak and sore, but it feels good to use my legs again. We walk together down the corridor until Mom stops outside a door and motions for me to go in.

"You're not coming?"

"I think you two should talk alone."

I'm reaching for the door when I'm hit with a wave of guilt. Meri wouldn't be in that hospital bed if it weren't for me. And the last time we talked, I said the absolute most terrible thing I've ever said to anyone in my entire life.

But in true Meri fashion, she meets my eyes and smiles as soon as I open the door. "Well, it sounds like I'll get out of two weeks' worth of lectures. Not a *terrible* deal."

And then I see Paul sitting in a chair in the corner of the room, sipping from a mini straw poking up from one of those little hospital Styrofoam cups. He smiles at me. "Hey, kid sister."

"Paul?"

"Good to see you, Cat," he says, then looks down in his cup. "Think I need some more juice."

He meets Meri's eyes and she smiles at him. He gives her hand a squeeze as he walks by her bed, then disappears out the door.

"Um, that's big," I say, sitting down in his chair.

Her face fills with a smile much too big for someone who *literally* just got hit by a truck.

"He came as soon as he heard about the accident. Even had a big game this weekend, but he told his coaches they either play the second-stringer or he's transferring schools."

I make my eyes wide, wanting to show my support and interest but also not wanting to make any assumptions. It's her life, and she and Paul need to figure it out for themselves.

But, not going to lie, it's good to see her happy.

"I'm sorry," I burst out. "About the accident. About everything I said on the phone. None of it was true."

She grabs my hand. Gives it a squeeze. "I know."

"Do you forgive me?"

"What do you think, Cat?" We hold each other's gazes, and a calmness settles over me. "So," she continues, "how are you taking it? The no-more-running thing?"

"I'm not sure it's really sunk in yet, but I know the doctor's right. I've been having dizzy spells again. A pretty bad one the day I called you, actually." I take a long deep breath. "State's next week. I really wanted you all to see me run, at least once."

She looks at me sympathetically. "I'm sorry, Cat."

I nod, feeling tears form, but I'm able to call them off. "What about you? How long until you're better?"

"Eh, it'll be fine. Just a couple broken ribs; they can't even really do anything about it. Just get to be waited on for a few weeks."

I feel my cheeks get warm. "This wouldn't have happened if –"

"The accident wasn't your fault, Cat. It was the other driver's. And you know what? Would Paul be here, squeezing my hand on his way out to refill his juice cup, if none of this had happened?" She holds my gaze with her dancing green eyes, and I think again how lucky I am to have Meri in my life. "I mean, I'm not saying I'd do it *over* again ..."

I run my hands along the armrests. "Do you believe there's a reason for everything?"

She shrugs. "It's nice to at least *pretend* to believe it, don't you think?"

I think about Lucy's red car pulling up next to me that warm June morning. Cheeto picking watermelons the day I went with Alma. Josie miraculously finding me along that deserted road at the precise moment I was about to give up.

"Yeah," I say, willing the hope inside of me to stick around.

**

If I had to pick a favorite season, it would be autumn. It's relatable, you know? Freezing cold one day, warm and colorful and bright the next. As much as I want to be a summer girl, it's just not who I am.

The day we all head home from the hospital is one of the warm and colorful and bright ones. Grandma's been watching Penny, and I can tell as soon as we walk through the door she's glad to have Mom back.

I walk into my room. The walnut trees out my window are crayon yellow, and with the sunlight streaking through the gaps in their branches it's like I'm about to have some sort of heavenly visitation. Definitely an improvement over the gloomy gray clouds I've been staring at outside the hospital window for the past two days.

A bunch of "get well soon" balloons bob in the corner; a bouquet of flowers and several cards are propped up on my nightstand: one from Coach and his wife, one signed by the whole team, one just from the freshies – with a picture of Richard Simmons on the front, of course – and one from Blythe.

I pick up the one from Blythe first.

We might be heading down different roads, Cat, but I will always love you like a sister.

It isn't the "I made a huge mistake, Tyler's a jerk and my friends are all fake, please take me back" message I might have hoped for several months ago.

But somehow, it's perfect. I guess sometimes you don't realize how much you need closure until you get it.

I set it back down and pick up the card from Coach when I hear the doorbell ring. A few seconds later, Mom calls out, *"Cat honey!"*

I come out of my room to see Mom waiting by the top of the stairs, wearing a grin that can only mean one thing.

What can I say? The woman loves love.

Cheeto has one hand in his jeans pocket. The other holds a small box wrapped in brown grocery sack paper.

"Hey," he says, blushing.

"Hey." I follow him outside and start to close the door, warding Mom off with my eyes before I shut it completely.

We wander over to the porch swing and sit down, swinging gently. Neither of us say anything.

Word must have made it around to him by now – I know how fast rumors fly in a small town. I think maybe he's come to say his goodbyes, to tell me it's probably for the best if we just be friends, which I would totally understand.

Instead, he takes one of my hands in his, lacing his fingers through mine. With the other, he reaches over and gives me the brown box.

"What's this?" I ask.

"Open it."

I let go of his hand and slowly unwrap the package. Inside is a small white box like you'd get at a jewelry store. I lift the lid to see a miniature wooden carving of a wolf attached with a gold clasp to a black cord necklace.

My breath catches in my throat. "Did you make this?"

He nods, looking somewhere between pleased and embarrassed.

I pull it out, holding it up close to my face. It's a work of art: the intricate detailing of the fur, the tiny paws, the way its head perfectly captures a wolf mid-howl.

I feel tears forming in my eyes. "It's the most beautiful thing I've ever seen."

"I wouldn't go *that* far."

I reach out and pull him into me, realizing how much I've missed his smell, the feeling of his body close to mine.

"No, really," I say, then pull back and meet his eyes. "Your dad would be so proud of you."

**

By Tuesday, Meri looks almost completely back to normal. She doesn't even wince when she's walking around.

Mom takes her to a follow-up appointment, where they tell her she can go back to college as soon as she's up to it. Which I'm sure means we *all* have to go back to school. Back to life. It's a prospect I'm not sure I'm ready for.

"Well, what do you think, Mer?" Dad says at dinner that night. "Should we take you up tomorrow? I can tell you're chomping at the bit to get back and hit the books."

She smirks and rolls her eyes. "Can't go tomorrow. We've got plans." She looks over at me. "It's State, right?"

"Yeah, but … I can't run."

"Shouldn't you be there to cheer your friends on?"

I shake my head. "No, it's okay, we don't have to –"

"You're part of the team, aren't you? Going to ditch them on the most important race of the year?"

I look at Mom and Dad, sure they'll back me up. Instead, they're both smiling.

CHAPTER 47

CAT

I leave my family in the stands near the finish line. Even if Meri were in any condition to run around, I doubt they'd be interested in pinballing around the course to watch random people they've never met before compete in a sport that they barely even knew existed until last week.

It's a beautiful day. There's a delicious chill to the air, and the vibrant autumn leaves are perfectly juxtaposed against the blue, cloudless sky. The park is packed. Groups of seven uniformed girls run past, warming up; clusters of excited parents and students with hand-painted posters are scattered around; coaches from competing schools shake hands and make small talk, feigning friendliness. It's like the invitational, but ... *more*.

I can't lie. Being here is harder than I thought it would be. My legs feel magnetized toward the start line, tugging the rest of my body like a puppy straining against its leash. I ache to feel the buzz of adrenaline, to have my stomach tangle up in the best kind of knots.

I hear someone call my name and turn to see Sophia, balanced on her crutches and waving. I feel a flash of anxiety but walk toward her anyway, steeling myself for what I assume will be the first of many awkward interactions today.

But my trepidation melts away as soon as I get close enough to see her face. There isn't an ounce of disgust or discomfort or even intrigue on her face.

"Oh, KitKat, we've missed you!" she says, pulling me in

for a long hug. "You're okay? What about your sister? Oh my gosh, everyone's going to be so excited you're here!"

"Yeah, we're both doing better. Thanks for the card." As grateful as I am for her concern, I'm eager to change the subject. "So who's all running today then?" I hope she can't hear the disappointment in my voice. Sophia is dealing with her own; if she can smile, I can too.

"Gretchen, of course. And then sweet Becca. She's a nervous wreck, but she's going to do great."

I wonder how that would be, running JV the whole season and then on the most important race of the year being asked to jump into the varsity race. I don't blame her for being nervous.

"So … is everything … good with you guys?" I ask, referring to the rift that was only widening the last time I saw the freshies.

A look I can't quite read passes over Sophia's face. "They will be."

I question her with my eyes, and she sighs. "I guess I might as well just tell you. It's not, like, a secret or anything, at least not anymore. Bea came out."

"Came out? Like …"

"Like, she's gay."

For a few seconds I'm confused, wondering what this has to do with the freshies' argument, but suddenly I remember Bea's very obvious dislike of Sophia's and Kyle's relationship, and the pieces fall into place.

My heart aches at the impossibility of the situation.

She gives me a knowing smile, clearly sensing that I understand. "She's my best friend, though, and both of us refuse to give that up. We're going to figure it out."

I nod. "Yeah. You will. We *all* will, together."

She takes a deep breath, lets it out slowly. "In the meantime … we've got a state championship to win."

We make a game plan to maximize our cheering potential, decide which turns and hilltops and back stretches of the course we think the team will need us most.

The announcer takes the field, and the whole park gets quiet. Goosebumps cover my arms and legs. I don't breathe.

My eyes find the bright blue of our jerseys at the start line.

CHAPTER 48

JOSIE

The starting line is a dam. A two-inch strip of white chalk, holding back a sea of ponytails and legs.

The weather seems like a good omen: 69 degrees, blue sky, slight breeze coming from the north. But then again, rain or shine, breezy or blizzarding, weather is the great equalizer. The control variable. Can't very well label it a blessing or a curse if it applies to everyone.

A hundred and forty girls on this starting line – a 20-colored rainbow – and the only other team I care about is, ironically, the only other team wearing blue. A different shade, of course; Plain City is deeper, denser royal blue, while Aspen Ridge is more of a shimmery cerulean, as if their jerseys are dusted with finely ground diamonds. That, or covered with hoarfrost.

There's a metaphor in there somewhere. Probably more than one.

Other than their ultra-fancy Lycra jerseys, a casual observer would likely find nothing extraordinary about Aspen Ridge. Just a typical high school cross country squad doing the same toe touches and hamstring stretches as everyone else on the line. But if you get close enough, you can see something missing from their eyes. Something tormenting every other runner on the field.

Fear.

The Aspen Ridge girls don't just *hope* they're going to win. Don't just *believe* it.

I, too, believe in the raw, intangible power of the mind. But this isn't a case study of *The Little Engine That Could*. This kind of confidence is rooted in biology, in physics, in hard data. I've run the numbers. With Cat and Sophia both missing, there's a 99 percent chance that Aspen Ridge will walk away with the state championship trophy.

But I'd give anything to prove them wrong. To shake their confidence.

No. *Obliterate* it.

A stocky man in khakis crosses the center of the field, holding a starter pistol in his right hand and a megaphone in the other.

I tune out the man's echoey speech: no pushing and shoving, stay between the spray-painted arrows and plastic cones, pacing will lead to disqualification. Rules each runner knows by heart, even if those rules aren't always followed.

The one thing I *do* pay attention to is how slowly the man seems to be talking.

Finally – the only four words I'm listening for: "Runners, on your marks!"

Emotion wells in the back of my throat as the seven of us – the Wolfpack, at least a *part* of it – elbow our way into position. Four months, three weeks, and two days of pain, sweat, and tears, and it all comes down to what happens in the next 20 minutes.

Better be more like 19, if we want to pull this off.

I've never bought into trite proverbs. Sometimes, winning *is* everything. More than everything, if you can pull off a win on a 1 percent chance.

But today, no matter what the scoresheet reads at the end of this thing, this team is walking away champions.

The man in khakis lifts the gun above his head. A crack pulses through the air.

The dam breaks.

CHAPTER 49

CAT

They weren't kidding when they said Aspen Ridge is a beast. Even though the first few seconds after the gun goes off are basically a stampede, their two top runners float into first and second place like ice in water. Josie holds her own in third, pumping up the hill just ahead of the next two Aspen Ridge girls.

Out of 140 runners, there are *four* of them in the top *five*. Insanity.

I remember Bea joking about the Aspen Ridge girls being robots, and I think I finally understand. Their faces reveal nothing – no pain, no struggle, no urgency. Definitely no joy. The way their lips are pinched together, sealed shut, makes me wonder how – *if* – they're even breathing.

After the top five pass, there's a big rush of runners. I spot Bea cresting the hill, definitely top 15, with Lucy close behind. It's a bottleneck as they merge onto the single-lane trail at the top, but both of them cut in expertly, asserting their position. Even though they have work to do and people to catch, they're in good shape.

Electricity ripples through me. I realize this is the first time I've ever actually watched a cross country race, and inexplicably, it feels almost more intense than running in one – a bird's-eye view exposing all the moving parts and variables that need to perfectly align in order for the team to win. When you're in the race, all you see is the ponytail swinging right in front of you.

Sophia and I stay there until the rest of the team goes by – Millie passes somewhere in the 20s; Alma, 10 or so places behind her. Gretchen and Becca, who both stepped up to fill the voids left behind by me and Sophia, are buried somewhere in the 50s or 60s. It seems high, but Sophia assures me that this is par for the course in a race like this. These are the best runners in the entire state.

It's that moment when I realize what a longshot winning actually is for us. I feel a flash of guilt when I wonder what might have happened if I were up there with Josie. How I might have given them a fighting chance.

"Come on, Jo's cruising," Sophia says, interrupting my thoughts before I can go down that rabbit hole. "Piggyback me?"

We're a scene, me wrangling the crutches with her on my back, the two of us nearly tipping over every five steps and laughing like we're five years old. But we make it to our next cheering spot right as the lead Aspen Ridge runner crosses the bridge. Her footsteps on the wooden planks are loud as gunshots. The spectators around me clap and cheer, clearly awed by her performance.

Awed, but not surprised. Not *inspired*.

The second runner emerges 10 seconds later, followed by Josie, who's drafting off her.

"You've got this, Jo! Catch them!" I yell.

Josie and I haven't talked since the night of the snowstorm. She didn't send me a card, didn't come over this week to check on me. But as her eyes flicker toward me now, I know we've crossed some sort of threshold. What that means, I don't know yet. I mean, I'm not expecting her to start inviting me to sleepovers, or that she'll leave me gel-pen notes decorated with little hearts inside our locker. But I feel pretty confident that things will be different from now on.

I'm mesmerized by her grace, by the way her legs seem to glide across the ground in a single fluid motion. I've run with Josie a hundred times, stared at her back for what feels like *hours*, but I've never truly seen her run.

Aspen Ridge's one and two might be faster, but there's no doubt in my mind that Josie wants it more.

She flies past us. When I glance back at the bridge to catch sight of the next clump of runners, my heart skips.

Bea's in sixth. And Lucy's right behind her.

"They're doing it, they're *killing* it!" Sophia shrieks, jumping up and down until I remind her she has a broken leg.

"Come on, Millie and Alma ..." I whisper into the air.

A few more faceless runners pass – if the jersey isn't blue, the runner might as well not exist right now – and then I see Millie. I've lost count, but she's in the high teens and looking strong.

"Come on, Mill!" I yell. "Bea and Lucy are six and seven! They need you up there!"

Her eyes flicker at the announcement. She gives us a determined nod and surges past the yellow-jerseyed runner in front of her.

We go wild.

There's only one scoring runner left, our fifth man, and barring any superhuman performances by Gretchen or Becca, it's Alma. I realize this is it – the moment she's been waiting for. Her chance to be a scoring runner. I think of our conversation by the watermelon truck that hot July day, hearing her express what it's like to feel invisible. To feel like you don't matter. I could relate; it's a variation on what I used to feel – sometimes consciously, sometimes not – with Meri. How no matter what I did, there would never be any way for me to measure up.

Cross country has helped me realize that while we're all in this crazy whirlwind called life together, we're all running different races. That your most important competitor is always yourself.

I see her coming, still lodged somewhere in the middle. I've lost count of what place she's in, but I know if we're going to win, it's a number we can't have on our scoresheet.

I don't want to send the message that what happens in the race today is all up to her – no one needs that kind of pressure. But at the same time I want her to know I believe she's capable of having the race of her dreams. That I *see* her. That she *matters*.

"You gotta get up there, Alma! We've got a chance to win this thing!" I don't actually know whether it's true or not, but I do know our chance drastically improves if she's not clear up in the 50s. "No regrets, Alma!"

It's a simple phrase, and truthfully, impossible to live by. I think of all the regrets I carry around with me daily.

But I don't think "no regrets" means "don't screw up." I think it means that doing the best you can in every moment is all you can do. And it's always good enough.

CHAPTER 50

JOSIE

Halfway there.

My mind is empty. No thoughts. No emotions.

I block out the screams and cheers. My eyes stay locked on the baby-blue jersey right in front of me.

I've visualized this scene hundreds of times. Knew that it would likely play out just the way it has – two blond ponytails swinging just out of reach, taunting me.

But as certain as I am that Brit and Jenna and the rest of the Aspen Ridge crew came to the race knowing they were going to win, there's also no doubt in my mind how this scene ends.

It's time to do what wolves do best.

Go hunting.

CHAPTER 51

CAT

At our third and final cheering spot, just half a mile from the finish, I see Lucy and assume it's all over.

There's a familiar gray tint in her face. Her head sags, and her fists are rolled into tight little balls.

I call out and she doesn't even look up.

I want to reach out and pull her off the course. Tell her it isn't her fault, that her being okay, that her *breathing*, is more important than a race.

But if I know Lucy like I think I do, she won't listen – not because of pride or stubbornness, but because she'd die before letting this team down.

She slows but doesn't stop. Several people pass her, and again I have the thought that maybe I need to intervene, that her health isn't worth this price.

But before I can make any sort of concrete decision, she disappears back into the trees for the final loop.

I cover my eyes with my hands and pace, sick with worry. It's too much.

It's only been 20 seconds or so when Sophia calls out, "Here they are!"

She pulls my arm down so I can see.

Alma has caught up to Millie, and the two of them are working together. They pass three people right in front of us, looking strong. It's the most confident I've ever seen Alma.

No regrets. She's doing it.

"Lucy's struggling!" I yell. "Get up there! She needs you guys! Half a mile left! Leave it all on the course!"

They disappear around the corner. The last we'll see of them before the finish line.

CHAPTER 52

JOSIE

I do it. I win.

Just like I knew I could. Like I knew I *would*.

I, Josie Romero, am the Colorado Girls 5A Cross Country State Champion.

It doesn't sink in, and I don't give it time to. I shrug off the people vying for high fives, eager to offer their congratulations. I don't even worry about catching Jenna's and Brit's reaction at the finish line.

None of it matters.

I hobble over to meet Coach, who's breathless and looking like a bag of nerves at the 200-meter line. He's probably sprinted way more than three miles cheering for us along the course. The guy deserves a medal of his own.

As soon as he spots me, he pulls me in for the best, most fatherly hug I could possibly hope for. When he pulls back I see tears in his eyes. "You did it, kiddo. I always *believed* you could, but you *knew* it."

I smile, feeling more relieved than anything. "How are we looking?"

He shows me the clipboard he's been using to tally everyone's places at different checkpoints, and I suddenly understand why he seems even more fidgety than usual.

My eyes go from his face to the clipboard and back to his face again.

"Don't want to jinx it," he says, "but I think we actually have a shot at this thing."

CHAPTER 53

CAT

The entire JV team has formed a human chute, like cheerleaders lined up for the tunnel entrance at a Broncos game minus all the pyrotechnics. It morphs into more of a V shape as we cheer Josie – yes, *Josie* – and the two Aspen Ridge runners trailing her into the finish line. As soon as she's across, we crane our necks back inward to watch for the next runners.

We wait, and wait, and wait. Finally, the fourth runner in a maroon jersey from some unknown school emerges from the trees.

Bea's five. We scream our heads off as she passes, our volume gradually subsiding for sixth, seventh, and eighth – an Aspen Ridge runner and two others. It's a straight-up battle between the three of them, and I'm riveted at the finish line until Sophia taps my arm. "Wait, is that … *Millie and Alma*? And Lucy!"

I turn back toward the incoming runners, and sure enough, Millie and Alma are sprinting, *flying*, toward us, synced up like two wheels on a single axle. They've moved up 10, maybe 15, places since the last time we saw them. Lucy looks beyond tired, but she's hanging on just a couple places behind.

Sophia and I look at each other, then exchange shocked glances with the rest of the team as we realize, at the exact same moment, what this means. Asking each other with our eyes the question we're too scared to say out loud.

Is this really happening?

CHAPTER 54

JOSIE

I look down at the chicken scratches on Coach's clipboard. Count. Count again.

Josie. 1.

Bea. 5.

Millie. 11.

Alma. 12.

Lucy. 15.

$1+5+11+12+15=44$

Then, I look at the numbers he's scrawled for Aspen Ridge.

$2+3+8+14+17=44$

The blood drains from Coach's face.

The blood drains from mine.

"I've never seen a state race come down to a tie," he says. "Which means ..."

He meets my eyes. "Which means it all comes down to the sixth runner."

CHAPTER 55

CAT

"What does it mean?" I say, frantic.

We're staring at the two equations scribbled on the back of some bell quiz Sophia had folded in her back pocket.

Two equations, one answer: 44.

"It means it all comes down to the sixth runner," Sophia answers. "Has Aspen Ridge's sixth runner crossed yet?"

It's that moment when I realize there are two very important pieces to this puzzle that no one has been paying much attention to at all: Gretchen and Becca.

I look up to catch the next batch of runners sprinting to the finish. Like everything else, cross country exists on a bell curve, and the slow trickling of finishers has now become a steady stream. I scan it for our royal blue.

And then I spot them. Their gaits are nothing like Josie's – slightly uneven, stiff. Clunky, you might even say. Their faces are tense with exertion, and it's clear that running doesn't come easy for them, isn't a natural state like it is for Josie and – if I'm being honest – me. The intensity of this race is requiring every ounce of grit they can salvage.

But they're helping each other. Running together. Following the Wolfpack code.

I don't know where Aspen Ridge's sixth runner is. I might have already missed her finish. It's possible this thing is over already.

But there's something beautiful – poetic, even – about the race coming down to this. Two girls who ran a whole season with hardly any recognition or praise, who joined cross country and stuck with it for no other reason than because they love this team.

It's the perfect ending to a perfectly imperfect season.

CHAPTER 56

JOSIE

The announcer begins the countdown. *"Fifth place ..."*

I search the stands. Find Mom, who is still shaking her head in disbelief. She meets my gaze and mouths, *I love you.*

"Fourth place ..."

Ziggy's standing next to her. He gives me two cheesy thumbs-up. I return them with a smirk and one of my classic eyerolls.

"Third place ..."

I find Sergio in the crowd. He smiles. The boys' race was just before ours. They came in second – best finish Plain City boys have ever had. I was so proud of them ... but also I can't wait to rub this win in for all of eternity.

"In second place, with a score of 44 points ..."

I look around at our girls, the JV team acting as human crutches for the exhausted State runners. Tears are already streaming down several faces.

"... Aspen Ridge High School."

I tune out the rest. Couldn't hear even if I tried due to the roar that erupts around me.

Yeah, winning might not be everything.

But it sure as hell is something.

CHAPTER 57

CAT

"Your turn," Josie says to me.

The trophy is made of granite and solid wood. Heavier than I expected, so I'm grateful for the other hands that help me prop it up.

Truthfully, it's not really mine. But if I've learned anything this year, it's that it doesn't have to be *mine* for it to be *ours*.

And as I pass it off to Sophia, holding her crutches with one hand so she can get a good grip, my other hand reaches up to my new necklace.

Yep, I think to myself. *Definitely lucky.*

COOLDOWN

CAT

One Year Later

"**D**id you *see* the way they looked at us when they jogged past during warm-ups?" Josie says to me, wide eyed. "If only they knew what a gift those scowls are to me."

I laugh, but she must sense that my nerves are getting the best of me.

"Hey, don't let them get in your head. Let them believe they're chasing us instead of the other way around. It's always better to be the hunter than the hunted."

I nod, take a deep breath. "Is Coach here yet?"

"Should be here any time."

"At least his new school's 4A so it won't feel like he's betraying us when he cheers them on."

We've staked out a pavilion next to the finish line. Millie is French braiding Alma's hair; Sophia and Bea are deep in a manic game of California Speed. Lucy, dressed in her street clothes – she elected not to run cross country this year because of her asthma – is helping some of the JV girls make signs that say things like "PACK ATTACK" and "BANSHEE TIME."

After nine months of going to therapy, meeting with online nutritionists, and regular visits to a new doctor in Lyman, Mom and Dad agreed that I could do cross country this year on a trial basis. There have been ups and downs – I've come to realize that's par for the course – but every day

I wake up grateful I don't have to keep my worlds separate anymore. And having my family there to support me at races has meant everything. Mom, who has basically taken on the role of unofficial team parent, even made everyone "Good luck at State" goody bags full of Gatorade, granola bars, and sparkly blue hair scrunchies.

"We ready, gals?" Our new coach, a former collegiate steeplechase runner named Cleo, who took the job in Plain City specifically to coach cross country and spring track, has become like a sister to us. "You better hustle to that line, ladies. The State train ain't waitin' on you."

The seven of us running today – me, Josie, Alma, Millie, Sophia, Bea, and Gretchen – get some last-minute hugs from Cleo, Lucy, and the JV girls, then start jogging toward the line. A few people in the crowd yell "Let's go, Wolfpack!" and "Come on, PC!" to which Josie responds with a few fist pumps in the air.

It's her senior year, which means this is her last cross country race as a Plain City silverwolf. At the pre-State team meeting yesterday, she – *Josie Romero* – got so emotional she actually *cried*. We're just as sad about her leaving as she is, though we know we'll be cheering her on in the Olympics one of these days. She signed a contract to go run on scholarship for the University of Washington in Seattle – said there was something about the gloomy weather that was calling to her.

I'm already stressed about finding a new locker partner.

We pass the boys, who have just begun their warm-up. The boys' race starts immediately after ours ends. "Hey, girls, break a leg," Jack says as the others crack up.

"Hey, boys, try winning this time," Josie responds, to which we add our own laughter and mocking cheers.

Cheeto, at the end of their line, catches my eye and winks. *You've got this*, he mouths.

I nod, grateful to know that whatever happens, he's got my back.

We find our spot on the line. The air is electric, humming with possibility. That's one of the five million things that's so great about this sport – the quintessential hopefulness of every starting line. For a few brief seconds, anything could happen. And as long as you keep putting one foot in front of the other, you'll make it to the finish line. One way or another.

The race official raises her arms into the air.

"Runners, on your marks!"

ACKNOWLEDGMENTS

First and foremost, thank you to Tobias Steed, Nicole Schroeder, Emily Rowlett, James Shannon, Mary Bisbee-Beek, and the rest of the team at Leapfrog Press for making my dream a reality. Your kindness, patience, and support has shattered every stereotype about the publishing industry in the best possible way.

Huge thank you to Becca Barnes for selecting *Wolfpack* as the 2024 YA/MG Leapfrog Global Fiction Prize winner.

Thank you to my many writing mentors and friends at both University of Nebraska-Lincoln and Weber State University, including Joy Castro, Timothy Schaffert, Pascha Sotolongo, Hope Wabuke, Siwar Masannat, Ryan Ridge, Siân Griffiths, Marisa Yerace, Sunni Wilkinson, William Pollett, and so many others. I am tremendously honored to have learned from and alongside you.

Thank you to Jenna Satterthwaite and Christine Nielsen, who both read earlier drafts of *Wolfpack* and gave me feedback that ultimately shaped what it became. I am forever grateful.

Thank you to my real-life cross country family, including (but not limited to) Art Hansen, Amber Tingey, Sunnie Hansen, Jerrica Hall, Danielle Retallick, Stephanie Wilson, and Annie Larsen, who showed me the magical alchemy of running and unconditional friendship. Truly, the strength of the wolf is the pack.

To my sisters: Thank you for your examples of powerful, brilliant, compassionate womanhood.

To my parents: I am who I am because of your constant support and love. You are, without hesitation, the best people I know.

To Ben: To say that I couldn't have done this without you is an understatement. Thank you for seeing me, hearing me, and loving me. We'll always be newlyweds.

Finally, to my kids: You are the reason I get up in the morning. I love you to the moon, past Jupiter and Saturn, beyond the stars and back again, infinity times infinity. Until the earth is done lasting.

ABOUT THE AUTHOR

Natalie Shaw Evjen is passionate about storytelling that builds bridges. She writes about faith, health, motherhood, and adolescence. She has a passion for sports, and *Wolfpack* was largely inspired by her experiences as a competitive long-distance runner as a teen and young adult. Her stories and poems have appeared in various literary journals and received several awards, including second prize in the Mari Sandoz/Prairie Schooner short story contest. Professionally, she teaches humanities and creative writing to secondary students, utilizing both a B.S. in history from Utah State University and an M.A. in English from Weber State University. When she's not writing or teaching, she is spending time with her family, gardening, or playing the piano. She has lived in Georgia, Virginia, and Nebraska, but was raised and currently resides in Ogden, Utah, with her husband, kids, and mischievous house rabbits.